MW00526804

# DEATH IN DALVIK

Before becoming a writer, Michael Ridpath used to work as a bond trader in the City of London. After writing several financial thrillers, which were published in over 30 languages, he began a crime series featuring the Icelandic detective Magnus Jonson. He has also written five stand-alone thrillers, including *Amnesia*, *Launch Code* and *The Diplomat's Wife*. He splits his time between London and Massachusetts.

You can find out more about him and his books on his website *www.michaelridpath.com* or on Facebook.

## ALSO BY MICHAEL RIDPATH

# DEATH IN DALVIK

MICHAEL RIDPATH

YARMER

First published in Great Britain in 2022 by Yarmer Head.

ISBN: 978-1-9997655-8-3

*for Sophie*

# PART ONE

# ONE

It was a gorgeous, crisp, clear November evening in the valley just outside Dalvík when Dísa came home from school to learn that her family would have to sell the farm.

Dísa's ancestors had tended the gentle slopes of Blábrekka for centuries. Five centuries: her grandfather could proudly and plausibly trace his descent to one Brandur Kolgrímsson who had purchased the farm in 1613. But the farm was much older than that – the ancient *Book of Settlements* reported its settlement early in the tenth century by one Ulf Blue Cheeks. Blábrekka stood a few kilometres outside the modern fishing village of Dalvík, at the base of a mountain overlooking the deep, dark waters of Eyjafjördur and the low island of Hrísey. The fjord pointed northwards to the Arctic Circle, which hovered invisibly thirty kilometres out to sea.

The sun had just slipped behind the mountain to the west; its rays painted the undersides of the clouds and the snow on the upper slopes of the surrounding hills a soft pink, with odd bruises of purple.

As Dísa walked up the snow-ploughed track to the

farmhouse, Bonnie and Clyde looked up and snorted over their fence, cocking their ears towards her while their breath misted in the cold. She waved, and it seemed to her that Bonnie nodded back. Bonnie was Dísa's horse and Clyde belonged to her younger sister, Anna Rós.

Who came tumbling out of the front door, coat flapping, tears streaming down her cheeks.

'Anna? What's up?'

'I'm going to see Clyde,' Anna Rós sobbed as she pushed past Dísa.

Dísa had thrown the odd tantrum in her time, but it was unlike Anna Rós to get upset over nothing. It must be *something*.

'Hi!' Dísa called out as she dumped her bag in the hallway and took off her hat, boots and coat. She entered the kitchen, which had been the warm heart of the farmhouse for centuries. Her mother looked up from the table with a strained face, and her grandmother clattered dishes in the sink.

Definitely something. 'What's up with Anna Rós?'

Grandma didn't answer, didn't even turn around. Mum looked into her coffee cup.

Dísa waited.

Mum glanced at the bent back of her own mother. 'Come with me. I've got something to tell you.'

'Is it Dad?' Dísa asked, her imagination leaping to her father hundreds of kilometres away in Reykjavík.

'No,' said Mum with a tight smile. 'And Grandpa's OK too. Nobody's ill. But I do have bad news.'

She led Dísa through to the living room. She sat on the sofa, and Dísa perched on the edge of her grandfather's armchair, eyeing her mother nervously.

'So what is it? What's Anna Rós freaked out about?'

'We're going to have to sell the horses,' Mum said. 'We can't keep them up any more.'

'Oh.'

Dísa wasn't exactly surprised. She had been aware of her family's money issues since she was a little girl. She dimly remembered a nice house in Reykjavík, and holidays to Spain and Greece, back when her parents were still married, before the *kreppa*, the financial crash that had ruined their lives as well as those of so many other Icelanders.

Her father had worked for one of the banks, where he had been seriously successful, until he wasn't. But he had broken some law that even now Dísa didn't understand, and had spent a couple of years in jail for whatever crime he had committed. There had also been a girlfriend in those heady days, an admin assistant at the bank, who had been uncovered along with the fraud. And a foreign-currency mortgage that had devoured the family's nice house in Fossvogur.

Mum had taken Dísa and Anna Rós, and run away back to Dalvík and her own parents' farm at Blábrekka.

Mum's family were rich – big people about town. Brandur's descendants had always been important landowners in the area. Mum's own grandfather had made plenty of money from Dalvík's fishing boom, as well as from the farm. The farmhouse itself was big by Icelandic standards, with a barn, built in the 1980s, large enough to house several hundred sheep.

But as she had got older, Dísa had realized that her grandparents were not as rich as everyone thought. Machinery wasn't fixed, a couple of outbuildings had been left to fall down, there was a leak in the roof of the garage, and paint peeled from the ceiling of the living room above her.

In the last couple of years, she had asked questions and divined some answers. Encouraged by Dad, Grandpa had sold his fishing quota and half of the farm's land to the big fishing company that now dominated Dalvík. With the proceeds, he had bought shares. Shares that had briefly gone up and then come crashing down. Also, Grandpa wasn't that great a farmer. He was a lovely man, but he just wasn't practical – Dísa could see that. Two outbreaks of scrapie in the valley in the last twenty years had taken their toll on the flock and the farm finances. If it wasn't for the labourer who came in most days to help, she doubted the sheep would make it through the winter.

Mum was a doctor, though, an anaesthetist at the hospital in Akureyri, and she made a decent salary, Dísa supposed. Enough to keep the farm above water. Dísa supposed.

'No wonder Anna's upset.' Dísa was spending less time on Bonnie these days, and she would miss her, but Clyde was everything to Anna Rós. And actually Mum loved riding as well. 'I'm sorry,' Dísa said.

Mum bit her lip, brushing a strand of her red hair out of her eyes. 'It's not just the horses,' she said. She swallowed. 'I haven't told Anna Rós this yet, but it's the farm as well.'

'What! Does Grandpa know?'

Mum shook her head. 'He should do. It's staring him in the face, but he refuses to see it. He hopes that if he ignores things, they will just get better of their own accord. *Thetta reddast* is his motto.' It was a phrase often heard on the lips of Icelanders: things will sort themselves out. A tear ran down her mother's cheek. 'There's a massive mortgage on Blábrekka. I've done my best to keep everything under control with my salary, but it's just not enough. We have to face facts. We're going to have to sell.'

'Can Dad help?'

'What do you think?' Mum said, her voice bitter. 'Dad has no money, you know that. The man's useless.'

Dísa flinched. Mum noticed, and Dísa could see she was considering apologizing, but decided not to.

A host of questions flooded Dísa's brain. Where would they live? Could they even afford a smaller place in Dalvík? What would happen to the animals? To the horses?

How would Grandpa take it?

Badly. Very badly.

'I'm sorry, Dísa.' Mum sniffed and a tear wriggled down her cheek. 'I've tried everything. I really have. You must believe me.'

'I know you have, Mum.' Dísa slipped next to her mother on the sofa and held her tight; Mum buried her head in her daughter's chest. Grandma drifted to the doorway from the kitchen, her face a mixture of anger and concern, and then she withdrew. She did as much work as Grandpa around the farm, probably more. She had put most of her life into the place. But Dísa knew it would be Grandpa whose distress would take precedence.

Dísa ran her fingers through her mother's hair. 'Maybe I can help,' she said.

The sobs turned into a chuckle. 'You're going to have to work for a hundred years at the petrol station,' Mum said, sitting up. Dísa did a few hours behind the counter there to earn some pocket money, in addition to the time she put in helping out on the farm. And her homework.

'How many hundred years? How much would it take?'

Mum closed her eyes. She hesitated.

'I'm sixteen, Mum,' Dísa said. 'I understand money. You can tell me.'

Mum smiled. 'Yes, you do understand money. I wish it had been you working at the bank, not your father, then we wouldn't be in this mess.'

Dísa fought back the sharp comment that this provoked. It was true, Dad had screwed up badly, but then so had Grandpa, from what Dísa could tell. Dad wasn't as evil as Mum constantly made out. Nor as useless.

'Ten million krónur to get us through next year. Probably twenty million to get rid of the mortgage and put the farm back on a commercial footing.'

'Whoa!'

'See what I mean about the petrol station job?'

Dísa did the sums in her head. 'Twenty-one years,' she said. 'Not a hundred.'

'We barely have twenty-one days.'

Dísa hugged her mother. 'Is Anna Rós still outside? I'll go and see her.'

Mum nodded. 'OK. But remember she doesn't know about the farm yet. The horses are bad enough for her.'

Dísa put on her boots, hat and coat and went outside. The sky had turned from pink to a deep, deep blue; blackness wasn't far away. She trudged through the snow to where Anna was hugging Clyde's neck in the field.

The snow on the slopes of the mountain glimmered a lighter blue in the gathering darkness. Blábrekka meant 'blue slope'. Grandpa said that the farm had been named that after the colour of Ulf's cheeks, or possibly his buttocks, but Dísa had always believed it referred to the colours of the hillside in the night.

A couple of hundred metres below, on the other side of

the road, the river lazily wound its way down towards the sea, pausing in pools of glimmering silver.

Dísa thought of all the generations who had pulled salmon out of those waters, who had rounded up the sheep every autumn from the great mountain above her, who had looked out at the wall of fells lining the far side of the fjord.

The farm wasn't for her, never would have been for her, but it had always been assumed by the family that Anna Rós would eventually take it over. She would do a good job – she loved animals and was willing to work hard at all hours to look after them.

Dísa opened the gate and approached her sister.

'Oh God, Dísa! I can't bear it! I'm going to miss Clyde so so much!'

Dísa pulled Anna Rós towards her. Even though she was probably fully grown by now, Anna Rós was fifteen centimetres shorter than Dísa's one metre ninety.

The two sisters were very different, but despite that, or perhaps because of it, they got on well. There was no rivalry. Anna Rós was pert and blonde and loved to laugh. She had plenty of friends, and, increasingly, male admirers.

Dísa thought of herself as mousy, albeit a very tall mouse. She was quiet, academic; nobody disliked her, but she was not exactly popular. She was sensible, pretty good at volleyball, very good at maths.

'Don't worry, Anna,' said Dísa. 'I'll sort it.'

'How?' said Anna Rós, her large moist eyes appealing with hope. She never underestimated her big sister. 'How, Dísa?'

Dísa smiled. 'I've got an idea.'

.  .  .

Dísa slipped upstairs to her room and flipped up the lid of her computer. She opened up the graph she checked at least once a day. Along the x-axis lay a series of dates, starting at 1 Jan 2017 and continuing along to 28 Nov, that day's date. Along the y-axis were a range of dollar numbers, rising from $1,000 to $10,000. A yellow, jagged line sloped inexorably upwards from the lower number towards the higher.

Bitcoin.

The price of one bitcoin at that instant was $9,815.

She switched to a simple spreadsheet. She owned 31.931 bitcoin.

Which at the current price was worth $313,403 or, and here she had to type in the current Icelandic exchange rate, thirty-three million krónur. That was up over twelve thousand dollars on the previous day.

Dísa smiled.

It looked like she wouldn't have to work in the petrol station for twenty-one years after all.

# TWO

Dísa had received her original five bitcoin only eleven months before, back in January when the price was still about a thousand dollars. It had been a gift from Dad.

He had summoned her to meet him in Akureyri for lunch. A secret lunch. Dísa had argued, but Dad had insisted. Dísa seriously hated keeping secrets from her mum. It was a Saturday, and she had had to lie that she was going shopping with her friend Kata, adding a hint that there might be boys involved. That was pure manipulation of her mother; Mum was worried that she didn't have a boyfriend yet, and had been dropping encouraging hints about how Dísa should be spending more time with boys. Mum liked Matti, Kata's new boyfriend, and wanted her daughter to find one like him.

It was a foul January day. The remains of week-old snow slopped around the pavements. A low, heavy, grey cloud squashed the fjord and obliterated the mountains around the town, even stooping to threaten the twin spires of Akureyri's dramatic church. Despite its northern location, Akureyri was supposed to be one of the sunniest places in Iceland. Not that day.

As Dísa walked from the bus stop to the restaurant on Skipagata where she was supposed to meet Dad, she wondered what his agenda was. Could it be that he had a plan for some kind of reconciliation?

Like so many kids of divorced parents, it was what Dísa wanted most in the world. She loved her dad, she loved Mum, memories of her early childhood of security and comfort warmed and nourished her.

She knew it was pointless to dream that dream; although she suspected Dad would have had a go, there was no way Mum was up for it. Mum was unforgiving, and there was plenty that would need to be forgiven. Dísa firmly believed that there had been a time when Mum loved Dad, and that she could remember it, but that time was long gone.

Yet, even though she knew it would never happen, Dísa consciously decided not to give up hope. It sustained her. It allowed her not to take sides, not to nod in agreement when her mother slagged off her father for the hundredth time, not to agree with her father about her mother's hard heart.

What else might it be? Some news he wanted Dísa to break to the family in her role as family mediator? Bad news? Was he ill? Cancer? Good news? Did he want to announce a girlfriend? A marriage? A *baby*?

Dísa's blood ran cold. That might be good news for him, but it would screw the chances of a reconciliation with Mum.

So it was with a touch of anxiety that she checked the restaurant for her father.

He was sitting at a table by the window, which overlooked the cloud-shrouded harbour and the fjord reaching into the murk beyond. He waved to her, and scrambled to his feet so he could give her a kiss.

A couple of years before, he had given himself a complete makeover. He had been a slim, sleek banker, with longish dark hair brushed back and gelled. Even in the two years he spent in Kvíabryggja minimum security prison he continued to look sleek. But on his release, he fell apart: the hair became longer and lanker, the chin unshaved, and a little belly appeared above his jeans.

He had found it difficult to get work during that time – the new, staid, boring banks didn't want the old flashy bankers. Dísa knew there had been drink, and guessed there had been drugs.

But tourism was booming, and eventually Dad had reinvented himself from Ómar Baldvinsson the smooth bankster, to Óm the hip, if slightly paunchy, tour guide, who could drive you into Iceland's rugged interior through gushing rivers and over treacherous glaciers. So he shaved his head, a tiny goatee dripped from his chin, an earring of one Viking rune dangled from his left ear, and a tattoo of another snaked up his neck.

But he was still Dad.

'Hi,' said Dísa, returning his grin despite her nervousness. She was always pleased to see him.

He had picked a nice restaurant – more expensive than the cheap cafés they occasionally met in – but they both ordered burgers. She and Dad always ordered burgers. And she got a milkshake.

He asked her about school, and her plans for the high school in Ólafsfjördur, the next fishing village down the fjord, that she would be attending the following academic year.

'You know they call the kids from Dalvík "potatoes"?'

He chuckled. 'That's not very nice. What do you call them?'

Dísa blushed. 'Something much ruder, I'm afraid. But it will be good to get to know a whole new set of people.'

She had made the local volleyball team, and he promised he would come and watch her next time he was in the north. Dad was good at asking questions. His interest in her and her life was always genuine.

But Dísa interrupted him, her curiosity demanding satisfaction. 'So what do you want, Dad?'

Dad took a deep breath, and smiled. It wasn't bad news, at least as far as he was concerned. A girlfriend, then. Or a wedding.

'Have you heard of bitcoin?'

That took her by surprise. 'Bitcoin? No.'

'It's a new kind of currency. A digital currency.'

'OK. Whose digital currency?'

'Nobody's. Or rather everybody's.'

'What do you mean?'

'It's not like the króna or the dollar, which is issued by central banks, and controlled by central banks. If the government runs out of dollars, they can just print more of them. Or they can make them worthless.'

'The American government would never do that,' Dísa said.

'Not now,' said Dad. 'But have you ever seen a Confederate dollar? Or those old marks they had in Germany before the war, when people were wheeling bundles of cash around in wheelbarrows? Just last year the Indian government scrapped all their large-denomination banknotes overnight. And our own króna only just survived the *kreppa*.'

'All right,' said Dísa, intrigued by the idea. 'But money

must be backed by somebody, surely? Some government promise, or a vault full of gold, or something.'

'Not necessarily,' said Dad, grinning. 'Bitcoin doesn't have any government or big corporation backing it.'

'Then how come it's worth anything?'

'It's worth something *because* of that. No government can mess with it. If you own a bitcoin, it's yours to keep. No one can change it. No one can take it away from you.'

'But what exactly is it?'

'It's an entry in a database called a blockchain, which cannot be manipulated by anybody. New bitcoins are produced every year, but the amount is strictly limited by the original code. So no one is going to create loads more.' Dad took a bite of his burger. 'It was invented by a guy called Satoshi Nakamoto in 2008. No one knows who he is, or even if that's his real name. But we do know he's a genius.'

'And can you buy anything with these bitcoin?'

'Not much yet,' said Dad. 'But that's going to change very soon. In a digital world, bitcoin is better than cash. You know how in Iceland no one really uses banknotes any more? We use these.' He pulled out his wallet and held up a debit card. 'Or nowadays even a phone. We're way ahead of most other countries, but they will catch up. But even with these digital payments, the big banks take a cut on every transaction. With bitcoin, there will be no banks.'

'So where is your money if it's not in a bank?'

'It's in the blockchain. You have a wallet address that's linked to your bitcoin in the blockchain database. To access your wallet, all you need is a private key.'

'A key?'

'Not like a metal key. It's a string of characters like a really long password that gives you access to your blockchain. Mine's on this.' He fished what looked like a stubby USB stick out of his trouser pocket. 'It's called a "cold wallet". With this I can access all my bitcoin.'

Dísa took a bite of her burger. 'So you have some of these bitcoin?'

'I do,' said Dad, his eyes twinkling. 'Rather a lot of bitcoin.' He gave her a long slow wink, just like he used to do when she was a little girl.

'How did you manage that?' Dísa said.

Dad was clearly pleased with her interest. 'Sharp gave me some a couple of years ago. Technically you are not allowed to buy bitcoin in this country, and you've heard of the exchange controls which mean Icelanders can't own assets overseas.'

'Sharp is your banking friend, isn't he? The one who didn't go to jail?'

'That's right. He lives in London. So he has set up a bitcoin wallet for me from over there.'

A suspicion occurred to Dísa. 'Why did Sharp give you the bitcoin? A birthday present?'

'Not exactly.' Dad put on his shifty face.

'He owed you something? For something you did for him?'

More shifty face. 'Maybe.'

'To keep him out of jail?'

Dad cleared his throat. 'Sharp is a good friend of mine and very smart. He helped me out. And since he gave me the bitcoin, the price has doubled. And I think it's going to double again. Suddenly the world is going to realize that bitcoin is the currency of the future, and everyone is going to want some.'

Dísa nodded. She still wasn't sure why he was telling her all this. Maybe he wanted recognition that he wasn't as useless as his wife was always saying. There was no way Mum would ever admit to that. But his daughter might.

Fair enough. 'Well done, Dad,' Dísa said. 'That was smart.'

Dad popped a chip in his mouth, sat back in his seat and grinned at his daughter. She was right; he was pleased with her compliment.

'The thing is, Dísa . . .' He leaned forward.

'Yes?'

'I'd like to give you some.'

'Some bitcoin?'

'Yes. Five bitcoin.'

'Well, thanks, Dad.' Five bitcoin didn't sound like much, and they seemed to be very fiddly to look after, but Dísa did appreciate the thought.

'The price is about one thousand dollars each today.'

'Oh.' Then Dísa did the sums. 'Oh! But that's five thousand dollars, Dad?'

Dad smiled. 'I know.'

'What do you expect me to do with it?'

'Nothing. Just sit on it. Invest it. Watch it turn into ten thousand.'

'Wow.' Dísa swallowed. 'Thanks, Dad, thanks a lot!' Then she frowned. 'What about Anna Rós? Are you going to give her any?'

'She's too young. She wouldn't understand. But I knew you would. You're good with numbers, and you get money, don't you?'

'I suppose I do,' said Dísa. She had had a semi-serious reputation within the family since the age of seven when she had earnestly announced that she was going to save 10 per cent of her pocket money, and had actually done so.

'And Jói?' Jói was Dísa's half-brother, Dad's son from a

previous brief marriage. He was seven years older than her. He used to stay with them at weekends when they lived in Reykjavík, and he had always been a loyal older brother to her, even after the divorce.

'Jói doesn't need the money,' Dad said. 'He's getting a good salary now with that games developer.'

Dad could see her doubts. 'Please take it, Dísa,' he said. 'You know how badly I feel, how badly I will always feel, about letting down you and Anna Rós and, yes, Helga. Mum. This is a small way, a tiny way, I can do something for you. It's really important to me. If this works as well as I think it will, if bitcoin doubles this year and maybe doubles again next year, then you'll have enough money for a start in life.' Dad sighed. 'And at least I will have given you that.'

Dísa wasn't sure that she completely understood this bitcoin, or that it was completely legal, but she knew her father. She could see how much this meant to him. How important it was to his pride, which had taken such a battering over the last few years.

To reject the bitcoin would be to reject him.

And that was something Dísa was determined not to do.

'All right, Dad. I'll take it. Thank you,' she said. 'It means a lot to me that you would do this for me.'

Dad beamed. He took out another USB stick, this one pink. Dísa flinched at the colour. He must have got one specially for his little girl. But she decided not to make a fuss.

'This is your cold wallet. It's called a cold wallet because it's offline – a hot wallet is online. Your wallet address and your private key are on here. I'll email you instructions for how to get access to your bitcoin.'

'OK.'

'Be very careful with that. Your wallet address doesn't

matter so much. It's like your address on the blockchain or your bank account details; you give it to people to tell them where to pay you. But if you lose the private key, you lose the bitcoin.'

'Can't I ask for another one?'

'No. Remember, no one is in charge of bitcoin. It's all down to you. Without the private key, no one can access your coin. Ever. So I suggest you make a paper copy of the key and hide that somewhere in case you lose the wallet – it's like a super-cold wallet. I've hidden mine at the summer house.' He chuckled. 'The hidden people can look after it.'

The summer house was a tiny cabin on the shore of Apavatn, a lake an hour and a half to the east of Reykjavík, which Dad had bought in the good days before the crash.

'Figure out a hiding place for the wallet and the paper back-up. You can password-protect the wallet; just hide the paper copy well.'

'I will.'

'And lastly, don't tell Helga.'

'But – Dad! I hate keeping stuff from her. Just like I hate keeping stuff from you.'

'I know, my love. But I simply don't trust her.'

'Seriously? Don't trust her? With what? The bitcoin?'

'Yes,' said Dad, nodding. 'It's a condition of me giving this to you. You must promise me.'

Dísa almost threw the USB stick back at him. A condition. Conditional love. Family distrust.

God, she was sick of it.

But it was five thousand dollars – half a million krónur – and that could come in very handy.

Dad was worried. He knew she might reject his gift. Reject him.

'OK,' said Dísa. 'But I have one condition of my own.'

'Yes?'

She held up the pink USB stick, the 'cold wallet' as Dad called it. 'Next time we meet you get me one of these in silver. Or gold.'

That evening, Dísa spent several hours on her computer getting to grips with bitcoin. There were a number of websites on which you could trade bitcoin, known as exchanges, and its price seemed to jump up and down wildly. Mostly up.

There were other coins too, known as 'cryptocurrencies'. These were even more volatile than bitcoin, and went up in price even faster. And there was a community of bitcoin enthusiasts all over the internet – more than enthusiasts: bitcoin lovers. According to their posts, they loved the cryptocurrency for one of two reasons – either because it was making them a lot of money, or because it demonstrated that individuals could now use a currency completely free of government interference.

Dísa was fascinated. She watched the price of her bitcoin spike up and then down every evening after school – mostly up. She read up on trading strategies: moving averages, trends, Fibonacci numbers, relative strength indices. All these indicators suggested that bitcoin was going up, up, up and would continue to do so.

But there were other cryptocurrencies that were moving up in price even faster. There was one called Ethereum, which people said was going to become just as important as bitcoin; it might even take over from it. In February she sold her bitcoin on an exchange and bought Ethereum, for a price of about thirteen dollars per Ethereum coin. Within a month, the price had doubled, and it kept shooting up. Dísa checked her phone several times a day, watching the price, cheering it on. By late spring the price of one Ethereum coin had risen to almost two hundred dollars.

That was literally fifteen times the price she had paid for it not even four months before. Fifteen times! Her Ethereum was now worth over eighty thousand dollars.

Dísa was transfixed. She watched the Ethereum price on her phone at school and then on her laptop in the evening when she got home. Some mornings she would wake up and the price had gone up 10 per cent overnight, and the whole day was good. Until, in the evening, the price plummeted 5 per cent. She could easily make or lose a thousand dollars between Mathematics first lesson in the morning and English last lesson in the afternoon.

The school year ended at the end of May. Her mother was disappointed with her report card, and so was she. Her mother and grandparents commented on how much time she spent on her phone, but, like most parents, they had no idea what she was doing on it.

In June, Dísa decided to take back some control of her life. She sold the Ethereum, and bought back the staid old bitcoin, vowing to limit herself to checking the price once a day, twice max. To her dismay, the Ethereum price continued to rise, breaking three hundred dollars, before slumping down to the price she had sold it for.

Thanks to the profits from her foray into Ethereum, her five bitcoin had now become thirty-two. The notional value of the digital codes stored on her little patch of blockchain was now approaching a hundred thousand dollars.

Which was a massive amount of money for a sixteen-year-old girl. She was rich!

But although she had enjoyed watching the value of her bitcoin grow – had become obsessed with it – she didn't really believe in it. Despite what the enthusiasts proclaimed, it wasn't like it was real money. You couldn't buy anything with it.

She didn't even know how she could turn it into krónur. Although the government had repealed the law about Icelanders transferring assets abroad, it was still technically illegal to buy or sell bitcoin.

So over the summer she still did a stint behind the counter at the petrol station. Earning fifteen hundred krónur an hour.

But while she was serving hot dogs, the price of her bitcoin was powering ahead. It broke four thousand dollars in the middle of August when she returned to school and six thousand at the end of October. It looked like it would reach ten thousand by December.

So yes, Dísa could save the family farm.

If only she could figure out how to turn the bitcoin into real money.

# THREE

Inspector Magnús Ragnarsson looked up at the open window, ten feet above the ground, and marvelled. How could people be so stupid?

He was standing at the back of a hangar-like building on the old US Naval Air Station right next to the international airport at Keflavík, which had been converted into a data centre. With its cheap geothermal energy and its even cheaper cold air for cooling, Iceland was developing a niche for itself as a place to store the ever-growing data produced by billions of smartphones and computers around the world. A video of baby Chung's first steps, an analysis of Jorge's browsing history, back-ups of Bloomfield Weiss's foreign exchange trades were all stored in sheds like these.

But this particular unit had housed 104 computers that were devoted to an altogether different purpose: mining bitcoin. Until the night before, when someone had driven out to this bleak spot, avoided disturbing the security guard playing solitaire on his phone, spotted a window open to let in air to cool the machines, found a ladder propped against a wall around the corner, climbed into the building and removed the servers. All 104 of them.

What made the negligence of the data centres more incredible was that a very similar break-in had taken place only the week before at another data centre up the road.

That too had involved computers dedicated to bitcoin mining. Which was something to do with solving cryptographic puzzles to create more bitcoin, the emerging currency of choice for drug dealers and peddlers of ransomware. Bitcoin was based on something called a blockchain. For the blockchain to work, each new bitcoin transaction had to be incorporated into it through solving these puzzles, which involved massive amounts of computer power, and a lot of electricity. The 'miners' were paid in new bitcoin created when their computers ground out the solution to the puzzle.

Magnus realized he was going to have to find out more about bitcoin and its miners.

But not right now.

'Can I leave this with you?' he said to Sergeant Vigdís, his colleague in CID. 'I've got the afternoon off.'

'Sure,' said Vigdís with a grin. 'And I hope it all goes well with Ási.'

It was a half-hour drive from the data centre through the black roiling lava fields to Álftanes, a little peninsula facing Reykjavík, where Magnus lived. Temporarily.

He parked outside the brown wooden house. A breeze was blowing cold damp air in from the Atlantic – nothing new there for Iceland. There had been snow in the north of the country, but the weather in Reykjavík was its usual changeable self, grey clouds scudding in, dropping diagonally falling rain and scudding out again, leaving glimpses of the sun and glimmering rainbows.

Cold weather for a little kid to be outside, Magnus worried.

Not an Icelandic kid.

He grabbed the plastic football he had bought that morning from the car's back seat and opened the front door of the house.

'Hi!'

'What the hell are you doing here?' a gruff voice replied from deep inside. 'Aren't you supposed to be at work keeping Reykjavík safe for its resident idiots? Or shagging your girlfriend?'

'And a good afternoon to you,' said Magnus, pouring himself a cup of coffee from the thermos and taking it into the living room where Tryggvi Thór, his landlord, was reading a book in English. *The Boys in the Boat*, Magnus saw, something about an American Olympic rowing team. Magnus planned to steal it off him when he had finished.

Tryggvi Thór grunted, furrowing his thick dark eyebrows as he read, the corners of his lips pointing downward in something close to a scowl. Magnus sat down opposite him and sipped his coffee.

'All right, I'll have a cup,' Tryggvi Thór said.

Magnus poured him one.

Silence.

'How's the rape case going?' Tryggvi Thór asked eventually.

'Not good,' said Magnus. That was another frustrating case, which he had been working on with Vigdís for most of the week.

'They're always tricky.'

'Yeah. It's the damn phones.'

'What do you mean?'

'It's a he-said-she-said. He says she gave consent; she

says she didn't. He says she's been sending him texts begging to see him; she says she did want to see him, but she didn't want to have sex with him.'

'Sounds familiar.'

Magnus sighed. 'His lawyer says she wants to see the victim's phone.'

'And the victim says no?'

'She says her phone is private and there are things on there she doesn't want anyone to see. Things that have nothing to do with the case. So she wants to back out of the prosecution. She says she doesn't see why, just because someone raped her, she has to lay out her entire personal life before a court of strangers.'

'Do you believe her? That the messages have nothing to do with the case?'

'I think so. I can't be sure. But I'm damned sure she's telling the truth. She said no and then the bastard raped her anyway. She scratched him on the neck – we've got the evidence for that. But unless we can persuade her to turn over her phone, the bastard will walk free. And that really pisses me off. We never used to have this problem, but now it's happening all the time.'

Tryggvi Thór shook his head. 'I always hated rape cases.'

Tryggvi Thór had been a policeman, a detective like Magnus, in the Reykjavík CID. He had been kicked out of the force under a cloud in the 1990s and had escaped to Uganda to run a school. But after the death of his African wife, he had returned to his late parents' home in Álftanes.

Magnus had returned to Iceland himself earlier that summer for a second stint with the Reykjavík Metropolitan Police – he had been away from Iceland for five years, back in his old job in homicide for the Boston Police Department.

Given the tourist boom and the season, it had been a nightmare trying to find accommodation in Reykjavík. Magnus had been investigating a robbery with violence at Tryggvi Thór's house when the retired cop had offered him a room. Magnus had accepted.

Three months into it, and the arrangement suited them both well. Tryggvi Thór was a grumpy bastard, and Magnus liked to be left alone. They respected each other's desire not to be bothered. Yet more and more they found themselves talking.

Magnus was coming to realize he actually liked the grumpy bastard.

The doorbell rang.

'Who's that?'

'A friend,' said Magnus, leaping to his feet. He corrected himself. 'Two friends.'

He opened the front door. A blonde woman wearing a cream-coloured woolly hat was standing there with a small boy clutching her leg. They both looked nervous.

'Hi, Ingileif,' said Magnus.

'Hi.' Ingileif hesitated, and then reached up to kiss him on the cheek.

Magnus squatted down on his haunches. 'Hi, Ási,' he said to the small boy whose bright blue eyes stared at Magnus from beneath a thatch of red hair.

'Do you remember Magnús?' Ingileif asked encouragingly.

The boy shook his head and clung more tightly to his mother's leg. A wave of disappointment washed over Magnus. It was two months since Magnus had met the little boy for the first and only time, by chance on a Reykjavík street with his mother. Magnus knew that the encounter would have meant much less to the boy than it would to

Magnus, but it hadn't occurred to Magnus that Ási wouldn't even remember him.

But then, why should he?

'I thought we could go for a walk?' said Magnus. 'It's not too cold, is it?'

The breeze was whipping Ingileif's blonde hair around her cheeks, which were blossoming pink in the chill.

Magnus couldn't help staring at her. Those cheeks were so familiar, the lips, her grey eyes. And that little nick on her eyebrow.

She stared back for a moment that was just about to become awkward when she answered his question. 'No. We're dressed for it.'

'Great. Look, come in from the cold. And just wait a sec while I get something for Ási.'

He ducked back into the living room to pick up the bright orange plastic football he had bought earlier. Tryggvi Thór was on his feet to greet Magnus's guests.

'Good afternoon,' he said to both of them. 'I'm Tryggvi Thór. Magnús is my lodger.'

'That's very brave of you,' said Ingileif.

'I'm a brave man,' said Tryggvi Thór. 'I take it you and he are old friends?'

'Old friends,' Ingileif confirmed.

'You don't look like the kind of girl who would be stupid enough to go out with a policeman?'

'Sadly, I was,' said Ingileif. 'Until I came to my senses.'

Tryggvi Thór looked at the little boy. 'My guess is until about five years ago?'

Ási was four.

'That's a very good guess,' said Ingileif, glancing at Magnus.

'Don't worry, he didn't say anything,' said Tryggvi Thór. 'I used to be a detective too. The boy looks just like him.'

'And I need to separate you two,' said Magnus. 'Before you discover all my secrets.' He put on his coat and hat. 'Come on.'

They left the house and Magnus led Ingileif and Ási down to the shore. A narrow beach skirted the peninsula, bordered by a sea wall of large rocks. Ducks fussed among the seaweed.

Ási clung on to his mother's hand.

'He seems like a miserable old git,' said Ingileif.

'He is, he is. I like him.'

'Just your type. In fact, I can imagine you becoming exactly like him in thirty years.'

'I'm not sure whether I'm supposed to be flattered or insulted by that,' said Magnus.

'Oh, insulted,' said Ingileif.

She sounded as if she was teasing – she was teasing. But there was a grit of truth there. And Magnus didn't know what to make of that hard, sharp grit.

Suddenly, his future widened out in front of him like a chasm. He felt a lurch of fear, teetering on its edge. Would his old age be spent in Iceland or America? Who would it be with? Would it be with anyone at all? Would Ási be a part of it?

Or when he was seventy would he still not know who he was, where he was from, whom he was to live his life with?

A bit like Tryggvi Thór then.

Ingileif seemed to read his mind. 'Sorry.'

'About what?' said Magnus, putting on a grin.

'You went all thoughtful.'

The beach was empty. The sand was a mixture of

yellow and black, with black pebbles scattered about, having been tossed by winds and currents this way and that in the several thousand years since they had been spewed out of some volcano. A faint smell from the seaweed draped over sand and rocks shifted in and out of Magnus's nostrils.

The Reykjanes peninsula stretched out to the west, into the Atlantic, a black mass of frozen folds of lava. The near-perfect cone of the small volcano Keilir pushed upwards just inland from the shoreline. Although it hadn't erupted for several millennia, it looked perfectly capable of putting on a performance at any moment.

No trees. If there had been trees there several thousand years before, and there probably had been, they had been smothered and choked by the lava, and had never had the opportunity to seed in the sterile landscape again. Only lichen and moss and the odd tuft of yellow grass could gain a foothold out there.

'How do you like it back in Iceland?' Ingileif asked.

'It's good,' said Magnus. 'I'm glad I came back.'

Magnus had been born in Iceland, but had moved to America to follow his father at the age of twelve. He had grown up there and, after the dreadful months following his father's murder which the local cops couldn't solve, had joined the Boston Police Department. When the National Police Commissioner of Iceland had come to the US looking for expertise in big-city crime, as the only Icelandic-speaking detective in the US, Magnus was the obvious candidate.

So Sergeant Detective Magnus Jonson became Sergeant Magnús Ragnarsson – Magnus's father's first name was Ragnar – as he spent three years attached to the Reykjavík police. His first stint.

Which was where he had met Ingileif.

They stayed together for most of those three years, but when they split up, Magnus had allowed his time in Iceland to come to an end. That was five years ago, now.

'Why did you come back here?'

'It wasn't the same in Boston. It hadn't changed; I had. You know how obsessed I used to be about investigations? I've lost that, or at least I had lost it in America.'

'Because you had solved your father's murder?'

'That's right,' said Magnus. Ingileif had always understood him, almost as well as he understood himself. Probably better. He had discovered the key to his father's murder had been in Iceland all along. Until that point, he had been driven to solve every homicide he came across in an ever-fruitless attempt to solve his father's murder, or if not to solve it, then resolve it. Which of course he never managed to do.

But after he had dealt with his father's death, he found the homicide investigations just depressing. And they produced ever-increasing quantities of information that had to be typed into computers.

'Are you happy now?'

Magnus glanced at Ingileif. Never afraid to ask direct questions.

'Yes.' His smile broadened.

Ingileif laughed. 'That was quick! You've only been back a few months. What's her name?'

'Eygló. She's an archaeologist.'

'She wasn't a witness on that murder case you were involved in, was she? The one that was in the papers?'

'Maybe.'

'Magnús! You must stop doing that! You know it's unprofessional.' That was how Magnus had met Ingileif.

'I know, I know.'

'Tell me about her.'

Magnus hesitated. His instinct was not to tell his former girlfriend about how wonderful his current girlfriend was. But on the other hand, if he was going to establish a successful long-term relationship with the mother of his son, he was going to have to get over the former-girlfriend bit.

So he did, describing how Eygló had her own eleven-year-old son, about her background as an archaeologist and how she had stumbled into the role of successful presenter of TV documentaries. He tried to avoid sounding too enthusiastic, but didn't entirely succeed.

'She sounds perfect for you. You really like her, don't you?'

'I do,' Magnus admitted.

'I'm glad,' said Ingileif. She sounded as if she really meant it. Yet somehow she sounded sad as well. Or was Magnus imagining that?

It was his turn to pry. 'Last time we met, you mentioned something about a guy called Hannes?'

They had only spoken twice since Magnus had been back in Iceland, and not at all when he had been in America. The first time, when they had bumped into each other on Borgartún and Magnus had learned of Ási's existence, Ingileif had mentioned a husband. The second time, over lunch, she had said the husband had gone off with another woman.

'Hannes wants to come back. Turns out I'm more interesting than his skinny model. Who'd have thought it?'

'Are you going to take him?'

'Don't know. Not sure.'

Magnus looked across at her. She was walking, head down. Was she avoiding his glance?

They continued on in silence for a bit. The wind

whipped in from the ruffled sea, shuffling the layers of white and grey cloud into streaks of blue. Magnus switched to English for the little boy's benefit. Or rather to exclude the little boy.

There was a question he needed to know the answer to. 'Does he know that Hannes isn't his father?'

'Oh, yes. He calls him Hannes, not Dad. But I have to say that Hannes is very good to him.'

'Does he know about me?'

'Who? Hannes or Ási?'

'Both.'

'I've told Hannes all about you. At the moment Ási thinks he hasn't got a dad. And I'd like to keep it that way.' She took a couple of steps. 'For now, at least.'

Ási had heard his name and looked up at his mother and Magnus.

'You're forty-one and a half,' he said.

Magnus grinned. Ási did remember him after all! They had swapped ages last time they had met. 'And you are four.'

'And a half.'

'And a half.'

Ingileif smiled at Magnus. 'What are you doing with that football? Are you taking *it* for a walk? Aren't you supposed to kick it?'

Magnus dropped the ball to his feet and dribbled it lackadaisically on the sand in front of him, small waves swishing against the shoreline a few metres away.

Ási watched closely, still clutching his mother's hand. When the ball drifted near Ási's toes, Ási gave it a poke and sent it skimming across the beach. Magnus scampered after it and passed the ball back to Ási, who let go of his mother's hand and ran after it.

An hour later, exhausted by all the running, kicking, falling down and laughing, Magnus hauled Ási up on to his shoulders and carried him back to Ingileif's car. On the other side of Álftanes the large white farmhouse, Bessastadir, that served as the President's residence stood alone with its church and its flagpole from which Iceland's flag proudly fluttered. Magnus had come to appreciate being in a country where the President lived on a farm.

'That was fun,' he said to her. 'Thank you for bringing him.'

'He enjoyed it. And it was good to see you playing, Magnús.'

Magnus lowered the boy off his shoulders and Ingileif strapped him into his car seat. Ási's eyelids were drooping.

'Can we do it again?'

Ingileif nodded. 'Sure. He'd like that. I'll text you.'

# FOUR

Dísa didn't get a chance to speak to her mother until the following evening, when Mum got back from her shift at the hospital. And she had to endure a tense supper where everyone seemed unhappy with everyone else. Even Anna Rós, who could usually be relied upon for some bubbly chatter.

Grandpa tossed some comments about politics on to the empty table. There had recently been an election and although Grandpa's party, the Independence Party, had the most seats, it looked as if the leader of the Left/Greens would become Prime Minister. A couple of days before, the conversation would have turned into a good-humoured skirmish of the generations, with Dísa taking on her grandfather, but that evening she didn't have the heart for it. She was bursting to tell them all about the bitcoin, but she knew she had to start with Mum.

'Can I show you something upstairs on the computer?' she said to her mother after they had put the dinner things in the dishwasher.

Helga sighed. 'What is it?'

'You'll see.'

She sat her mother down on the bed next to her, opened her laptop and showed her the graph of the bitcoin price.

'What on earth is this?'

'It's bitcoin. It's a cryptocurrency. Have you heard of it?'

'I think so. It sounds dodgy to me.'

'Dad gave me some. In January.'

'What! When?' Anger flared in Mum's eyes.

Dísa had expected this. 'I saw him in Akureyri. He made a trip up just to see me. To give me the bitcoin.'

'And you didn't tell me?'

'No.'

'Dísa! Why on earth not?'

Dísa tried to fight the impatience rising within her. 'Because you'd have gone apeshit.'

'Damn right I would have gone apeshit. In fact, I can feel myself going apeshit now.'

'OK. OK,' said Dísa, realizing she had gone about this wrong. 'Just hear me out first. And then you can get as angry as you want.'

Dísa watched her mother struggle to control her temper. She didn't usually lose it, but Dísa could feel the pressure of the money worries, see it in the tightness around her mother's eyes and lips.

'All right,' Helga said. 'So how many bitcoin did he give you?'

'Five.'

'Five! What's that worth? Five dollars? Fifty? That's not going to make much difference.' Then a thought struck her. 'Don't tell me, they're worth nothing. Your father really is useless.'

'They were worth five thousand when he gave them to me.'

'Really?' Helga raised her eyebrows. 'And now?'

'And now, thanks to a bit of trading I did in another cryptocurrency, the five bitcoin have become thirty-two.'

'That *sounds* good.' Mum was nodding her head.

'Take another look at this graph.' Dísa pushed her laptop in front of her mother.

Mum took another look. 'Is that nine *thousand* dollars?'

'It is.'

Helga was an anaesthetist; she could do arithmetic perfectly well. Her mouth dropped open.

'But that's about three hundred thousand dollars?'

Dísa grinned. 'Three hundred and thirteen.'

Anger was replaced by a flash of hope in her mother's eyes. Almost greed.

'But that's ridiculous, Dísa. That can't be right. And it's all yours?'

'It is,' said Dísa. 'Thanks to Dad.' The point had to be made.

'He was just lucky,' said Helga. 'Where did he hear about this bitcoin?'

'He's got a friend called Sharp from his banking days who lives in London. Sharp told him about it and fixed it up for him.'

'I remember Sharp,' said Mum. 'He was always smarter than Ómar. Managed to keep himself out of jail, for a start. Why didn't you tell me about this?'

'I wanted to, but Dad made me promise not to.'

'He made you promise?' The anger was back. 'You know you don't have to keep your promises to your father! He never kept any of *his* promises.'

'Mum! I've got three hundred thousand dollars! Thirty million krónur. Enough to keep the farm. If I can only get it out of bitcoin and into real money. I'm not sure how you do that.'

'Dísa, that's your money. You don't have to give it to us.'

Dísa smiled. '"Us". You said "us". Who do you mean by "us"?'

Helga looked confused. 'Well . . . Me. Grandpa.'

'You mean our family. Me, you, Anna Rós, Grandpa, Grandma?'

'Yes, I suppose I do.'

'Well, as far as I am concerned, it is ours. Dad gave it to me because he felt guilty about how he had let us all down, and he thought I could look after a good investment. But this is a way for him to help us when we really need it.'

'But it's *your* money.'

'It's *our* money.'

'Does Ómar know you are planning to give it to us?'

Dísa shook her head. 'He doesn't know about the problems with the farm. Or at least I haven't told him.'

Helga was about to lay into her ex-husband again when she stopped herself. Dísa could see the confusion in her mother's eyes. She knew her well enough to understand what she was feeling: anger with her ex-husband, excitement at the unbelievable amount of money that Dísa had somehow accumulated, relief that her money worries might be over, and doubt. Doubt that it was all too good to be true – too unreal.

Mum's eyes welled up with tears, and she gave Dísa a confused smile of desperation and happiness.

'I can't believe this! You are such a clever girl.'

She opened her arms and pulled Dísa to her, as they both sobbed with relief and joy.

# FIVE

Blábrekka cheered up. Grandpa and Grandma were told that Dísa had conjured up a fortune from the internet, and Grandpa had insisted on a long explanation of what exactly bitcoin was. Anna Rós was just very happy that Clyde wasn't going anywhere. Mum, too, suddenly became fascinated by how bitcoin worked, and how Dísa had managed to make so much money from the Ethereum coin.

Dísa was happy to see those lines around her mouth and eyes soften, and the warm smile that she loved so much return.

There still remained the problem of how to turn Dísa's bitcoin into krónur and get it into Helga's bank account in Iceland. But Helga said she had been able to borrow enough money to keep the farm going until they figured that one out.

They agreed that the best idea was for Dísa to ask Ómar, and to do it face to face, but to warn him in advance so he had time to find out how to sell the bitcoin and get the proceeds back to Iceland. To her intense frustration, Mum insisted that Dísa not tell her father about her plans to bail out the farm. Mum was worried that Dad wouldn't help Dísa sell her bitcoin if he knew what she was planning to use it for. Dísa thought the opposite, that he would be pleased, but she reluctantly accepted her perennial role as her parents' lying go-between.

It was a seven-hour bus trip from Akureyri to Reykjavík, which would take Dísa most of Saturday getting there and most of Sunday getting back. Plenty of time to do the homework that was backing up. But it seemed worth it, especially since Dad said he had an idea that required Dísa seeing him in person.

Dad met Dísa at the bus terminal in Mjódd and drove her back to his dilapidated flat in Nordurmýri in the centre of Reykjavík. He was bubbling – Dísa had never seen her father so excited – and it was all about bitcoin.

'Did you see what happened yesterday?' he said. 'The price smashed through ten thousand. Can you believe it? I *told* you it would go up.'

Dísa smiled. 'You said it would double this year, Dad. Actually, it went up ten times.'

'OK, OK. I was wrong.' He turned and grinned at his daughter. 'But I was *so* right.'

'Thanks, Dad. I can't thank you enough.'

'It's no problem,' Dad said. But she could tell from his smile he was pleased with her thanks. 'The best decision I ever made to give you that bitcoin. And your Ethereum trade was genius. I *knew* you would get this stuff.'

Dísa nodded happily. She was pretty pleased with herself, truth be told.

'But now you want to sell?'

Dísa nodded. 'The price can't keep going up forever. I think it's time to take my profits.'

'What will you do with the money?'

'Just put it in the bank,' Dísa lied. 'At least for now. Maybe I'll invest it in something else later.'

Dísa *hated* lying. So why did she always end up doing it anyway? It was her parents, of course. She never lied to anyone else. One day she would give up lying for them. One day soon.

'But I need to figure out how to sell the bitcoin and change it into krónur.'

'OK. Well, I've got an idea about that. Sharp's over from London.'

'The guy who put you into bitcoin in the first place?'

'That's him. And he's got a new idea. It's called Thomocoin. There's a presentation this evening and we should go.'

'But I don't want to buy some other cryptocurrency. I want to sell.'

'It'll be worth seeing, I promise you.'

Dísa frowned.

'Trust me. Aren't you glad you trusted me before?'

'I am,' Dísa acknowledged.

'Well then?'


The Thomocoin presentation took place in the underground auditorium of one of Reykjavík's large hotels. It wasn't exactly what Dísa had imagined a sober investment presentation would be like. There was loud music, expensive lighting and a real buzz among the hundred or so people who were there.

Dísa was intrigued.

The presentation was begun by a dark-haired Icelandic woman of about thirty named Fjóla who seemed almost comically overexcited. She demanded audience participation, and got it, encouraging cheers at the mention of Thomocoin, and rapturous applause as she introduced 'Iceland's foremost financial brain and Thomocoin's CEO', Sharp.

Sharp bounded on to the stage. He was a tall man, pretty cute, Dísa had to admit, with short fair hair, a square jaw, and bright blue eyes that danced enticingly before settling on his audience in a thrilling stare.

He admitted that his real name was Skarphédinn Gíslason and got the audience laughing when he explained how difficult that name was for foreigners outside Iceland. He explained that he had had a younger brother named Thomas who had died of leukaemia at the age of ten, and Thomocoin was named after him.

He then told the audience all about Thomocoin.

The problem, he said, with bitcoin and Ethereum and all the other cryptocurrencies was that they had been set up as digital currencies to rival the old-world offline paper currencies. What was needed was a new cryptocurrency that was designed to slot into the regulations and payment systems of the real world, yet keep the anonymity and trustworthiness and freedom from government interference. And it would be a way for people without bank accounts all over the world to receive their wages and pay their bills easily, something billions of people needed desperately.

Thomocoin was that currency.

He cut to a video of an old Swiss guy with a pointy grey beard who talked about regulation, then a smooth Ugandan with a pointy black beard who talked about how Thomocoin would revolutionize village life all over Africa, and then a Chinese woman with no beard whatsoever who talked about how a billion Chinese were itching to buy Thomocoin.

Finally Sharp asked the question that had been bothering Dísa. Why, with all those billions of people demanding to buy Thomocoin all over the world, had Sharp bothered with Iceland?

The answer he gave was that Iceland was the most advanced country in the world in digital payments, and, he said, Icelanders were the smartest people.

The crowd loved that. They knew he was being ironic, yet they believed he secretly meant it at the same time.

Thomocoin was going to be launched in two weeks, in time for Christmas. They had decided to launch it to the smartest early investors before they had an exchange set up ready to convert it into hard currency, and before they had the regulatory approvals, because that would give a chance for the guys who got in early to make a fortune. All they would need was a bit of patience and a bit of belief.

It all sounded pretty good to Dísa.

Afterwards, Dísa and Dad went up to the hotel bar to meet Sharp, who was there with Fjóla, a couple of young guys in T-shirts, and a few Icelandic admirers. Sharp seemed genuinely pleased to see Dad, and gave him a warm embrace.

'This is my daughter, Dísa,' Ómar said. Dísa glowed from the pride in his voice.

Sharp turned his piercing eyes on her. 'Hi, Dísa. You're the young woman who bought the Ethereum last winter, right? Your dad told me about you.'

'That's right,' Dísa said. 'It's all back in bitcoin now.'

'And now you want to take your profits? You know bitcoin is shooting up even faster now?'

'I know,' said Dísa. 'But from what I've read that means the price is getting near the top. I don't know where the top is, but I've made enough for now.'

Sharp grinned. 'Smart girl. Take a look at Thomocoin. Do your research. Check out the white paper on our website – it will tell you all you need to know. If you like what you see, use your bitcoin to buy Thomocoin when it comes out in a couple of weeks. Then wait until we set up the exchanges and get the regulatory approvals, and sell it. If you want. My guess is Thomocoin will prove to be just as good an investment as your Ethereum.'

'When will the exchange be ready?'

'Hard to say. It takes time and we want to do it properly. Six months? A year, max. In the meantime, talk to Fjóla. She's in charge of launching Thomocoin in Iceland.'

Fjóla smiled and handed Dísa a card emblazoned with the Thomocoin logo.

'Thanks, Sharp,' Dísa said. And then: 'I'm sorry about your little brother Thomas. Or Tómas,' she corrected herself, using the Icelandic version of the name.

Sharp paused. Frowned. And then nodded in acknowledgement.

'What shall I tell Krakatoa?' Fjóla asked her boss, pulling out her phone. 'He wanted to know how it went.'

'Tell him it went well,' said Sharp. 'Don't you think, Dísa?'

'Who's Krakatoa?' she asked.

'My partner,' said Sharp. 'He's the brains behind the operation.'

'Is he an Icelander too?'

'I think he's from Canada,' said Fjóla. 'Isn't he?'

'Vancouver,' said Sharp. 'But after this, we may make him an honorary Icelander.'

Dísa thought Thomocoin sounded good. It sounded very good. She'd check it out online, but it looked like it might be a good option for her bitcoin.

'Yeah,' she said. 'Tell him it went well.'

But one thing she had heard didn't quite ring true. Dísa wasn't totally convinced that Thomas, or Tómas, was real. Not that that mattered.

Or did it?

# SIX

Magnus looked down at the spiky blonde head on his lap, or what he could see of it behind the covers of a book. Something about trolls in the medieval north.

The set-up was both uncomfortable and very comfortable. It turned out Eygló liked to read and so did he, and they liked to read together.

Work was busy. To Magnus and Vigdís's frustration, the rape victim had withdrawn from her case, unwilling to give up her mobile phone's secrets. But the data-server heist had exploded. There had been two more break-ins; the value of the equipment stolen was now counted in the hundreds of millions of krónur. Magnus had been investigating the sales channel the thieves had used to offload the servers, and trying to track down any bitcoin transactions with which they could have been paid. More promising was a CCTV image of a suspicious blue van taken near one of the break-ins.

Some progress, but not enough. The pressure was on: the news websites were all over the story.

They were in Eygló's small flat in Kópavogur. Bjarki,

Eygló's eleven-year-old son, was playing *Football Manager* in his bedroom as usual. He had explained at great length to Magnus how he was managing Macclesfield Town, some tiny place in England, and powering it up to the English Premier League. Magnus didn't know much about English soccer, although he was trying to keep up with Bjarki's passion for Liverpool.

Frankly, Magnus couldn't give a damn about Macclesfield Town.

He was trying to get Bjarki interested in the Red Sox. He reckoned he'd snare him in the end with the statistics, but so far Bjarki was only showing polite interest in baseball.

Eygló looked on with wry amusement.

Soccer wasn't a bad game. Magnus had been pretty good at it when he was a little kid, playing at the Snaefell club in Stykkishólmur in the west of Iceland. Although they played it a bit at his middle school in Cambridge in Massachusetts, he had taken up real football. American football.

Ási had shown some early talent on the beach. Would he play for his own club team eventually? Icelanders were pretty good at soccer.

It was three weeks since Magnus had kicked a ball around on the beach with his son, and he couldn't help thinking about it. He didn't really understand why. Until a couple of months before he hadn't really thought about children. But now?

He couldn't wait to see Ási again. Christmas was coming. Could he get him a gift? Something small, or it would be weird. After all, Ási thought of Magnus as no more than a friend of his mother.

Ingileif had promised she would text, but she hadn't. Magnus was beginning to fear she wouldn't.

Patience! All he needed was patience.

'What's up, Magnus?' said the head on his lap, putting down her book. 'You're fidgeting.'

'Sorry.'

Eygló sat up. 'Are you thinking about Ási?'

Magnus nodded. 'I'm worried Ingileif isn't going to contact me.'

Eygló sighed. 'Then call her.'

'Should I send her a text?'

'No. Call her. Talk to her. Then you'll know what's what.'

'All right.' Magnus took out his phone as Eygló tactfully withdrew to the kitchen.

Magnus found Ingileif's number and called it. It rang and then went to voicemail.

He put the phone down, disappointed. He was just wondering whether to assume she was avoiding him when his phone buzzed.

It was her. 'Hi, Ingileif,' he said.

'Hi.'

'I was just calling to see how you were. And Ási.'

There was silence on the other end of the phone.

Uh-oh.

'Magnús. I know I said I would bring Ási to see you again, but now I don't think it's such a good idea.'

Magnus's blood went cold. 'Why not?'

'Hannes came back.'

'So what? You said Ási knows he isn't his father.'

'Yes. But Hannes says that if the three of us are to operate as a family, then you shouldn't be part of it. It will confuse Ási.' Ingileif hesitated. 'It will confuse *me*.'

'What do you mean?'

Ingileif sighed. 'On the beach at Álftanes I told you that Hannes had gone. I gave you a chance to come back. But you didn't want to. I respect that, I really do. But I need to make a clean break. I *need* to.'

'But . . .' Magnus was at a loss for words. 'But – but how could you take him back? He went off with another woman!'

'You took me back,' said Ingileif.

'Yes. But that was different.'

'Was it?' Ingileif said.

Magnus pulled back from the retort that was forming on his lips. 'I told you I have a girlfriend and I'm very happy with her,' he said. 'Can't you tell Hannes there is no chance of anything between us? I want to see Ási. I *need* to see Ási.'

Magnus was surprised by the strength of feeling as he uttered these last words. But he meant them.

'I'm very sorry, Magnús. The answer is no. I owe it to you to be crystal clear on that. No.'

'But I have a right to see him. And your sleazy husband doesn't have any right to stop me!'

Now anger flared in Ingileif's voice. 'You have no right, Magnús. You didn't know Ási even existed until three months ago. Even then, I didn't want to tell you. He's *my* son, and I want to bring him up in a stable family. With the man I love. Who, by the way, isn't you.'

'But – Ingileif! You have to let me see him. You *have* to.'

'No, I don't, Magnus. And don't even think of trying to force it.'

The line went dead. Magnus stared at his phone.

He fought to control tears welling up in his eyes. Where the hell did *they* come from?

Two hands rested on his shoulders, and he felt lips kiss the back of his head.

'I'm sorry, Magnús. I couldn't help hearing that.'

'She said no.'

'I heard.'

'I don't know why it bothers me so much,' said Magnus, turning to Eygló. 'But it does.'

'You need a family,' said Eygló. 'We all do.'

Magnus reached up to kiss her. 'I'm very glad I've got you.'

# PART TWO

**– 2020 –**

# SEVEN

He lay on his stomach at the brow of the hill, looking down the valley towards the fjord. A low, flat island floated close to the near shore. The cluster of white buildings that was the village of Dalvík squeezed itself between its mountain and the water, while a large blue trawler edged its way into the harbour.

It was a chilly September morning, but he was dressed for it. Rays of sunshine sprinkled the waters of the fjord, and the river winding down towards it. A tight black ball of moisture was rolling along the valley to the south-west in his direction.

A bit of rain would be good. A lot of rain would be better.

Enough to wash away evidence that he had been here.

Then he saw it. A lone figure on a horse, picking its way up the hillside towards him, at least a kilometre away.

He edged backwards until he was out of sight, and then hurried down the reverse slope along the path. The spot he had picked was in a kind of hollow created by a stream tumbling down the hillside, invisible from anywhere but above, high on the summit. And there was no one up there. Just a pair of ravens circling, their loud croaks echoing off the rocky walls across the valley.

He sat, removed his glasses – they were expensive and he didn't want to damage them – and grabbed his ankle, allowing himself to slump crookedly against a stone, a small day pack by his side.

He waited.

The horse appeared over the brow of the hill, a short, tough-looking animal with a reddish coat and a thick pale mane. The rider was preoccupied, and took a moment to spot him, even though he was only fifty metres away.

He waved and cried out. 'Hello!'

The rider saw him, and set her horse down the gentle slope at a fast trot, or rather a weird kind of smooth run he had never seen before.

He winced.

The rider pulled the horse up next to him and said something to him in rapid Icelandic.

'I've hurt my ankle,' he replied in English. 'I think I might have broken it.'

The rider jumped off her horse. 'I'm a doctor,' she said. 'Let me take a look.'

'Thank you.' He smiled, moved his leg, and then let out a short cry of pain.

The woman crouched down next to him. She was in her forties with thick red hair and a warm, comforting smile. Quite attractive, he thought.

'Let me take off your boot,' she said.

As she bent over his foot, he shifted his right hand out from beneath the day pack by his side and swung the knife hard into her stomach.

A moment later, he was hurrying along a path back up the side of the mountain, her riderless horse whinnying as it dashed in the opposite direction towards home.

# EIGHT

'Want some coffee, Petra?' Dísa asked. 'I've just made some.'

The girl blinked, pushing back her thick dark hair. She was wearing pyjamas and had just emerged from Jói's room. It was nearly eleven, but it was a Saturday. Jói was a night owl anyway – he usually worked late into the small hours of the morning, and his girlfriend was happy to do things his way.

Petra was happy pretty much all the time. Dísa envied her. She was Australian of Greek heritage, about Dísa's age, and had met Jói the year before when she had been a student at the university. She had decided to drop out of Australian uni, stay in Reykjavík and start a career as a barista. This suited her. She didn't seem to Dísa to do anything when she wasn't working except lie around next to Jói fiddling with her phone.

Jói seemed just as happy with that arrangement. Petra was attractive in an exotic way for Iceland: large and soft, with olive skin, sleepy black eyes and dark hair.

Dísa was in her first year at the university. She was studying economics and had planned to share a place with

Kata, her friend from Dalvík, who had signed up for English Literature. But then Kata's boyfriend Matti had suggested that he and Kata live together in Reykjavík – he was starting at the same time – and Dísa had released Kata from her obligation to share a flat with her.

Which meant Dísa was stuffed. Jói allowed her to stay with him and Petra in his flat in Gardabaer until she sorted herself out. At least six months of the coronavirus pandemic had kept the tourists away from Reykjavík, removing some of the pressure on housing.

'You won't have to put up with me much longer,' said Dísa. 'I think I've found somewhere.'

'No worries,' said Petra. 'You're good here.'

Dísa smiled, knowing Petra meant it. It was a lovely modern flat built just before the crash; large, triple-glazed windows looked out over the bay towards the President's residence on Álftanes. Nice, but not very big. Dísa was occupying Jói's study, and since he was working from home in the pandemic, fiddling about on his computer with whatever he did for the games company, that was a bit tight all around. Dísa tried to spend as much time as she could at the university. Jói seemed to do most of his work at night in the living room while she was asleep.

'Thanks, Petra.'

'Did you say you'd found somewhere?' Jói said, emerging from his bedroom, yawning.

'I hope so. I saw a girl last night. She's offered me a place in her flat. I need to see it first, but it sounds OK. She's on my course, but I don't know her very well. She seems nice.'

'Great,' said Jói. He gave her his habitual vacant smile. His fair hair coiled in tight curls around his brow and his round cheeks were so pale they were almost translucent. He was twenty-seven, but he had a look of mild innocence about him that made him seem much younger. Dísa sometimes thought he looked like an angel – an angel after a rough night, perhaps.

'Thanks for letting me crash here,' she said.

'No, it's been good,' said Jói.

'Yeah.' And it had. Dísa had always liked Jói and had resented the way their parents' domestic arrangements had kept her away from her brother. She hoped the month they had spent together would forge a bond they could keep as adults.

She wasn't certain how Jói felt about it; her intuition was he felt the same.

Her phone buzzed. She checked it.

'Hi, Anna Rós,' she said.

For a moment there was silence. Then the sound of a sob.

Dísa darted a look of panic towards her brother, who was pouring himself a bowl of cereal.

'Anna?'

'It's Mum. She's dead.'

'What!'

'Someone's murdered her. Stabbed her. I found her out here on the mountain. The police are on their way. It's horrible! You've got to come home, Dísa. You've got to come quick!'

# NINE

Magnus ladled chunks of lobster and scallops on to the linguine piled high on two plates and carried them to the table.

Tryggvi Thór poured two glasses of Sauvignon from the bottle. 'This looks great,' he said.

'I used to make it back in Boston,' Magnus said. 'There was always plenty of lobster around.'

'You should spend more Saturday nights here.'

'I might just do that.'

Tryggvi Thór glanced at his lodger. 'Eygló kicked you out, has she?'

'No, nothing like that,' said Magnus. 'I don't know. I just want to keep my independence, that's all.'

'Because I wouldn't be surprised if she had kicked you out.'

'She hasn't kicked me out.'

'Kicked yourself out?'

Magnus watched the old man's alert dark eyes watching him under black eyebrows.

'Not really,' said Magnus.

'Hm.' Tryggvi Thór slurped up his pasta. 'You know, I thought I'd be rid of you one of these days. It's been three years.'

'I know, I know,' said Magnus. For most of that time he had spent the majority of his evenings and weekends at Eygló's place, keeping his stuff in his room at Tryggvi Thór's house, paying rent, and occasionally showing up, especially when Eygló was travelling for her work. Everyone seemed content with that relationship: Magnus, Eygló, Tryggvi Thór and even Bjarki, who had stayed with him on Álftanes sometimes when Eygló was away.

Or at least he had thought everyone was content. Now he wasn't so sure.

That morning, Magnus had sent Ingileif a text:

*Hi. I hope you are all OK. Any chance I could see Ási some time?*

He hadn't received an answer yet.

His phone rang. He checked it: Detective Superintendent Thelma, head of Reykjavík CID, and Magnus's boss.

'Hi,' he said, putting down his fork. The linguine was good: he hoped he would get to finish it.

'I want you on the first plane to Akureyri tomorrow morning,' Thelma said.

'What is it?'

'A murder in Dalvík. Female, forty-seven. Doctor at the hospital in Akureyri. Stabbed while out riding this morning.'

'Isn't Ólafur the senior investigating officer?' Ólafur was the inspector in charge of the small CID in Akureyri. Murders were rare in Iceland, and it wasn't surprising that reinforcements would be sent up from Reykjavík, but

Magnus and Ólafur were the same rank, and Magnus knew Ólafur would object to Magnus showing up.

'Apparently, there is a cryptocurrency angle. Financial Crimes are not interested, so I decided that you are our cryptocurrency expert and I'm sending you. I don't care what Ólafur thinks, I'd like you to keep an eye on things.' Thelma didn't trust Ólafur any more than Magnus did.

'But I know virtually nothing about cryptocurrencies,' said Magnus.

'You know more than any of the rest of us.'

Magnus had eventually arrested the gang behind the bitcoin mining thefts, and it was true that during the investigation he had learned a bit about the cryptocurrency, though he would hardly call himself an expert.

But he definitely wanted to be involved in the Dalvík investigation, so he wasn't going to argue.

'All right. I'll be there.'

He hung up and turned back to his linguine.

'Was that your boss?' Tryggvi Thór asked.

'Superintendent Thelma, yes. Your old buddy.'

'Huh.' Tryggvi Thór glared at him under his thick eyebrows. Tryggvi Thór and Thelma pretended not to know each other, although Magnus had once spotted them together. Every now and then Magnus wound him up about it, although he had no idea what their relationship, if any, was. Tryggvi Thór certainly wasn't going to tell him.

'I'm going to the north tomorrow. Dalvík. There's been a murder.'

'Dalvík? Huh. Stinks of fish.'

# TEN

Grandpa was waiting for Dísa in the white terminal building in Akureyri. The instant she saw him she ran to him and threw her arms around him.

She pulled tight; she wouldn't let him go.

'Oh Dísa, Dísa,' he whispered in her ear. 'I'm so sorry. I'm so sorry.'

'I know, Grandpa, I know.'

Eventually, Dísa released him. He took her suitcase and led her out to his car.

'What happened?' she asked.

'Your mother was riding out on Takki on her usual route along the mountainside. She was alone.' Grandpa sighed. 'It looks like someone attacked her. Stabbed her with a knife.' He stared at the road ahead, a tremor running along his jawline. Dísa waited for him to continue. 'Takki came back to the farm in a right state, without her, so Anna Rós rode out to look for her with Gunni.' Gunni was a neighbour who kept a horse at Blábrekka. 'They found her just lying there.'

'Oh, my God! Poor Anna! Do they know who did it?'

'Not yet. The place is crawling with police. The inspector in charge is confident they will find the murderer.'

'Do they think it's someone local?'

'They don't know. They've been asking about Thomocoin.'

'Thomocoin?'

'I'd like to talk to you about your mum's Thomocoin later.'

'Sure,' said Dísa.

Her phone rang. 'Hi, Dad.'

'I heard what happened to Mum,' said her father's voice. 'Jói told me. I can't believe it.'

'I know.'

'Jói said you were going straight up to Dalvík?'

'I'm in Akureyri now. Grandpa's just picked me up from the airport.'

'That's good. Tell him I'm very sorry for him. And you. And everyone.'

Dísa glanced at her grandfather. 'Dad says he's sorry about Mum.'

'Tell him thanks.' Grandpa had no time for Dad after the way he had treated Helga, but Dísa knew he would put that behind him, at least for a few days.

'And how are you?' said Dad.

'I don't know. My brain has just been whirling since I heard. Jói was great. But I don't think it's sunk in yet.'

'It's good you're there,' Dad said. 'Give Anna Rós a hug from me. And look after her. And yourself.'

'I will.'

'I'd better stay away. But let me know when the funeral is; I'll come to that.'

'OK, Dad. I love you.'

She didn't often say that to her father, but God she meant it.

'I love you too, Dísa.'

It felt good to be back in the kitchen at Blábrekka with her family.

They had had their supper, but they gathered around Dísa as she ate her grandmother's lamb soup: Grandpa, Grandma, Dísa and Uncle Eggert, Helga's brother, who worked in the town hall in Akureyri.

Grief had struck them hard. Dísa, her grandparents and her uncle were stunned by it. Anna Rós was shattered. Sadness was alien to her, so it was disturbing for the others to see her face racked with such grief.

Grandma fussed with the soup, with the dishes, with Dísa's suitcase. Many more times than necessary, she asked the question on everyone's mind: Who could possibly have done this?

Grandpa said little, but patted Anna Rós's hand, and then Dísa's, and then reached for his wife's but she withdrew it, eager to keep moving.

Uncle Eggert was full of ideas about what the police might or might not do. Unsurprisingly, they had spent the day at the farm and were due to return tomorrow morning. He had watched way too many British crime dramas on TV.

Dísa liked her uncle. While most adults naturally gravitated towards her prettier, bubblier younger sister, Uncle Eggert had always seemed to be more interested in what she was up to. He had played volleyball himself when he was younger, and occasionally he would come and watch her matches, which was more than her mother ever did.

He was a couple of years younger than Helga. He had never liked the farm work he had had to do as a boy, and had escaped to Reykjavík, with a spell in California, before returning to Akureyri. There he had married, started a career in local government, bought a house and produced three children – Dísa's cousins – the oldest of which was eight. There was long-standing tension between him and Grandpa about the farm and Eggert's lack of interest in it. Dísa's theory was that neither one of them was a natural farmer, but at least Eggert realized it. In recent years the tension had thawed, and Eggert had even helped Grandpa with his computer, without which it was hard to run a farm in the twenty-first century.

They had been staring at each other all day, so Dísa's arrival was an opportunity for a change of subject. They asked her about university and the COVID virus in Reykjavík, how people were responding, how the case figures were beginning to rise again after falling to almost zero, and how she had to wear a mask to lectures – so far, in the pandemic, Icelanders had rarely worn masks. After an early surge in cases in the spring, Iceland had got the virus under control, to the extent that in the summer life had gone on almost as normal, apart from the lack of tourists. Then, in July, the government had let the tourists back in, and with them had come the virus, so that by now in September cases were ticking up.

It gave them all something to do, something to talk about.

At about ten o'clock, Eggert said he should be going home. Grandma and Anna Rós went up to bed, leaving Dísa with her grandfather.

'Dísa?' he said. 'Do you think you could get into Helga's Thomocoin account? I don't know how to do it.'

Dísa smiled weakly. 'Yeah. I set it up for Mum. I know where she keeps her wallet, and I set up her password.'

'Will you be able to give them instructions? To sell the Thomocoin?'

'I guess so,' said Dísa. 'Is the exchange running yet?'

Dísa had transferred all her bitcoin to Mum three years before. With Fjóla's help, she had set up a Thomocoin wallet for her mother and used the bitcoin to invest in it. Which had worked out well. The end of 2017 had been a wild ride for bitcoin. The price had doubled to almost twenty thousand dollars in December before crashing off, at one point falling 25 per cent in a single day. The new Thomocoin that Helga had bought had retained its value, and indeed the price had grown slowly but steadily over the following three years.

But in order to convert Thomocoin into real money, there needed to be an exchange through which to sell it.

'Not yet,' said Grandpa. 'The haters are still managing to stall it. But approval from the Icelandic government is very close.'

'I didn't know you knew much about Thomocoin,' said Dísa.

'I have to,' said Grandpa. 'The future of the farm depends on it. And I bought some myself, you know? Not nearly as much as your mother, but enough to make a nice little return.' He chuckled to himself. 'A lot of people in town bought it. And Eggert. And some of Helga's colleagues at the hospital.'

'I didn't know that,' said Dísa.

'Oh yes. Mind you, it was good for your mother. She got a cut of all the Thomocoin sold, a kind of commission for herself. Half in Thomocoin, half in bitcoin. Which she used to buy more Thomocoin.' Grandpa smiled. 'She had quite a pile.'

Dísa wasn't sure what to make of Grandpa's interest in her mother's crypto-fortune. Anxiety about the viability of the farm was certainly fair enough. But there was a flash of greed in his eyes, the same flash that she had seen occasionally in her mother's.

And why hadn't Mum told her that she had been persuading all and sundry to buy Thomocoin?

Dísa suddenly felt very tired. 'Don't worry, Grandpa. I'm sure I can get into Mum's wallet. But I'll do it later, OK?'

'OK,' said Grandpa, relieved.

'I'm off to bed now.'

Dísa lay on her bed, staring at the ceiling, thinking of her mother. Her smile. Her unruly red hair. Her infectious laugh. Her warmth. There was something about being hugged by your mother that nothing – no one – could replace.

She tried to think of her first-ever memory of her. Was it in that house in Fossvogur? No, it was being dropped off at nursery and screaming her head off at the fear that she was going to be abandoned. She had sat on her mother's lap and Mum hugged her. Then Mum had stayed with her as they both watched the other kids playing.

Eventually Mum had left Dísa, and it had been OK because Dísa felt strong.

How old had Dísa been? Three?

The tears came. She sobbed.

Then, later, spent, she waited for sleep to come. But it wouldn't.

Thoughts of Thomocoin drifted into her consciousness and she hung on to them as a distraction. There wouldn't be a problem logging into Mum's wallet, would there? She knew the password for Mum's cold wallet, and she knew where it should be. *Should be.* What if Mum had put it somewhere different?

Well, then she knew where Mum had hidden the paper copy of the private key. In a box under a stone at the back of the farm, next to the rock where the hidden people had lived for centuries.

Most farms in Iceland had a family of hidden people living with them, usually in an identified rock or mound. Neither Grandpa nor Grandma put much store in them, but Dísa remembered her great-grandmother had been a firm believer. In fact, just after Mum had been born, a hidden woman had come to her great-grandmother in the night to tell her the new baby should be named Helga.

Helga it was. You didn't argue with the hidden people. And you certainly didn't argue with Great-Grandma.

Dísa had suggested the hiding place, remembering what Dad had told her about how he had stashed his private key at his summer house, which was supposed to be inhabited by the local hidden people. She and Mum had selected a stone by the rock where the Blábrekka hidden people lived, and dug a little hole underneath it, together.

Sleep didn't come.

Dísa got up and went down the landing to her mother's room, switching on the light. She stood there, silent, her gaze drifting over the bed, the bedside table, the wardrobe. Mum had made the bed that morning, but there was underwear strewn on a chair. And there were photographs. Of Anna Rós, of Grandpa and Grandma. Even of Great-

Grandma. And one of Dísa, aged about five, laughing in her mother's lap.

The cold wallet USB stick should be at the back of the bottom drawer under her mother's sweaters. Dísa opened it, and felt around. Nothing.

What now? Should she search the whole room? Maybe it would be in the desk by the window?

She couldn't face it.

The sensible thing to do would be to wait until it turned up somewhere, as it probably would once they started going through Mum's things. But Dísa didn't want to wait. And she liked the idea of looking in the secret hiding place she and her mother had dreamed up together for an eventuality like this.

So she pulled on jeans and a sweater, crept downstairs and out of the back door, making sure not to awaken Hosi, the farm sheepdog.

It was a cool, fresh night. The sky was clear, and a three-quarter moon illuminated the mountainside above the farm in a shimmering blue. Dísa stared at it, allowing her eyes to adjust. Blue slope. Blábrekka.

A dim, glimmering curtain of green swished and swayed in the sky above the horizon to the north, over the fjord. She had missed the northern lights in Reykjavík. They were much less visible there with all the ambient light from the city, whereas here in the valley the heavens were dark and clear, and the aurora could perform in all its glory. When there was no cloud, of course.

She knew that the large barn would be full of a warm, seething mass of wool. The week before, Grandpa and the other farmers in the valley had ridden up to the mountain with their dogs to bring the sheep down for the winter. Many would be sent off to the slaughterhouse at Blönduós, but the survivors would be shorn and spend the winter indoors until right after their lambs were born the following spring.

The elves' rock was fifty metres higher up the slope from the barn, over rough ground. Dísa found the stone, the largest of a group scattered next to it.

Dísa didn't believe in hidden people but, nevertheless, she felt compelled to announce her intentions.

'Good evening,' she said to the stone. 'I'm sorry to disturb you. I just need to get something of my mother's. She died yesterday.' Dísa looked up and along the hillside to where Anna Rós had found Mum. 'But you know that, don't you?'

She listened for a response. There wasn't one.

For a second she felt foolish. Yet she thought of her ancestors on the farm, going back countless centuries, who had communicated with the hidden people by this very rock.

It wasn't so dumb.

She knelt down and lifted the flat stone. Underneath was the shallow hole and the clear plastic food-storage box she had watched Mum place there, a folded sheet of paper dimly visible inside.

She carried it indoors.

Back in her bedroom, she flipped open her laptop and logged on to the Thomocoin site, carefully typing out the string of characters of the wallet address and then the private key which her mother had copied out on that scrap of paper three years before.

Wow.

At the current Thomocoin price of $338, Mum's total holdings were worth $2.6 million!

Wow.

Dísa scrolled over the transaction history. Mum's initial purchase was there at the Thomocoin launch price of a hundred dollars. So the price had more than tripled over three years. Not a bad result since during that time prices of all the other cryptocurrencies had fallen sharply and had only recently recouped their losses. As Grandpa had said, more Thomocoin had been added to the wallet over the years with the label 'commission', and Mum had made a steady series of top-up payments, presumably with the bitcoin she had also received for selling Thomocoin to all her friends.

For a small town, Dalvík contained quite a few wealthy people, Dísa knew. Throughout the twentieth century, it had been a big fishing port, its harbour crammed full of small fishing boats, which meant that when in the 1980s fishing quotas had been granted to every fisherman based on his catch in the year 1983, it had been a bonanza for many of the town's inhabitants. Over the years, almost all the fishermen had sold their quotas on to the large fishing company which now dominated the town and its harbour. The bright little fishing boats had disappeared, to be replaced by large trawlers fishing the consolidated quotas with brutal efficiency. As a result, Dalvík's former fishermen had serious money to invest. As did their heirs.

Mum had known them all.

For the first time, Dísa wondered what would happen to all her mother's money. She didn't know if Mum had made a will, but she knew that under Icelandic law the children inherited most of it anyway. Which meant her and Anna Rós.

With $2.6 million they should be able to secure the future of Blábrekka.

Yet another tear ran down Dísa's cheek.

Mum would like that.


The back streets of Dalvík were dead. Which was just how they should be at 1 a.m. in the middle of a pandemic. They had probably been just as dead at 10 p.m., but he wanted to be safe.

He always wanted to be safe.

He was walking uphill out of town towards the ski lift, which was dimly discernible in the moonlight. Behind him the horizon shimmered green – the northern lights. He paused for a moment to admire them, then left the road to skirt the village along the lower slopes of the mountain.

As he approached the church, silhouetted against the fjord, he counted back to figure out which was the house he wanted.

It was large by Icelandic standards, a simple rectangular structure made of concrete with a corrugated metal roof, a double garage and a shed. He had decided to try the shed first, around the side of the house.

It was unlocked. He couldn't see anything inside, but he avoided risking the flashlight on his phone until he had shut the door behind him.

The shed was full but well organized. A snowmobile took pride of place in the centre, and two sea kayaks leaned against one wall. Shelves stacked with tools, tarpaulins and fishing equipment lined the back wall. Bags of salt, shovels and spades crowded the front wall near the door.

He stood and thought. He needed a good hiding place, but not one that was *too* good.

His eyes alighted on the kayaks.

Perfect.

He unslung the day pack from his shoulder and took out

a plastic bag. He extracted the item with his gloved hands, and dropped it into the kayak, out of sight a little way down from the seat, at about the place where your feet would go.

Then he turned off the flashlight on his phone and slipped out of the shed into the Dalvík night.

# ELEVEN

The aeroplane descended as it approached Akureyri, following a broad valley with mountains pressing in on either side until it passed over a small airport and banked 180 degrees above the town to head back towards the runway at the head of a fjord. Although Akureyri was the largest town in Iceland outside the Reykjavík area, it was tiny by American standards: fewer than twenty thousand souls clustered around a twin-pronged church on a hill at the head of a long thin fjord that pointed due north towards the Arctic Ocean.

Magnus searched for the settlement of Dalvík halfway up the western shore, but it was hidden by a kink in the fjord. He remembered he had stayed there once with his father and little brother on one of their joint trips back to Iceland from Boston when he was a teenager, but he couldn't recall much about it, except there were a lot of fishing boats.

As the plane landed he checked his phone. One missed call. Eygló.

He considered skipping it, but if he was going to call her

back, now was the time to do it, before he became fully embroiled in the investigation.

'Hi, Magnús,' she said as she picked up.

'Hi.'

'I got your text that you won't be here tonight. When are you expecting to get back?'

'Hard to say. You know what it's like. If we crack the case today, then maybe tomorrow night. But it could be longer, maybe even a week or more.'

'Oh.'

'What is it?'

'I need to talk to you.'

'Can it wait?'

'Not really. I got an interesting email on Friday,' Eygló said.

'Oh yes?'

'It was from an English university. Southampton. They want to talk to me about lecturing there.'

'That's good.' Magnus hesitated. 'Would they want you to move?'

'Not right away. I can do it on Zoom from next term. But they would like me to move there next academic year, if I get the job. Next September.'

'I see.'

'I think I'm going to say "no", but I wanted to speak to you first.'

'Would it be good for your career?'

'Yes. It's a good university. And it will make the TV documentaries easier to do if I am living close to London.'

'What about Bjarki?'

'A couple of years in British schools would be good for him.'

'Sounds to me like you should at least go for the

interview,' Magnus said. 'Or talk to them on Zoom or something.'

Silence. Although she was hundreds of kilometres away, Magnus could feel Eygló's expression. Not good.

'Eygló? What is it?'

'Don't you know what it is?'

Magnus knew. But he didn't know what to say.

'Bye, Magnús.' And she was gone.

Magnus stared out of the aircraft window as it taxied towards the terminal.

On the surface, all was well with his relationship with Eygló. But for almost a year now, she had been signalling she wanted more. She wanted more permanence. She wanted Magnus to actually live with them. She wanted to get married. She wanted to have a child with him.

And he didn't. Not really.

He didn't understand his lack of enthusiasm, and neither did she.

After all, he had been searching for permanence for years, for a family, for a place he could call home, and Eygló was offering that. He and she got on well together. She understood him. Small, lithe and sexy, she was undeniably attractive, in an impish way.

He loved her.

Didn't he?

He said he did.

In which case, why didn't he leap at Eygló's suggestion that they build a life together?

Magnus hadn't given her an answer. He hadn't even really acknowledged the question. He was hiding from it. Which was why he had spent the first Saturday night in weeks at Tryggvi Thór's house.

But now Eygló was framing an ultimatum. Did Magnus

care whether she went to England? Either he did or he didn't. And if he did care, what did that mean?

The plane came to a halt and the passengers scrambled to their feet, eager to be released.

At some point very soon Magnus would have to answer that question.

But not now. Now he had a murder to solve.

Árni's police car roared into Dalvík, lights flashing. Magnus tried not to shut his eyes as kerbs flew by and pedestrians stared. When he had picked Magnus up from the airport, Árni had said it was important to get to Ólafur's morning briefing in time, but Magnus knew Árni just liked to drive police cars fast. The journey along the flat straight road running along the side of the fjord from Akureyri to Dalvík had been exhilarating.

It had been good to see Árni's goofy grin again. He wasn't the world's greatest detective, but he and Magnus had worked together in Reykjavík for three years, and Árni had once taken a bullet for Magnus, literally, ending up in hospital. He had married, got promoted to sergeant and moved up to Akureyri, his wife's town. Magnus didn't see much of him now, although they had worked successfully together three years before on a murder at Glaumbaer a little further west along the north coast, the case on which Magnus had met Eygló.

Árni screeched to a halt outside the police station, a low scruffy white building – little more than a shed – with a green metal roof just back from the harbour. Between car and station, Magnus caught a whiff of fish, just as Tryggvi Thór had predicted. They were late, but only by a couple of minutes.

Inspector Ólafur was taking the briefing. He had been in charge of CID in Akureyri since Magnus had first arrived in Iceland. Now in his late forties, tall and lean, he was one of the old-school Icelandic policemen and had been suspicious of Magnus and his foreign methods when they had worked together in the past.

Magnus doubted he had changed.

Ólafur interrupted himself when he saw Magnus and Árni enter the crowded room. 'Magnús? I'm surprised to see you here. I was expecting someone from Financial Crimes.'

'I'm afraid you've got me,' said Magnus.

'We asked for someone to look into the critto-currency angle.'

'I can do that.'

Ólafur allowed his furrowed brow to rise a couple of millimetres. 'Good. I was just running through what we've got so far.'

Magnus recognized two of the detectives whom he had worked with on the Glaumbaer case three years before. There were also a number of uniformed officers, presumably from Akureyri as well as the locals from Dalvík and nearby Siglufjördur, and Edda, head of the forensics team in Reykjavík. She would have been called up right away.

Ólafur described how Helga had been found by the victim's daughter, Anna Rós, and Gunnar Snaer Sigmundsson, a neighbour who stabled a horse at Blábrekka. It appeared that the victim had been stabbed once in the stomach with a large hunting or fishing knife. No sign of clothing removal or sexual assault. Nothing stolen. The only relevant forensic evidence so far was a partial footprint a few feet away from the body. They might learn more that afternoon after the autopsy had been done.

No obvious suspects as yet.

Helga seemed to get on well with her parents at Blábrekka. She had a daughter at home and another at university in Reykjavík. There was an ex-husband in Reykjavík and a stepson. No current relationship, at least none that had emerged yet – an angle which had to be looked into further. Ólafur assigned a detective to interview her colleagues at the hospital.

Only one sighting of anyone on the mountain so far. Gunnar – the neighbour who had found the body – said he had seen someone walking alone down from the mountain towards the road when he had taken his dog for a walk before driving to Blábrekka. He had never got close, and so Gunnar couldn't give much of a description, apart from the fact that the walker was wearing glasses and a blue woolly hat, and carrying a small backpack.

They needed to find that man. Door-to-door interviews at the scattered houses and farms between Blábrekka and Dalvík. Ólafur would talk to the press. The police would put an appeal up on the local Dalvík Facebook group, which was already buzzing with gossip.

Helga didn't have enemies, as far as they knew so far. She had, however, sold a 'critto-currency', as Ólafur called it, to a number of locals. Thomocoin. It had done very well and a lot of people had made good money out of it, but the police needed to find out more. Which is why Ólafur had asked for help from Financial Crimes.

That with a pointed look at Árni and Magnus.

'They didn't want to know,' said Magnus. 'That's why Superintendent Thelma sent me.'

'Why didn't they want to know?' Ólafur asked.

'That's a very good question,' said Magnus. 'I'll find out.

And I'll find out more about this Thomocoin. Can Árni help me? I could use some local knowledge.'

Ólafur nodded and doled out tasks for the day.

As the team broke up, Ólafur approached Magnus. 'Good to have you on board,' he said with a stiff smile. 'We can always use help here.'

'I'll do what I can,' said Magnus.

Ólafur nodded. 'Just remember that I am the senior investigating officer. Don't do anything without clearing it with me first. Understood?'

'Of course,' said Magnus. 'Árni and I will talk to Helga's family to get a better idea about her involvement in this Thomocoin. And I'll see what I can get out of Financial Crimes.'

'Go do it.'

# TWELVE

Dalvík was a prosperous little town of well-maintained white houses, schools, playgrounds and kids on bicycles. Its harbour hosted an impressive array of sheds, concrete wharves, trucks and shipping containers. There were few actual fishing boats in port: most of the smaller boats had sold their quotas to the big trawlers long ago.

A large white church with blue trim overlooked the village, and above the church rose a steep boulder of a mountain, the summit of which was bizarrely emblazoned with the number seventeen in last year's snow.

Blábrekka stood a few kilometres outside Dalvík on the slopes of a broad, green, rather beautiful valley. Magnus was reminded of the famous phrase in *Njal's Saga*, one of his favourites, where the great warrior Gunnar decides not to follow Njal's advice to run away from his farm, despite the danger from his enemies: *How fair the slopes are.*

It didn't end well for Gunnar.

The farm had the usual accoutrements: a green 'home meadow', half a dozen horses in an adjacent field, a large barn for the sheep to spend the winter in, huge round white plastic bales of hay and bits of machinery scattered around. From a distance, Blábrekka looked prosperous, but at close quarters it was clear there was a lot of work to be done. Paint peeling, broken doors and fences, old harrows rusting, a 1970s Land Rover that wasn't going anywhere.

Interesting.

They parked next to Edda's forensics van and a couple of police cars. A woman of about seventy answered the door, small anxious eyes, lines pointing down a mottled red face, her dark hair hanging wildly around her cheeks. She was wearing a traditional patterned lopi jersey with buttons at the top.

She introduced herself as Íris and led them through to the kitchen, where they were greeted by a sheepdog and a tall, bald man, also in his seventies, with a stoop and a matching sweater.

'Hafsteinn,' he said. 'Hafsteinn Eggertsson. I'm Helga's father.'

His wife fussed about getting Magnus and Árni coffee and some cinnamon rolls, which Árni grabbed unnecessarily quickly.

'I'm sure you have spoken at length to my colleagues yesterday,' Magnus began. 'I've come to ask you about Helga's dealings in Thomocoin. I understand that Helga had invested in it herself, and that she sold it to a number of friends and neighbours?'

'She did,' said Hafsteinn. 'Including me and her brother. But if you want to talk about that kind of stuff, Dísa is the expert. My granddaughter.'

'I'll get her,' said Íris, leaving the room, and a minute later returning with a very tall, nervous-looking girl with light brown hair.

Hafsteinn and Íris seemed proud of their

granddaughter, and with good reason. She gave a clear explanation of what Thomocoin was and how she had introduced it to her mother. Then she fetched her laptop, logged into her mother's wallet, and showed Magnus her holdings.

'Am I reading this right?' said Magnus. 'Two point six million dollars. Not krónur?'

'Dollars,' said Dísa.

'Jesus,' said Magnus. He turned to Árni. 'Does Ólafur know she had that much Thomocoin?'

'We only discovered it last night,' said Hafsteinn. 'When Dísa checked. We knew she had a few hundred thousand. Enough to pay off the mortgage on the farm. But not *that* much.'

'I have to ask this,' said Magnus. 'Who inherits? Did Helga have a will?'

'I'm due to see our lawyer tomorrow,' said Hafsteinn. 'I know she made a will right after the divorce, and I assume she left it all to Dísa and her younger sister, Anna Rós.'

'Mum was going to use the money to bail out the farm,' said Dísa. 'And if I inherit it, that's what I'll do with it too. And so will Anna Rós.'

'And how old is Anna Rós?'

'She's sixteen.'

'She found the body,' said Árni to Magnus, with knowing emphasis.

Dísa spotted it. 'You don't think Anna Rós did this?' she said with a look of horror. 'That's just mad. Totally crazy.'

Árni had picked up the wrong end of the stick and started waving it around the room. 'No, not at all,' said Magnus. 'I know how devastated both you and she must be about your mum. But in a murder investigation everyone gets asked difficult questions.'

He smiled. Dísa was watching him. She seemed to trust him. 'All right.'

'Is it easy to sell this Thomocoin?' Magnus asked. 'Is it quoted on one of the cryptocurrency exchanges? Coinbase or Binance, for example?' He had checked his notes on the bitcoin-mining heist on the plane to refresh his memory about cryptocurrency.

'That's a very good question,' said Dísa. 'The answer is no, or at least not yet.'

'Any day now,' said Hafsteinn.

Dísa ignored her grandfather. 'Thomocoin was launched almost three years ago, in December 2017. They said then they were working on an exchange that would allow investors to sell their Thomocoin for dollars or euros or even krónur, and it'd be ready in, like, a few months. But it still hasn't been set up.'

'Why not?' asked Magnus.

'They say that the regulators are taking their time.'

'It's the haters,' growled Hafsteinn.

'Haters?'

'Yes. The big banks. The central banks. The governments. They all need to keep control of money. Thomocoin scares the crap out of them. If we all use Thomocoin, then who will need dollars? Who will need banks? So they've launched a global PR campaign to discredit cryptocurrencies, especially Thomocoin.'

'What do you think?' Magnus said, turning to Dísa.

She glanced at her grandfather, who was glaring at her.

'Maybe,' she said diplomatically. 'I know Mum was worried about it. She called me last week to ask me what I thought. To be honest, I haven't been following Thomocoin that closely. I gave Mum all my bitcoin three years ago. But it is a bit odd that it's taken so long.'

Hafsteinn snorted.

Magnus wondered where Dísa had got her bitcoin from. Drugs? Very unlikely, looking at her. Bitcoin mining? A relative?

'The thing is,' Dísa went on, 'if there is a problem, it wouldn't just be for her. I didn't realize it until Grandpa told me last night, but Mum persuaded all kinds of people in Dalvík to buy Thomocoin.'

'And at the hospital,' Hafsteinn added.

'And if the exchange never materializes, presumably they'll all be in trouble?' Magnus raised his eyebrows. Dísa knotted hers.

'The exchange will happen,' said Hafsteinn firmly.

'Did Helga ever say anything about her worries to you?' Magnus asked the old man.

'Not really,' said Hafsteinn.

'Yes, she did, Steini.' His wife spoke for the first time. 'That's why she went to Reykjavík last week. To speak to Ómar about it.'

'Ómar?' Magnus asked.

'Helga's ex-husband,' said Hafsteinn.

'He was the one who originally told me about Thomocoin,' said Dísa. 'A friend of his set it up. I didn't know Mum came to Reykjavík last week, Grandpa,' she said to her grandfather. 'Why didn't she come and see me?'

'Flew down and back in the day,' Íris said.

'Is he the one you originally got the bitcoin from?' Magnus asked Dísa lightly.

'Er . . .' Dísa bore the expression, so familiar to Magnus, of an honest person who has just incriminated herself.

'Never mind,' he said. Buying bitcoin was still illegal in Iceland, as far as he knew; he wasn't sure about Thomocoin.

But he wanted Dísa's help and trust, not her confession. 'Can you give me your father's details?'

After he had written them down, Magnus asked for the names of people Helga had sold Thomocoin to. Hafsteinn reeled off a list of a dozen names that he knew about, including himself, his son Eggert and Gunni Sigmundsson. Dísa explained that Helga had received a commission from every sale, and that she had in turn bought the Thomocoin from a woman called Fjóla Rúnarsdóttir.

'Multi-level marketing,' said Magnus.

'What's that?' Hafsteinn asked.

'More commonly known as a pyramid scheme. You get a commission on every product you sell to your friends. It could be vitamin supplements. Or cleaning products. Or a new cryptocurrency. Then when your friends sell the product to *their* friends, you get a cut of their commission on that. So the higher up the chain you are, or the closer to the top of the pyramid you are, the more money you make.'

'Yes. I think that's the way it worked,' said Hafsteinn. 'Sounds clever to me.'

'Until eventually, someone ends up with lots of cleaning products and no one to sell it to. Or lots of cryptocurrency.'

Dísa was watching Magnus closely. 'Maybe Mum was right to be worried.'

'Did Helga keep a complete list of those names?' Magnus asked.

'I don't know,' said Hafsteinn.

'She will have done, knowing Mum,' said Dísa. 'It'll be on her computer. You took that yesterday.'

Magnus turned to Árni, who nodded.

'What about the password to your mother's Thomocoin account? Can you give us that, please?'

'It's called a private key.' Dísa looked at her laptop, open to her mother's wallet on the Thomocoin website. 'Don't you need a warrant for that?'

'We've got a warrant for her computer,' said Árni. 'We can easily extend that to her passwords.'

'Then do that,' Dísa said. 'The thing is, if you've got the private key, then you can take all her money. Just like that.'

'Don't you trust the police?' said Árni, bristling.

'I think it would be smart to have a judge or someone like that involved,' said Dísa nervously.

Magnus smiled. 'You're quite right. We'll get a warrant. And we'll ensure that a judge is around when the private key is first used.'

# THIRTEEN

Magnus and Árni headed back to Akureyri to interview Eggert, Helga's brother.

'What was all that about the warrant for the private key, or whatever it's called?' said Árni as he was driving along the shore of the fjord, only slightly more slowly than he had been going earlier that morning. 'There's a good chance our existing warrant will cover it.'

'Dísa's right: we need to be careful about that. With the private key, anyone can just transfer the money to their own wallet.'

'But we're the police!'

'There was a big case in the States a few years ago. They took down Silk Road, a kind of eBay for drugs on the dark web. Two separate law-enforcement officers stole bitcoin from Silk Road during the investigation, once they got their hands on the private keys.'

'But that's America,' said Árni. 'This is Iceland. No one here is going to steal anything.'

'Probably not,' said Magnus, although he wasn't convinced. In his experience Icelanders could become a little complacent about their honesty and probity – until the next scandal came along. 'Dísa is a very smart girl, and she can be useful to us. The thing is to win her trust. And accusing her little sister of murdering her mother isn't the best way of going about it.'

'You always say we should think outside of the box,' said Árni. 'Anna Rós found the body. She had the motive. Dísa herself said the farm needed saving.'

'She also said her mother intended to use the Thomocoin to do it.' Magnus had indeed once told Árni he should think outside the box. He regretted it; Árni mostly needed to do more thinking *inside* the box.

From the car, Magnus called Vigdís back in Reykjavík and asked her to interview Ómar, Helga's ex-husband.

Then he called Sigurjón, a sergeant in Financial Crimes with whom he had worked a couple of times, on Sigurjón's mobile.

'Hello?'

'Hi, Sigurjón, it's Magnús Ragnarsson. Sorry to ring you on a Sunday. I'm in Dalvík, working on the murder. Thelma asked me to take a look at the Thomocoin angle.'

'Oh, yes?' Sigurjón sounded hesitant.

'She said you guys didn't want to know.'

'That's true.'

'Why?'

'I can give you the official version.'

'What's that?'

'Thomocoin is an unregulated cryptocurrency. As such, it is not the Icelandic authorities' responsibility. If Icelandic citizens invest in it, it's entirely their own decision; they can't expect any help from us if it goes wrong. Once we start investigating, we're saying we accept responsibility for regulating it, and that's something we definitely don't want to do. Orders from the minister.'

'Which minister?'

'That's a good question. It's not entirely clear. Finance? Justice? The Prime Minister?'

'Is it going to go wrong?'

'Maybe.'

'Has it already gone wrong?'

Silence for a moment. 'Maybe.'

'All right. What's the unofficial version?' Magnus was glad Sigurjón wasn't in the office; it would be easier for him to speak out of turn at home.

'It's a political hot potato. Some politicians want Iceland to embrace cryptocurrency as tomorrow's financial technology. Others want to have nothing to do with it. There are certain politicians who are lobbying for Thomocoin to be recognized as an official currency. Other politicians, and my bosses, think we shouldn't touch it. Especially after the MLATs we've received from the FBI.'

MLATs were mutual legal assistance treaty requests for information.

'What are they investigating?'

'Thomocoin. An Icelandic national, Skarphédinn Gíslason, who lives in London.'

'Investigating for what?'

'The usual. Conspiracy to commit securities fraud and money laundering.'

'That doesn't sound good for Thomocoin,' said Magnus. 'Or its investors.'

'No. Or anyone who was supposed to be regulating it. Which is why my bosses don't want to get involved.'

'How many Icelanders have bought it?'

'Don't know. We've heard of a few. But we're not counting.'

'Shouldn't you be? If it's fraud.'

'That's what the Americans say, not us. Some of our politicians still think it's the future of money. It's a minefield, Magnús.'

'OK. I get it,' said Magnus. 'But I'm investigating a murder. I need answers.'

'And I get that.'

'Have you got the names of the FBI agents who sent the MLAT?'

'Yeah, but I'd need to log on to the system at the station. They'll be closed today anyway. I can send you the details first thing in the morning.'

'Thanks, Sigurjón. That would be great. Investing in Thomocoin isn't illegal then?'

'No. That's precisely what the fuss is about.'

'But bitcoin is?' Magnus remembered Dísa had mentioned she used to own some.

'It's a grey area. You can own it, but you can't buy it or sell it under the Foreign Exchange Act. Although I wouldn't be surprised if they change that. Mining it always has been legal, of course. All the programs chugging away on those servers out by the airport. But you know all about them.'

'Indeed I do. Thanks, Sigurjón.' Dísa's ownership of bitcoin might be a useful stick to prod her or possibly her father with at some point in the future.

'No problem. I'm sorry we can't do more. And Magnús?'

'Yeah.'

'Let me know what you turn up. Unofficially. I have a feeling our policy is going to change on this all of a sudden, and when it does it would be useful to have a jump on it.'

## FOURTEEN

Eggert Hafsteinsson lived in a house of green concrete up the hill from the police station in Akureyri, with a wife, three kids, a cat and a view through trees to the fjord. He had just taken one of his kids to basketball practice when Árni and Magnus showed up outside his house.

He was long-limbed, with thinning mousy-brown hair and small round spectacles, and he was wearing a disconcertingly bright orange long-sleeved T-shirt.

He led Magnus and Árni through to a living room. The smell of roast lamb for Sunday lunch wafted in from the kitchen. A small, wan woman wearing an apron appeared, introducing herself as Eggert's wife Karen, and offered coffee.

There were clear signs of distress and concern on Eggert's face, but he seemed willing to speak to them.

'How's it going? Do you have any suspects yet? I thought the first twenty-four hours were the key?'

'There's some truth to that,' said Magnus, not answering Eggert's first question. 'We'd like to ask you about Thomocoin.'

'Do you think that has anything to do with Helga's murder?'

'That's what we want to find out,' said Magnus. 'I understand you bought some from her?'

'Well, not directly from her. From Thomocoin itself. But Helga said she would get a commission. Which was fine with me. I think I get one too if I persuade any of my friends to buy it.'

'And have you?'

'No. That's not my thing.'

'Why did you buy it?'

'It seems like a great idea. It was Dísa's, really. Have you met her? Helga's daughter?'

Magnus nodded.

'I think her father Ómar told her about it. He used to be a banker, but he got caught out after the *kreppa*. I'm not sure exactly what he did, but he ended up in jail for it. Thomocoin is legal, isn't it?'

'It's not illegal,' said Magnus, remembering his conversation with Sigurjón.

'How much did you buy?' asked Árni.

'A lot,' Eggert replied. He took a deep breath and lowered his voice, possibly so his wife in the kitchen couldn't hear. 'Three million.'

'Dollars?' said Magnus, raising his eyebrows.

Eggert laughed. 'No. Where would I get that kind of money? Krónur. That's, what, twenty thousand dollars? That's a lot of money, don't you agree? I mean, Thomocoin sounds like a good investment, but it's clearly risky. My investment's worth nearly sixty thousand dollars now, according to the latest price. So it's done well.'

There was something about Eggert which reminded Magnus of his niece, Dísa. It wasn't just the lanky awkwardness and the brown hair; it was also the shy intelligence.

'Do you have any concerns about it?' Magnus asked.

'Thomocoin?' Eggert paused. 'Well, it sounds like a good idea to me. Digital currency must be the future, and the blockchain must be the way to go. But they promised there would be an exchange where investors could sell their Thomocoin for real money and that hasn't happened yet. That's got to be a question mark.'

'Did you talk to your sister about the exchange, or lack of it?'

'Oh yes. Last time was about three weeks ago.'

'And did she seem concerned?'

Eggert hesitated. 'Not exactly. But she seemed less confident than she had been.'

'Did that worry you?'

'No. I was pleased. I hoped she'd find out what was going on. Why? Should I be worried?'

Magnus didn't answer that one. 'Did you ever meet a man called Skarphédinn Gíslason?'

'Sharp? He's the CEO of Thomocoin. I knew him when I was working in Reykjavík many years ago, but not since then. I've seen him on Thomocoin videos. Impressive guy. He used to work with Helga's ex-husband Ómar at a bank.'

'Do you know Ómar?'

'I did. Back when they were married. I went to their wedding, of course, and I used to go and see him and Helga sometimes when I lived in Reykjavík. He acted the hot-shot banker in those days. But then he went to jail and they got divorced. Now he's a dumpy bald guy with a dodgy tattoo on his neck. Sad, really.'

'Were you and your sister close?' Magnus asked.

'Not super-close,' said Eggert. 'We're very different

people. Although she went into medicine, she always loved the farm. Whereas I hated it.'

'Why?'

Eggert ran his fingers through his sparse brown hair. 'When I was about twelve I realized that I would have to spend the rest of my life working on that farm where my father had been born and his father and his father, going outside on freezing winter mornings to wade around in sheep shit. I had no choice, or so my father wanted me to believe. I didn't like that.

'And, eventually, I summoned up the courage to tell him. He wasn't happy. He talked about centuries of inheritance coming to an end. I told him I just didn't care. We didn't speak for years, although we get on better now Helga lives at the farm.' He stopped himself. Looked down at his hands. 'Lived.'

He looked up and laughed ruefully. 'I wanted to see the world and make my fortune. I went to university in Reykjavík and spent a year at college in California studying engineering, so that was something, I suppose. Then I got involved in the whole dot-com thing and tried a start-up in Reykjavík. That's where I met Sharp – Ómar introduced him to me. At one point I thought we were going to hit the big time, but the crash came and it didn't get anywhere, so I work for the town council now. Recycling. And I only live forty kilometres from Blábrekka. It's a pretty dull life, but I like it. It's *my* choice.'

'I see,' said Magnus.

'So I was pleased when Helga came back to Blábrekka from Reykjavík after the *kreppa*. It took some of the pressure off me. That's when Dad and I started talking again. And they have Anna Rós lined up to take over the farm eventually.'

'Are you happy with that?' asked Magnus.

'Why shouldn't I be?'

'Well, it's a large farm. It must be worth a lot.'

'From what I understand, it has an even larger mortgage. Blábrekka is a liability, not an asset.'

'Did Helga say anything to you about bailing it out?'

'Yes, she did. She asked me to help out a few years ago, but I said sorry. I mean, the idea of me bailing out Blábrekka is ludicrous.'

'Was she upset when you refused?'

'She said she was, but I didn't believe her. She always knew there was no chance. And then Dísa did some bitcoin trading or something, and suddenly this Thomocoin appeared. Helga said she would use that to save the place.' He shook his head. 'I don't know,' he muttered.

Magnus raised his eyebrows. 'You don't know what?'

'I mean, she made a fortune with her daughter's help,' Eggert said. 'And now the farm is going to swallow it up. That farm will swallow us all up in the end. She should have kept the Thomocoin. For herself.'

'Did you tell her that?'

'I did,' said Eggert. 'She wasn't having any of it.'

'Do you know how much Thomocoin she had?'

'No idea. But it must have been a lot if she was going to pay off the bank. She always acted like it was a lot, but I never asked her.'

Magnus wrapped the interview up. 'Thank you, Eggert,' he said. He handed Eggert his card. 'If you do think of anything else that might be useful, give me a call.'

Eggert held the card and stared at it. He was thinking.

Long experience had taught Magnus that when witnesses stared at his card like that they had something else to say.

Árni got to his feet, but Magnus stayed seated.

He waited.

Eggert glanced up from the card, indecision written all over his face.

Magnus smiled gently.

Eggert looked up at the ceiling. 'My sister told me something once. In confidence. I've never told anyone,' he said. 'Not even Karen.'

He nodded towards the kitchen where a fan was whirring in a vain attempt to keep the smell of the lamb under control.

'If I tell you, can you keep it to yourselves?'

'Probably not, Eggert,' said Magnus softly. 'At least not if it's relevant. But if it *is* relevant, if it helps us solve your sister's murder, then you should definitely tell us. Shouldn't you?'

Eggert took a deep breath and nodded.

'It was a few years ago,' he said in a low voice. 'Maybe 2015? Or 2016? Helga came to see me; she was really upset. It turned out she was having an affair. With a married man, who lived in Dalvík. She had given the man an ultimatum to leave his wife or Helga would finish things between them. The man had called her bluff. She wanted to know whether she should call it off, or just accept the situation.'

'And what did you say?'

'I didn't know what to say,' said Eggert. 'I more or less said it was her choice.'

'Did she leave him?'

'She said she did when I saw her later. Or at least she said it was over. I don't know which one of them ended it; I suppose it may have been him.'

'Was it usual for her to discuss that kind of thing with you?' Magnus asked.

'No. I'd asked her about boyfriends once or twice since she split up with Ómar and she hadn't volunteered anything. But it was clear she needed to talk to someone, and I think she may have thought I had guessed they were up to something.'

'Why was that?'

'I'd seen them together many years before when she was still living in Reykjavík, holding hands.'

'That was a bit of a giveaway, wasn't it?'

'Yes, I suppose so. I didn't say anything to her then, I just acted like I hadn't seen anything.'

'So the affair started in Reykjavík?'

'I guess so. The guy was an MP back then, and spent a lot of time down there.'

'Who is this man?' Magnus asked.

'Gunni. Gunnar Snaer Sigmundsson.'

'The man who found Helga's body with Anna Rós?' Árni said.

Eggert nodded. 'Yeah. Him.'

# FIFTEEN

Dísa sat on the end of Anna Rós's bed, listening to Taylor Swift and fiddling with her phone. Anna Rós was fiddling with her phone next to her.

Dísa had been in touch with Jói, who had been calmly sympathetic, but she was mostly communicating with Kata at the university in Reykjavík, who was also supportive. Kata said she would definitely be in Dalvík for the funeral, and insisted that they should go back to their original plan of living together – Matti wouldn't mind.

But now Dísa and Kata were exchanging dumb texts about Beth in *The Queen's Gambit*, a TV show they had both fallen for.

Anna Rós had plenty of friends, but Dísa wasn't sure they were entirely constructive. Lots of hysteria rather than support seemed to be coming her way.

But it was nice to be in her little sister's bedroom: pictures from Anna Rós's early teens of boy bands and horses covering most of the wall space.

She heard a car pull up outside and a moment later the deep rumble of a male voice.

'That's Gunni,' Anna Rós said. 'I should go downstairs and thank him. He was so nice to me yesterday. I don't know what I would have done if I had found Mum by myself.'

'I'm glad he was there.'

'But I don't really want to see anyone.'

'Then stay here,' said Dísa. 'With me.'

Anna Rós smiled at her sister and went back to her phone, letting Taylor Swift's tears ricochet between them.

After a few minutes they heard Grandma's feet on the stairs and a knock at the door. 'Dísa? Gunni wants to talk to you. It's about Thomocoin.'

Dísa exchanged glances with her sister, slipped off the bed and went downstairs.

Grandpa was supposed to be a big man about town. Gunni really was a big man about town. He wasn't particularly tall, but he had square shoulders, a square face, a barrel chest and tough blue eyes. He had grown up a fisherman but, like most of the others, he had sold his trawler and the quotas he had accumulated to the big local fishing company fifteen years before, to become an MP. He had eventually retired from that, claiming he didn't like to spend so much time in Reykjavík. Ever since Dísa could remember, he had kept a horse at Blábrekka, which he rode occasionally. His current mount was a black stallion called Fálki.

Everyone liked Gunni. But everyone was just a little bit afraid of him.

'Hi, Dísa.' He smiled with a mixture of warmth and sadness. 'I am so sorry about your mother. As is Soffía.' Soffía was Gunni's glacially beautiful wife, who never said anything to anyone.

Dísa nodded in acknowledgement.

'I have some questions about Thomocoin I'd like to ask you. Maybe we can go for a walk?'

Dísa glanced at her grandparents. It would certainly be easier to talk without Grandpa's true-believer interruptions. And Gunni was a canny businessman – ruthless even. It would be interesting to hear what he thought was going on with the cryptocurrency.

'All right,' she said.

They put on their coats and left the farmhouse. Gunni set off along the hillside, towards the spot where he and Anna Rós had found Mum.

'Do you mind if we don't go that way?' said Dísa.

'No,' said Gunni. 'No, not at all.'

They changed direction, walking along the road for a couple of hundred metres until they came to a path down to the river. The air was fresh, but sunlight gently brushed their cheeks. It was good to be outside. The valley was alive with the cries, chirps, peeps and warbles of countless birds. They turned off the road and followed a stream tumbling down to the water meadows below. A pair of wagtails hopped from stone to stone next to them.

'You may not know this,' said Gunni. 'But I bought some Thomocoin as well.'

'Grandpa told me.'

'The truth is, I'm a bit worried about it.'

The warmth had gone out of Gunni's voice.

'About the exchange?' said Dísa.

'Yes. I'm beginning to wonder whether there will ever be an exchange,' he said. 'Or if there ever was going to be one.'

'I'm sure they're trying,' said Dísa. 'They just haven't succeeded yet.'

'Are you really sure?'

'Yeah. I saw Sharp give a presentation at the launch three years ago.'

'You see, I wonder if Thomocoin is worth anything at all?'

'Of course it is,' said Dísa. 'I checked the price on the screen this morning: three hundred and thirty-eight dollars.'

'I can check the screen too. But is that a real price? Maybe it's just a number some guy in Thomocoin makes up?'

'That can't be right,' said Dísa. She thought about it a moment. 'It must be a real price. It's the price that investors pay to buy more Thomocoin. If you logged on and bought some today, you would pay three hundred and thirty-eight dollars.'

'Sure, if I *bought* some. But not if I tried to sell some.'

'But that's only because there isn't an exchange yet.'

'Precisely.'

A pair of snipe shot up into the air from tufts of grass in front of them, chirping angrily and zigzagging on sharp, pointed wings. A group of horses trotted across the field on the other side of the stream to check them out: there were as many horse farms as sheep farms in the valley.

They walked on. Gunni was leaving time for Dísa to think. And she was thinking hard.

'You're a smart girl, Dísa. You know what I'm saying. If there never is an exchange, if you can never actually sell any Thomocoin, then it isn't worth anything.'

Dísa wanted to argue, but she did see what Gunni was talking about. She wasn't sure he was right – but she feared he might be.

'Did you speak to Mum about this?' she asked eventually.

'Yes, I did. A couple of weeks ago. She said she'd go down to Reykjavík to ask your dad about it.'

'She went, apparently,' Dísa said. 'Although she never told me. Did Dad have any answers?'

'I don't know. I called her a couple of times, but she didn't answer. I was planning to speak to her about it yesterday morning when I came up here to ride.' He took a deep breath. 'But I never got the chance.'

Dísa glanced at Gunni. He looked worried. He also looked angry.

She felt a surge of panic. What if he was right and Thomocoin was a complete con from start to finish? And Dísa had then made her mother buy it? And her mother had encouraged people in the village to buy it too?

'I believed Helga,' said Gunni.

'You don't think she knew it was a fraud?' The moment she spoke the words, she regretted them, admitting as they did that there was something rotten about Thomocoin.

'No. Your mum really did believe in it,' Gunni said. 'Which is why I lent her so much money to keep the farm going. And why I invested so much myself.'

'I knew she borrowed money,' Dísa said, surprised. 'But I assumed it was from the bank, not you.'

'No, it was me. No bank would lend against Thomocoin. But I did. Twenty million krónur. I've got notes from her to prove it. And then, when I saw the price going up, I bought some Thomocoin myself.'

'Not a lot, I hope?' said Dísa.

'A lot,' said Gunni. 'Three million dollars' worth. Which is supposed to be worth five million now. But may be worth nothing.'

Dísa could feel herself blushing. It was ridiculous. It wasn't her fault at all. She had never told Gunni to buy any

Thomocoin – she didn't even know he had. Gunni was a grown-up businessman; he could make his own decisions about investments.

But she could easily believe that Mum had urged him on.

And together with the Thomocoin she was due to inherit, she felt she had inherited her mother's guilt as well.

They had reached the river, which here paused to form a broad pool among the water meadows. Two swans drifted towards them. They turned and retraced their steps back up the slope towards the farm. From down here, Dalvík was out of sight, but the ever-present island of Hrísey sunned itself out in the fjord.

'I want the money back, Dísa. I want it now.'

The voice was low and urgent and commanding.

'What?'

'I want you to repay your mother's loan.'

'But I can't,' said Dísa. 'You know Mum had no cash. That was why she had to borrow from you in the first place.'

'You have the private key to her Thomocoin,' Gunni said. 'Helga told me once she'd told you where it's hidden. Don't deny it.'

Dísa considered doing exactly that. But instinct told her the way to beat Gunni wasn't to lie to him.

She stopped and turned to face him. She was a good six inches taller than him. But he was powerful and used to intimidating men bigger than her. He looked up at her, his square jaw thrust towards her. He took a step forward.

'Yes, I do,' she said.

'In that case, transfer two hundred thousand dollars' worth of Thomocoin to my wallet now.'

Dísa swallowed.

'No,' she said.

'What do you mean, no? Your mother owed me the money. I want it back.'

'Have you spoken to Grandpa about this?'

'No. But I will if necessary. I am sure he can be made to understand the right thing to do.'

He probably could, thought Dísa. Grandpa would crumble.

But she wouldn't.

'It's Monday tomorrow. Grandpa is going to see the lawyer about Mum's estate. I'll go with him. If you are right and you can prove you lent Mum the money – and I believe you, by the way – then you can talk to the lawyer about how to get it back from the estate. Only then will I transfer the Thomocoin.'

'But that's why I'm talking to you now. You could do it just like that.' Gunni clicked his fingers. 'On your phone.'

'No,' said Dísa, looking right into Gunni's hard blue eyes. 'Anyway, why do you want Thomocoin if it's worthless?'

'I'll get what I can take,' said Gunni. He jabbed a short finger at Dísa's face. 'I liked your mother. But if she is responsible for losing me three and a quarter million bucks, I swear I won't rest until I've got it back. From you.'

Dísa kept her voice calm. 'I understand we owe you the money you lent Mum. But if you decided to buy that much Thomocoin, that's your problem. Not mine.'

Anger erupted in Gunni's eyes. He dropped his arm and his fingers clenched into a fist. For a moment Dísa thought he was going to hit her. She wanted to flinch, close her eyes, raise her arm, duck her head, but she didn't.

She forced herself to stare into that anger.

'Stupid bitch,' he muttered and turned on his heel. Dísa swayed as she watched him stride back towards the farm.

She needed to find her mother's USB stick and put the paper copy of the private key back in its hiding place.

But if Gunni was right – and Dísa feared he was – it wouldn't matter if all her mother's Thomocoin was stolen. It was all worthless anyway.

She looked up the valley to Blábrekka, standing proudly on the lower slopes of the mountain. That would be gone.

And it wouldn't just be Gunni who would lose money. People all over Dalvík had trusted her mother and trusted Thomocoin. Dalvík was a small place and people had long memories. In twenty years' time, people would pass Dísa in the street and think she was the woman who'd lost them or their family their life savings.

They would be just like Gunni. They wouldn't forgive.

Why, oh why had her mother been so stupid, so greedy, as to pull in all those other people? All she'd needed to do was sell the bitcoin Dísa had given her, pay down the mortgage and forget cryptocurrencies.

And why borrow money from Gunni, of all people?

Probably because he was the only one who would lend it to her.

Mum had really screwed up. And then left Dísa to clear up after her. For a second, maybe two, Dísa felt a flash of anger towards her mother, followed by a cold wave of remorse.

Mum was dead. Despite that fact taking up all the space in her head, she still couldn't quite believe it.

A tear leaked out of her eye. Dad had warned her. 'Don't tell Helga,' he had said.

But she had.

It was Dísa's fault. It was all her fault.

# SIXTEEN

Krakatoa stared at his laptop screen. He was kind of enjoying this. Even though he knew the shit was about to hit the fan big time.

TUBBYMAN: What about $361 for the price tomorrow? I think the guys need a bit of good news. And bitcoin's going gangbusters.

KRAKATOA: OK Tubs. Go for it. But give them a hiccup in a couple of days. Don't want to make it too easy for them. How are sales?

TUBBYMAN: Uganda's going crazy. We sold $1m+ yesterday.

KRAKATOA: Nothing from the States?

TUBBYMAN: Nothing for a week.

KRAKATOA: That's good. We need to shut down in the States.

TUBBYMAN: The Netherlands is still going strong. And Poland.

KRAKATOA: Good to hear. Thanks Tubs.

She was good, Tubbyman. She had a real feel for market psychology; she should have been a trader in some bank somewhere – she would have made a fortune. She knew just when to give the Thomocoin investors a little encouragement and when to give them those down days that added the element of danger that kept them playing.

She was the one who set the Thomocoin price every day. Although she went by Tubbyman, she was actually an extremely thin thirty-four-year-old American woman called Jessica who lived in Berlin. Thomocoin was the ultimate 'working from home' organization; coronavirus lockdowns had no effect on business. Krakatoa employed people all over the world. He paid them well – in bitcoin usually, or Thomocoin if they preferred. He insisted on knowing who they really were. He also insisted that they should never know who he was, just that he lived in British Columbia and worked odd hours.

And that they should never cross him.

TECUMSEH: Job done.

KRAKATOA: Where did you hide the knife?

TECUMSEH: The shed by the side of the house. In a kayak.

KRAKATOA: Good work. I'll transfer the bitcoin now.

TECUMSEH: Shall I go to the airport?

KRAKATOA: No. You'll never get back in if they tighten the tourist restrictions further. But get out of Dalvík. Go back south. Lose yourself in Reykjavík.

TECUMSEH: I'll need $1500 a day waiting time.

KRAKATOA: $1000.

TECUMSEH: Those are my rates. I prefer to leave the country now. And there's a risk staying here.

KRAKATOA: OK. $1500. Wait for my instructions.

Fifteen hundred seemed steep for doing not much, but Krakatoa could afford it. And he might need Tecumseh to act quickly in the next few days.

He logged into one of the four crypto-exchanges where he held bitcoin and transferred sixty thousand dollars' worth to Tecumseh's wallet.

Tecumseh had been an exception to Krakatoa's employment rules. He had insisted that he wouldn't tell Krakatoa anything about himself, other than he had served in the German KSK. Which was fair enough.

Krakatoa didn't believe that Tecumseh had been in the German special forces. He doubted he was even German. But Tecumseh had a high rating and good reviews on the dark web and that was good enough for him.

And so far Tecumseh had provided a good service.

# SEVENTEEN

The police station in Akureyri was a miniature version of police headquarters in Reykjavík before they had tarted it up, squatting in its parking lot behind a high, forbidding wire fence. Árni found Magnus a desk, and they set to some serious googling. They needed to find out about Thomocoin and they needed to find out fast.

Thomocoin's website was slick, a little glitzy, but friendly. 'Welcome to our community' was the vibe. Join a band of smart investors all over the globe who could see how the world was changing. Do something good for the countless millions without a bank account and make some money while you are at it. Stay two steps ahead of the game.

Skarphédinn Gíslason, or 'Sharp' as he was mostly referred to on the website, was the chief executive, an international banker living in London, 'originally from Iceland'.

The site boasted that there were over four hundred thousand investors in Thomocoin from all over the world. A 'white paper' described the workings of the cryptocurrency in some technical detail. There were pages of investor education, graphs, charts and a number of videos of rousing events where Sharp or the darkly good-looking head of global marketing, Jérôme Carmin, fired up crowds of enthusiastic investors. The graphs looked financial; the videos looked like a cult.

Magnus tried to pin down where Thomocoin was actually located. There seemed to be an address in High Holborn in London, but that didn't look like a company headquarters. There were occasional references to Thomocoin Holdings SA in Panama.

That figured.

Magnus scanned the section on regulation. This stated in several different ways that Thomocoin was confident it would get approvals to set up exchanges in London, Singapore and Iceland. Apparently, Iceland was the perfect place for the world's first cryptocurrency as legal tender since it was already almost cashless, and forward-thinking politicians there were eager to promote Iceland as a world leader in digital currencies. Iceland would serve as 'proof of concept' for Thomocoin. Once it was seen to work there, it would be rolled out all over the world.

Which explained the pressure Financial Crimes was under.

Given what he had read on the website, Magnus was surprised by how little there was in the international press. There were two interviews with Sharp in major magazines, but that was about it.

'Got anything interesting, Árni?'

Árni was poking about in the dingier corners of the web, looking for scandal.

'Not really. There are guys on Reddit forums who think

Thomocoin is all a scam, and there are others who say Sharp is a genius. No real evidence one way or another. It all seems to boil down to whether Thomocoin is serious about an exchange or not.'

'It *sounds* serious,' said Magnus.

'There's a guy called Krakatoa mentioned in a couple of places. He's supposed to be the brains behind the operation. There's some speculation about who he really is. A bunch of Thomocoin true believers think he is Satoshi Nakamoto, the guy who invented bitcoin.'

'Really?' said Magnus.

'Someone else thinks he's George Soros. Or a Rothschild. Thomocoin is going to take over the world's banks. Wait a moment! Here's someone who thinks he's from Wuhan and he started the coronavirus.'

That's what you get from looking at the internet, Magnus thought. PR, hype and conspiracy theories.

Magnus's phone buzzed. A text from Sigurjón. Turned out he had the FBI agent's details after all. Agent Ryan Malley at the New York Field Office.

Magnus dialled the number and left a message for Agent Malley to get back to him. That probably wouldn't be until Monday morning New York time at the earliest.

He needed to talk to a real person before then. Someone who might know about Thomocoin as an investor, maybe.

Ollie!

Magnus and his younger brother had been extremely close when they were growing up but had fallen out when it transpired that Ollie had played a part in their father's death. Ollie had done time as a result of Magnus's testimony against him in a Massachusetts court.

He had been out of prison for several years now and

lived and worked in the Boston area. Or lived and got involved in shady deals in the Boston area.

Putting an ocean between him and his newly released brother had been one of the reasons Magnus had moved back to Iceland three years before, but from the safety of Reykjavík, he had tentatively got back in touch.

And Ollie had tentatively responded.

Thomocoin was just the kind of money-making scheme on the edge of legality that would attract Ollie. And if he didn't know about it, he would know someone who would.

So Magnus called him.

'Magnus?' Ollie's voice was groggy. 'Do you know what time it is?'

Magnus checked his watch. 'Eight-thirty?'

'On a Sunday! It's Sunday morning, Magnus.'

Magnus winced. He should have waited another couple of hours.

'Yeah, sorry, Ollie. How're you doing?'

'You woke me up to ask me how I'm doing? I'm sleepy, Magnus, and just a little bit pissed off. How are you?'

'I'm working on a murder investigation.'

That might impress some people, but not Ollie. 'Course you are.'

Magnus decided to cut the small talk. 'And there's something called Thomocoin involved. A cryptocurrency. Have you heard of it?'

'Yeah, I heard of Thomocoin. I even looked into it last year.'

'And?'

'And it's a piece of shit.'

'Why's that?'

'Classic crypto-Ponzi. They get new investors in to pay off the old investors, or in this case, give them the cash to pay commissions. They make up a price every day on some website. They talk about the coin becoming tradable on an exchange but it never happens. Like I said. A piece of shit.'

'So how much do you think a Thomocoin is really worth?'

'Nothing. Zero.'

'Nothing at all?'

'Nothing at all. Now, if you'll excuse me, Magnus, I've got someone to see to.'

Magnus heard a female giggle and then Ollie was gone.

At least that was clear.

And not good news for Dísa. Or her family. Or the people of Dalvík who had bought Thomocoin through Helga.

His phone rang. Vigdís.

'Did you see Ómar?' Magnus asked her.

'Just finished with him.'

'And?'

'He has an alibi for yesterday morning. Spent Friday night with a woman. Bumped into a neighbour on his way home in the morning. He is certain the neighbour will remember.'

'Girlfriend?'

'"Occasional friend", Ómar called her. I checked with the neighbour on the way out. She did see Ómar at about nine a.m. Saturday morning.'

'Pretty much when Helga was killed in Dalvík. Did he say anything about meeting Helga last week?'

'Yes. They met at the Kaffitár on Borgartún. She wanted to talk to him about Thomocoin. She was worried that the currency would never be approved to trade on an exchange. He said he thought it would, but she wanted him to check with a guy called Sharp. A banker friend of his in London.'

'Did he do that?'

'He did, after Helga left. Sharp said that there would definitely be at least one exchange approved by the end of the year, and Ómar called Helga the next day and told her that.'

'Did she believe him?'

'Ómar thinks she didn't. He says she was pretty upset.'

'Does Ómar believe this Sharp?'

'He says he does.'

'Has he invested in Thomocoin himself?'

'I don't know. I didn't ask him,' said Vigdís.

'That's OK. Did he have any idea who might have killed Helga?'

'No. He seemed genuinely upset about it, though. For what that's worth.'

Magnus knew what Vigdís meant. In murder cases, most people seemed upset, even the perpetrators. It was unprofessional for a detective to set much store in that. But it was the response you wanted to see from a human being.

'Thanks a lot, Vigdís.'

'I'll send you my report. Say hi to Árni for me.'

'Vigdís says hi,' said Magnus to Árni as he hung up. He was relaying the rest of what Vigdís had told him when his phone buzzed again.

A New York number.

'Inspector Jonson,' said Magnus, reverting to the American version of his name. His father had been Ragnar Jónsson, which meant that Magnus had been Magnús Ragnarsson in Iceland, but when he moved to America as a kid, his father had simplified his son's last name to Jonson, and the accent had slipped off 'Magnús'.

'Hi. This is Agent Ryan Malley of the FBI. I came into

the office this morning to catch up on some stuff and I saw your message.'

Magnus grinned, pleased with Agent Malley's work ethic. 'Thanks for getting back to me, Ryan. I'm investigating a murder here in Iceland, and there might be a Thomocoin angle. I know you sent us an MLAT about it recently. Can you give me some details?'

'Haven't heard squat from Reykjavik,' said Malley gruffly.

Magnus had learned from long experience in Boston that the FBI could sometimes be very helpful, and they could sometimes be very unhelpful. It all depended on how you started off with them. And bullshitting them was never a good idea.

'I don't think you will hear back from them,' said Magnus. 'Or at least nothing useful. Apparently, the whole subject has gotten political here, know what I'm saying? But maybe we can come to an arrangement.'

'An arrangement?'

'I tell you things. You tell me things.' Magnus left unsaid that any information exchanged in this way could not be used as evidence, but he was sure Malley knew that.

'You speak pretty good English,' Malley said.

'I worked for the Boston Police Department for fifteen years,' Magnus said. 'Homicide.'

'Oh really? You know Harry Spaventa, then?'

'Yeah, I know Harry,' said Magnus. 'He retired last year.'

'He and I worked a case five years back.' Magnus waited while the FBI agent thought. 'OK. What do you want to know?'

'What has Thomocoin been up to? And do you have

anything on a guy called Sharp? Skarphédinn Gíslason. He's the CEO.'

'Thomocoin is a Ponzi scheme, pure and simple. They use existing multi-level marketing teams to recruit investors. They sell them "Thomocoins" with the promise that the investors will be able to sell their Thomocoins one day at a large profit for dollars or euros or whatever. It's never going to happen.'

'Don't the investors get impatient?'

'They do. But these guys are plausible, especially Sharp, and a French guy called Jérôme Carmin, who is head of marketing. There'll come a time, though, when they won't be able to keep the plates spinning in the air, and then they'll all come crashing down. And we think that time is pretty soon now.'

'Are you going to shut them down?'

'We've shut them down in the States. We're working on a red notice for Sharp and Carmin, but we don't have the evidence yet. And there's a guy goes by the name Krakatoa. We don't know who he is. Sharp is CEO, but he's just a front man. Krakatoa runs the operation.' Malley sighed. 'So that's why it would be kind of nice if you guys got back to us.'

'What do *you* want to know?' said Magnus.

'Where Sharp is at. Is he in Iceland?'

'I don't think so,' said Magnus. 'Not that we know of, anyway. I've heard he lives in London. I'll probably need to question him myself.'

'Can you hold off until we've gotten the arrest warrant?'

Magnus could see this getting messy. An Interpol red notice would call for Sharp's arrest with a view to extradition to the United States. If Sharp was a genuine suspect for Helga's murder, Magnus might want access to him first, before the FBI had grabbed him. But Sharp wasn't a suspect yet. The best way of getting the cooperation of the FBI for an interview, if they did succeed in arresting him, was to get his cooperation in first.

'I'll do what I can. I'll ask if anyone knows where Sharp is and let you know. And if we need to interview him, I'll talk to you first. Can you tell me when you've got him?'

'Sure,' said Malley. 'What's your murder investigation? How's Thomocoin involved?'

# EIGHTEEN

'I've got some bad news,' Magnus said. He and Árni were sitting opposite Dísa, Hafsteinn and Íris at the kitchen table at Blábrekka.

The family waited, faces strained.

'It looks as if Thomocoin is a scam. There will never be an exchange.'

'Oh my God!' said Dísa.

'How do you know?' Hafsteinn asked.

'I can't say.' Magnus was reluctant to let them know that the FBI were suspicious in case Sharp was somehow tipped off. 'But I have heard it from at least two sources.'

'So Mum's Thomocoin is worthless?' Dísa said.

'Looks like it,' said Magnus.

'It's the haters,' said Hafsteinn. 'The Thomocoin haters. They've got to our police now.' He grabbed his daughter's hand. 'Don't worry, Dísa. Have faith. It's just a sign that Thomocoin has got them scared.'

Dísa withdrew her hand. 'But that means all those people Mum sold Thomocoin to will have lost their money too?'

Magnus nodded. 'We found Helga's list on her computer.' Árni produced two sheets of paper with a list of twenty-two names. 'Do you know these people?'

Árni shoved the list over to the other side of the table.

Hafsteinn picked it up and scanned the list. He nodded. 'I know at least half of them.'

'Some of them will be her colleagues at the hospital,' Íris said. 'We won't necessarily know them. But I recognize the Dalvík names.'

'Are these the amounts they bought?' Dísa said, leaning over her grandfather's elbow to look.

Magnus nodded.

'Gunnar Snaer Sigmundsson bought fourteen thousand?' Dísa asked.

'That's right.'

'So that's worth about five million dollars now?'

'Yes. Gunnar was by far the biggest investor.' Most of the other investments were for a hundred or two Thomocoin, although there were two purchasers of a thousand Thomocoin each.

'Gunni?' said Hafsteinn. 'He's a smart guy, that Gunni.'

'Grandpa!' said Dísa. 'Don't you see? He's not smart at all! He's going to lose all that money.'

'No, he's not, Dísa, dear,' said her grandfather.

'Do you have any reason to think any of these people knew that their investment was worthless?' Magnus asked.

'It's not worthless!' said Hafsteinn. 'You may say it is, but I want proof and you haven't given me any.'

'All right,' said Magnus. The old man was correct: Magnus hadn't offered any proof. And neither, really, had the FBI. 'But did any of these people have any suspicion that Thomocoin might be worthless?'

Hafsteinn folded his arms and shook his head. 'No.'

Dísa looked down at her thumbs and bit a nail.

'Dísa?' Magnus said gently.

'Gunni came around here this morning after you left,' said Dísa. 'He said he wanted to talk about Thomocoin. We went for a walk.'

Magnus waited. Hafsteinn glared at his granddaughter.

'He told me he was afraid there would never be an exchange. He said he had told Mum this and that was why she went to Reykjavík to see Dad. To ask him about Thomocoin.'

'Was Gunni angry?'

'He is now,' said Dísa. 'Very angry.'

Magnus and Árni returned to the police station in Akureyri, where they briefed Ólafur. Ólafur decided to bring Gunni in for questioning the following morning and search his house and computer.

Afterwards, Árni brought Magnus back home for supper.

Árni's family was chaotic. He had two extremely naughty little daughters, who ran him and his wife ragged. Neither seemed to mind. His wife, a small, round woman named Greta with a long dark fringe, seemed, if anything, to egg them on.

Supper was feeding time at the zoo, pasta flying and tomato sauce splattered everywhere. But the pasta was delicious and they were all having fun. Once Magnus had overcome the temptation to arrest the lot of them for insurrection and riot, he enjoyed himself too.

Eventually, Greta took the kids upstairs for a noisy bath time and stories.

Árni and Magnus stuffed plates into the dishwasher.

'They'll be at least an hour,' said Árni. 'Would you like a Scotch?'

Árni had a decent Macallan and poured them both a glass.

'A good day's work,' said Árni.

'It was,' Magnus agreed. 'We'll see what Gunni has to say for himself tomorrow.'

Magnus's phone buzzed in his pocket. 'Excuse me,' he said as he examined the screen.

He smiled.

'Who is it?' said Árni.

Magnus glanced at him. 'Ingileif.'

'Ingileif? I didn't know you were still seeing her?'

'Haven't seen her for three years. But I asked her if I could meet Ási again, and she said yes. Haven't seen him for three years, either. He'll be seven now.'

'Why wouldn't she let you see him?'

'She has her own family now. She thought me seeing him would disrupt it. I guess she has a point. I don't know. I'm just glad I'm getting to see him. I don't know why it's so important to me.'

'Oh, I do,' said Árni. 'I don't know what I'd do if I couldn't see my girls.'

'You've done well, Árni. I like Greta.'

'And she likes you, Magnús, despite all I've told he about you.'

Magnus grinned as he sipped his whisky. It was a shame Árni had moved to Akureyri.

'I take it you are still with Eygló, then?'

Magnus hesitated. 'Yes.' He wasn't sure whether Árni picked up on the hesitation.

'Now you two really were made for each other. I can

imagine the conversations about mud in saga times you must have.'

'It's fascinating stuff, Árni.'

'I'll bet.'

Suddenly, Magnus wanted to ask Árni his advice. Árni knew how to find a woman, start a family, run around after little kids. Be happy.

Magnus didn't. But it wasn't that he didn't know the answer that was stopping him. He didn't know the question.

He loved Eygló, he thought. He certainly liked her. He respected her. He was attracted to her. He liked spending time with her. He liked her son.

So what was the damn problem?

Ingileif was the damn problem. Or Ási. Or both of them.

Which was goddamned stupid. They weren't his family. Ingileif had kept Ási's very existence from him for four years. If there was a family, it was Ingileif, Ási and her husband Hannes, and Magnus had no part of it.

There was another family beckoning: Eygló and Bjarki.

Why couldn't he just accept that? Just say yes. Marry Eygló. Move in. Have another kid.

Because somehow that would be dishonest.

How? Why?

Magnus didn't want to be dishonest with anyone, let alone Eygló.

'Are you OK, Magnús?'

Magnus finished his whisky. 'Yeah, I'm fine. I ought to head back to my hotel now. Thanks for dinner and the whisky.'

As soon as he got back to his hotel room, he sent Ingileif a text explaining he would love to see Ási but he might not be back in Reykjavík for a few days.

He fell asleep waiting for a response.

# NINETEEN

Magnus had never conducted an interview with Ólafur before. It was an important one; Gunni was firmly in the number-one-suspect slot. Though technically he was not yet a suspect but a witness, which under Icelandic law meant he didn't have the right to a lawyer. At least not yet.

The three of them were in the interview room in the Dalvík police station. After the morning briefing, two constables had gone to pick up Gunni. While Gunni was being interviewed, Árni and two uniformed officers were searching his house and seizing his computer.

They had agreed that Magnus would start the interview in a low-key way, and Ólafur would pile on the pressure when he judged the time right.

Magnus started with silence, while he sized up the man opposite him. Gunni was short, compact, powerful, his body tense with barely contained energy. He seemed impatient and angry rather than anxious. Magnus was expecting bluster, maybe even threats – Gunni was a big man in the area and would have big friends.

Gunni glanced from one detective to the other. 'Well?'

he said, raising thick grey eyebrows.

Magnus paused before speaking. 'Tell me about Thomocoin, Gunni.'

'You tell *me* about Thomocoin,' said Gunni. 'Is it a fraud? Are you investigating it? You should, you know.'

Magnus smiled thinly. 'No. We are investing Helga Hafsteinsdóttir's murder, and we think Thomocoin may have something to do with it.'

'And how is that?'

Magnus ignored the question. 'Have you invested in Thomocoin, Gunni?' he asked.

'I have.'

'How much?'

'A lot.'

Magnus raised his eyebrows

Gunni sighed and briefly lowered his eyes, as a hint of shame passed through them. 'I've invested over three hundred million krónur.'

'And how much is that worth now?'

'According to Thomocoin's website, it's supposed to be worth just over five million dollars. So it's up seventy per cent. If you believe the website.'

'And you don't?'

Gunni hesitated. 'I'm not sure,' he admitted.

'I see. Who first told you about Thomocoin?'

'Helga.' Gunni described how Helga had enthused about the cryptocurrency. At first, he hadn't invested himself, but after a year or so, during which time the price had risen steadily and Helga had boasted of her own profits, he had bought some. He had started off small, ten thousand dollars' worth, but had soon invested more. He had listened to Helga, read the information, watched the videos, done his research. He had believed in it.

'Did you lend any money to Helga during this time?'

'Yes, I did. In 2017, maybe early 2018. She needed it to keep the farm afloat.'

'How much did you lend her?'

'Twenty million krónur.'

Magnus whistled. 'That's a lot of money.'

'It certainly is,' said Gunni. 'But I knew she had at least that much in Thomocoin, so she would be able to repay me.'

'You must have trusted her?'

'I do. I did.'

Magnus wasn't sure whether Gunni no longer trusted Helga just because she was dead, or because she had let him down.

'You asked me whether Thomocoin is a fraud,' said Magnus. 'Do *you* think it is?'

'I think it may be,' said Gunni with defiance.

'Why?'

Gunni described his growing suspicions that the promised exchange on which it would be possible to sell all the Thomocoin he had accumulated might never be set up, how he had discussed these fears with Helga, and how she had spoken to her ex-husband about it.

'So let me get this straight,' said Magnus calmly. 'You lend Helga twenty million krónur that she's going to repay once she has sold her Thomocoin. On her advice, you invest a further three hundred million krónur in Thomocoin yourself. And then you discover that all this Thomocoin might be worthless. Which means not only is Helga unable to pay you back, but you have lost it all.'

'That's about right,' said Gunni. 'And I want it back. If not from Helga, then from her estate.' His eyes were burning.

'I bet you do. In fact, I bet you were pretty angry with Helga.'

'I was.'

Magnus stared at him in silence. He was pleased that Ólafur was content to watch, at least for now.

'Sure, I was angry with her,' said Gunni, realizing where Magnus was going. 'But I didn't kill her.'

'Tell me about your relationship with Helga.'

'She was a neighbour. I've known her all her life, since she was a little girl.'

'A little girl? How much older than Helga were you, Gunni?'

'About ten years, I think.'

'I see. But Helga was more than a neighbour, wasn't she?'

Gunni hesitated. 'Yes. She was a friend. I've stabled a horse at Blábrekka for years. We used to go riding together.'

'Riding?' interrupted Ólafur with a sneer. 'And what kind of riding was that?'

'What do you mean?'

'I mean were you riding her or was she riding you? Or a bit of both?'

Magnus had to hand it to Ólafur; he did know how to be annoying.

And Gunni was annoyed. 'I don't know what you're talking about,' he growled through clenched teeth.

'Hah!' said Ólafur with an unpleasant grin. 'You bet you do. You were screwing each other.'

'What?'

'I mean you and she used to have sex together. In Reykjavík when you were a member of parliament down there, and then back here in Dalvík.'

'What makes you think that?'

'She confided in someone,' said Magnus. 'In 2015 or 2016, when she was trying to decide whether to break up with you.'

'You and she had an affair over many years,' said Ólafur. 'And then she broke it off. And you were angry with her. And then the Thomocoin that she told you to buy became worthless and you were even angrier with her. Weren't you?'

For a moment, Magnus thought Gunni was going to leap over the table, grab Ólafur and pummel him. But Gunni took a deep breath and leaned back in his chair. 'All right. I did have an affair with Helga when she lived in Reykjavík. And then again when she came back north. But I was the one who called it off.'

'So you say,' said Ólafur.

Actually, it fitted with what Helga had told Eggert, Magnus remembered.

'So I say,' said Gunni. 'My wife was suspicious. In a small town like Dalvík it's impossible to keep these things quiet. She guessed I was having a bit on the side, although she didn't know who with. She told me I had to stop or she would leave. So I promised I'd end it, and I did.'

'*You* promised *you* would end it,' said Ólafur in disbelief.

'Yes,' said Gunni, meeting the detective's eyes. 'Helga didn't like that. She was angry with me, rather than the other way around. But after a frosty few months, we managed to treat each other as friends again.' He paused. 'I admit I did feel guilty about it. And that may have been why I lent her the money. I liked her. I like her parents. I like Blábrekka. I didn't want them to lose it.'

'When was the last time you had sex with Helga?' Ólafur barked.

Gunni looked at Ólafur steadily. 'Four years ago,' he replied. 'Not since then.'

'I don't believe you!' said Ólafur, slamming his palm down on the table.

Gunni wasn't intimidated. He shrugged, his blue eyes firm. 'It's true.'

He shook his head. 'I *am* angry I lost money because of her. But I'm devastated she died. Devastated. Her poor daughters.' He looked from Magnus to Ólafur, doubt in his eyes now. 'I'm angry that someone killed her. In a way, I'm angry with her for being killed. I know that doesn't make much sense, but I think it's true. I'll miss her. I'll miss her a lot.'

Magnus paused to see if Ólafur would push it further, but the other detective fell silent and nodded to Magnus to continue.

'All right,' said Magnus. 'Take us through again what you did on Saturday morning from when you woke up.'

There was a window when Gunni could just possibly have killed Helga. He had said he had taken his dog for a walk before driving out to Blábrekka; that was when he had claimed to have seen the lone hiker on the mountain. Magnus had begun probing exact timings when there was a knock at the door.

It was Árni. He signalled he wanted to speak to both detectives and he looked excited.

'What have you got?' Ólafur asked him in the corridor.

'A fishing knife. With blood on it. We found it in a kayak in Gunnar's shed.'

'Human blood?'

'Don't know. I'm getting it checked now. But if it was fish blood on that blade, why would the knife be hidden in a kayak?'

# PART THREE

# TWENTY

LINDENBROOK: Hi Krak.

KRAKATOA: Hi.

LINDENBROOK: Did you see what the British FCA put up on their website this morning? 'Investors are warned that they may lose the entire value of their investment if they buy Thomocoin.'

KRAKATOA: I saw that. It's just the UK. And the FCA always says things like that. Have you had any pushback?

LINDENBROOK: Yeah. There's pushback. We've got a ton of UK investors.

KRAKATOA: Tell them the usual. It's dinosaurs and haters.

LINDENBROOK: I can do that. But we need an exchange. At the very least we need approval for an exchange.

KRAKATOA: We'll get it. Iceland is the place. All we need for now is an indication from some regulator, any regulator, that they are looking at it seriously.

LINDENBROOK: We're working on that. But people want to see an actual functioning exchange.

KRAKATOA: It's ready to go. Tested. Bugs ironed out. All we need is approval and we can flick the switch. And once it's going in one country, then everyone will be happy to wait. I tell you, Iceland's the key.

LINDENBROOK: All right. I'll fend them off. Have you heard anything about the FBI investigation?

KRAKATOA: They've gone quiet. Now they've shut us down in the US, they've lost interest. We're not their problem any more.

LINDENBROOK: Let's hope the UK don't start investigating.

KRAKATOA: Yeah. Are you ready to scramble?

LINDENBROOK: Do you think I'll have to?

KRAKATOA: No. But things can change. And with COVID it's a lot harder to travel. If you're going to Panama, you need to plan to avoid the US. No Miami stopover.

LINDENBROOK: I've got it all worked out. Madrid is the key. They still have flights to Panama.

KRAKATOA: OK. Good.

LINDENBROOK: It's bad about Helga. Do they know who killed her?

KRAKATOA: I heard they arrested a local. Gunnar Snaer Sigmundsson. He's one of our investors.

LINDENBROOK: Any link back to us?

KRAKATOA: No. We're OK. He invested through Helga.

LINDENBROOK: Do you know when the funeral is?

KRAKATOA: Yes. Tuesday next week.

LINDENBROOK: Are you going?

KRAKATOA: Yes. Yes, I'm going.

## TWENTY-ONE

Dísa's left hand hurt as her sister's fingers gripped it.

They were gathered around the graveside overlooking the valley in which generations of Dísa's and Anna Rós's ancestors were buried. It had been raining for most of the morning, but as Mum's coffin had emerged from the church on the pallbearers' shoulders, the grey clouds had rumbled away towards the mountains to the east, allowing weak sunshine to wash over the large crowd of mourners that filled the graveyard and spilled over into the surrounding meadow. Two pillars of a rainbow shimmered softly beside the mountain. The valley's birds provided a requiem of joyful chirps and warbles.

As the priest intoned a prayer, Dísa's eyes settled on the elegant figure of Soffía, Gunni's wife, tall, blonde, beautiful even in her fifties, standing towards the back, alone. It was good of her to come – brave of her to come. Her husband was locked up in jail while the police gathered evidence. Rumours were flying: the police had found a knife with Mum's blood on it, Gunni had invested hundreds of millions in Thomocoin and, worst of all, he had had an affair with Mum. Inspector

Ólafur had confirmed the first two to the family, but remained silent on the third, at least in front of Dísa.

She refused to believe it.

The coffin was lowered into the ground. Anna Rós emitted a strangled wail, and a sob thrust its way up from Dísa's chest as her eyes filled with tears. Again. She gripped her sister's hand and leaned into her father's shoulder next to her.

It was horrible. It was all so horrible.


The farmhouse at Blábrekka was big, but not nearly big enough for everyone who came. All the rooms downstairs were full, and people spilled outside.

Dísa hoped none of the mourners had COVID, as the bodies pressed together. The virus had disappeared from Iceland almost entirely during the summer, but it was making a stealthy comeback, and case numbers were rising. The university insisted on social distancing and face masks, and there was talk of new restrictions coming in. But in Dalvík, no one seemed to care, at least not for a funeral.

Her mother would have been horrified. As an anaesthetist, she had been caught up in the first wave in Akureyri in March and April and had wrestled with the disease at first hand.

Dísa recognized most of the crowd. Half the town of Dalvík had come, as well as several of Mum's colleagues from the hospital and a few of her friends from her time in Reykjavík. Dísa couldn't see Soffía; she must have slipped away. Mum's medical friends looked as if they were about to follow her.

Dad had come, thank God. Dísa and Anna Rós had

been so relieved to see him. Mum's death had hit him hard, as Dísa always knew it would. Grandpa and Grandma seemed to understand and were polite, even warm to their former son-in-law. Dísa had done her best to support them through their grief over the last ten days, but she needed her one remaining parent.

'Hey, Dísa, how are you doing?'

It was Kata, who had arrived from Reykjavík in time for the closing of the coffin the day before. It was good to have an old friend around.

'I'm OK,' she said, although she clearly wasn't.

'That must have been tough. The burial.'

'It was,' said Dísa. 'But it's good at the same time.'

'There are so many people here,' said Kata. 'She had a lot of friends, your mum. A lot of respect.'

'I know.'

Kata smiled up at Dísa. She was a good six inches shorter, dark-haired, slightly plump, with a bright smile that lit up a crowd, especially of men. And at that moment it warmed Dísa.

Jói elbowed his way through the pack, his blue eyes clouded with sadness and sympathy. Dísa grabbed her brother and clung on hard. He wrapped his arms around her.

'I'm so sorry, Dísa,' he said.

She stood back as Jói hugged his father and Anna Rós.

'You remember Kata, Jói?'

'Of course! But I haven't seen you for years.'

Kata turned her smile on him. 'Yeah. Not a great way to meet up again.'

'Kata says I can stay with her when I get back to Reykjavík, Jói,' Dísa said.

'That's good,' said Jói. 'I don't mean I want to get rid of you, but at least you'll be with someone you know.'

'I'll look after her,' said Kata, putting her arm around Dísa and squeezing. Dísa smiled back gratefully.

'They've got the guy that did it, I hear?' said Jói.

'Yes. Gunni. Did you ever meet him?'

'Yeah, I remember him. He kept a horse here, didn't he?'

Mum had invited Jói to stay at Blábrekka a few times even after the divorce. She knew that he and Dísa were close, and she had always liked him herself.

Dísa lowered her voice so in the hubbub only Jói could hear what she was saying. 'There's a rumour going around town that Mum had an affair with him.'

'With Gunni?'

'That's what they say. That can't be right, can it?'

'No, it can't be,' said Jói with a reassuring smile. 'It's small-town gossip. Don't believe a word of it.'

'All right,' said Dísa. 'I won't believe a word of it.'

That was what she had wanted Jói to say. It was what Kata had said. And yet Jói hadn't seemed as shocked by the idea as he should have been, as Kata had been.

Dísa banished the suspicion from her mind.

'Are you going back to Reykjavík tomorrow?' said Dísa. 'I am. Kata's giving me a lift in her car. I'm sure there's room for you.'

'That would have been nice, but I'm getting an evening flight with Dad right after this.'

'Do we have to talk about Thomocoin?' Dad's voice broke through the din, loud and irritated.

Dísa turned. Her father was speaking to Uncle Eggert. Ómar used to look good in a suit in the old days, with his slick black hair brushed back, but no more. The hair was shaved off, a tattoo crawled up his neck above the white collar of his shirt and his tummy hung over his too-tight trousers.

'It's a fair question,' said Eggert. 'A lot of people here have a lot of money riding on this.'

'Not at her funeral, Eggert. Not at her funeral.'

Some of the mourners closest to them had overheard Ómar and were turning towards him, curious.

'I have no information,' Ómar said. 'Neither good nor bad. I just don't know.'

'Maybe *he* does,' said Eggert, looking over Ómar's shoulder.

Ómar turned, as did Dísa. A tall figure was weaving through the crowd, which parted respectfully. The level of noise in the room fell two notches.

Sharp. Now he did look good in a suit.

At least half the crowd recognized Sharp from his Thomocoin promotional videos and they shut up and stared.

Sharp nodded at the sea of people he didn't know and headed straight for his friend Ómar.

'Hey, man, I'm so sorry,' he said, putting his arm around Ómar. 'She was a special woman.'

Ómar nodded. 'She was.'

Sharp hugged him tightly.

'Hi, Dísa,' he said, flashing her a quick smile. 'My condolences.'

'Thanks,' Dísa said, pleased that he had recognized her.

Eggert was glaring at Sharp. Sharp smiled and held out his hand. 'Eggert, isn't it? Good to see you again.'

'I'm surprised you showed up here,' said Eggert icily.

'Helga and I were good friends, back in the day,' said Sharp. 'I wanted to come.'

'You know your Thomocoin is the reason why she was killed?'

'We don't know that,' said Ómar.

'I know Helga was worried,' said Sharp to Eggert. 'Ómar told me. But it's going to be fine. That's why I'm in Iceland. To speak to the government. Dot the i's and cross the t's on an agreement for an exchange here.'

'Here?'

'Yes. Iceland's the natural place to start. No one uses cash any more, so the infrastructure is in place for non-cash payments. We won't go straight to Thomocoin being used in shops, but the first stage is an exchange where you can convert Thomocoin into krónur. The Icelandic government gets that. I've got a meeting at the Central Bank in a couple of days.'

'I told you, Eggert.' It was Hafsteinn. 'See, Dísa? What did I tell you? Thanks for coming all the way from London, Sharp.'

'I wouldn't have missed it.'

The man had charm, Dísa was forced to admit. He *looked* trustworthy. Dísa could see Eggert was beginning to doubt his scepticism.

But this exchange was years, *years,* late. For three years Thomocoin had been taking in real money with the promise that the fake money they gave trusting people in return would be worth something very soon.

Well, it wasn't.

Grandpa was going to lose everything. Including Blábrekka. They had all grown up here: Dísa, Mum, Grandpa and their ancestors going back generations. Dísa had tried to save the farm, had come very close to saving it, but she had failed.

The sadness of that fact, on top of the greater sadness of her mother's death, was overwhelming.

Dísa didn't know why Gunni had killed Mum. She suspected that Uncle Eggert was right and it had something to do with Thomocoin. Half the people in the room had trusted Helga, who had trusted Dísa, who had trusted Ómar, who had trusted Sharp. And now they were all going to lose everything.

Dísa was acutely aware of her and her mother's position in that chain.

She felt responsible.

And she also felt angry.

'Dad?'

He ignored her, listening to Sharp.

'Dad?' She tugged his sleeve.

'Yeah?'

'Can we talk for a moment?' She looked at the crowd. 'Outside? You're going back to Reykjavík right after this, aren't you?'

Ómar's frustration with his daughter flared. But then he nodded.

She led him out of the back door and a few metres up the slope towards the rock where the hidden people lived, watching over Mum's private key. A key to nothing.

'Dad. You've got to pay them back. You and Sharp. Pay them all back.'

'Pay who back? Your grandfather? Eggert?'

'Not just them. Everyone in Dalvík who invested in Thomocoin. And Mum's colleagues at the hospital. All of them.'

'And why would I do that? *How* am I going to do that? Where am I going to get the money?'

'They paid good money for their Thomocoin. Where is

that? OK, maybe you don't have it, but Sharp does. And he needs to pay it back.'

'You heard him. He says there's going to be an exchange in Iceland soon.'

'He's always said that and it's never happened. He sounds good, but I don't believe him. Do you? Do you believe him?'

Ómar looked up in frustration and then back at his daughter. 'I don't know.'

'Right,' said Dísa. 'Listen, it's our responsibility that all these people are going to lose so much. You. Me. And Mum. Grandpa's going to have to sell Blábrekka. You know that, don't you? It will break him. And Grandma. And you know how Mum would have felt about that, how much the farm meant to her. We need to do this for Mum.'

Anger flared in Ómar's eyes. 'I warned you not to get your mother involved in this, didn't I, Dísa? Don't you remember? When I first told you about the bitcoin in the restaurant in Akureyri?'

Dísa nodded.

Ómar's frustration spilled over. 'I loved your mother, but she was greedy, you know that? When stuff was going on at the bank that shouldn't have been, back before the crash, I had decided to blow the whistle. I spoke to Helga about it. And she talked me out of it. She said I should trust Sharp; Sharp knew what he was doing. She said we needed the salary, we needed the bonuses.'

He shook his head. 'We didn't need the bonuses. We didn't need a Discovery *and* a Mercedes. But your mum wanted them.'

'Dad!' Dísa could feel her face reddening. 'How can you say that! You lost us everything.'

'I did,' said Ómar. 'And I will always regret that.'

'So do something about it! Give the money back. Or get Sharp to give the money back.'

'I don't have it,' said Ómar. 'And I can't make Sharp give it back. You heard him. He really does believe there's going to be an exchange.'

'Figure out a way, Dad,' said Dísa.


Ómar watched his daughter stride back into the farmhouse.

He couldn't face going back in there.

He walked up the hill, hauled himself on to a rock and looked out over the broad green valley.

It really was a beautiful place, his wife's childhood home. The fjord stretched northwards, its mountain walls eventually coming to an abrupt halt as its waters opened out to the broad horizon of the Arctic Ocean. The flat island of Hrísey floated just a few kilometres offshore, a smattering of white buildings at its southern tip.

He smiled as he remembered how he and Helga had spent a July day out there, the first time he came to Blábrekka to meet her family. They had wandered through the summer houses and found a field of bright purple lupins. Helga had insisted that no one could see them there; Ómar thought the whole fjord could and, besides, there was a stiff breeze coming from the sea. Then Helga had crouched down, wriggled out of her clothes and asked him what he was waiting for, there was no wind down here.

He had loved her then. Her thick red hair, her wicked smile, her sense of adventure.

She had been proud of him, her hot-shot rising-star banker husband. She enjoyed being a doctor, she felt good fixing sick people, but she liked it even more if there was a banker's salary to help things along. And that salary was shooting up, together with bonuses, as the bank found ever more creative ways to make money.

For the hundredth time, Ómar wished he had stopped the merry-go-round when he could have. It was true that he had asked Helga for her opinion and she had told him to go along with Sharp and the others. But he was the banker. He was the one who knew that secretly lending money to shell companies to buy stock in the bank wasn't financial genius, it was morally wrong and probably illegal.

He accepted his responsibility for what had happened. He had accepted that he had broken the law and deserved to go to jail, along with four others. They could have taken Sharp down with them, who was then working for the bank's London branch, but they chose not to.

And, actually, that had worked out. Especially when Sharp had given him the bitcoin and the price had gone up. And he had given some to Dísa, who had traded it so well.

Then another poor decision. Trusting Sharp on Thomocoin. Ómar still hung on to the hope that he hadn't misjudged his friend, but he knew in his heart he was kidding himself. Dísa saw it. Dísa was smart about these things.

He wasn't going to lose much. Unlike Dísa and Helga, Ómar had sold most of his bitcoin through Sharp – he needed the money to spend. Sure, he had invested some in Thomocoin, but not everything. Nothing like Helga's investments.

He *knew* she'd screw up. That's why he had given the bitcoin to Dísa. Even at fifteen, she was a better bet than Helga.

Helga.

He had loved her passionately. Even when he had gone to jail and she had ditched him, he'd loved her. Even just before the crash when everything was going so well and he had started that stupid affair with Bryndís at the bank, he had loved her. Bryndís was another mistake.

Helga had stopped loving him, he knew that. And that had been his fault. He knew that too.

Dísa wanted him to atone for all those mistakes. And he'd like to if he could. But he had very little money himself. And he had no chance of persuading Sharp to cough up.

His best bet – Dísa's best bet – was to hope that Sharp could conjure something out of nothing with the Icelandic government.

He felt alone. He wanted Helga. The old Helga he had fallen in love with, not the more recent one who demeaned and dismissed him, who knew him for what he really was.

A loser.

Sitting on the rock, looking out over the valley she had grown up in, he felt a tear run down his cheek. And then another.

For three minutes he sobbed.

It felt good.

Then he slid off the rock and headed back to the farmhouse to fetch Jói and take him back to Reykjavík.

# TWENTY-TWO

Magnus's expenses from his trip up north didn't add up. No matter how hard he stared at the damn screen, 4,500 krónur were missing. He knew from bitter experience that he had to make the numbers add up eventually.

Fudging expenses was a major crime in CID.

His phone rang. He picked it up. 'Magnús.'

'It's Jón from the front desk. I've got a young lady here who wants to see you. Dísa Ómarsdóttir.'

'I'll come down.'

Dísa looked tired and washed-out. And angry.

Magnus led her up to CID via the coffee machine and sat her down next to his desk. She responded to his attempt to chat with one-word answers. He gathered that she had returned to Reykjavík the day before, after her mother's funeral.

Magnus was sympathetic. His father had been murdered when he was about her age. He had been tired, washed-out and angry too.

'All right,' he said with what he hoped was an encouraging smile. 'What can I help you with?'

'I want you to arrest Mum's murderers,' said Dísa.

'We've done that,' said Magnus. 'Gunnar Snaer Sigmundsson is in custody. My colleagues in Akureyri are building a good case against him. They are confident of a conviction.'

The DNA analysis of the blood on the knife found in Gunni's shed had come back with a match for Helga. There was a window of about an hour when Gunni was supposedly walking his dog when he just about had time to get up the mountainside and kill her. Motive wasn't completely clear yet, but Ólafur's strategy was to let the suspect stew in solitary confinement in prison at Hólmsheidi until they had gathered overwhelming evidence against him and then use that to get him to confess.

'I don't mean Gunni. I mean the people who *really* killed Mum. The people behind Thomocoin.'

Magnus nodded. He noticed Dísa's northern accent was more obvious here in Reykjavík than it had been when he had seen her in Dalvík. 'I see. But we're not even sure that Thomocoin is the reason Gunni killed your mother.'

'Of course it is. What other motive might there be?'

Dísa was staring hard at Magnus, daring him to answer.

Magnus paused. This was one of the things he hated most about murder investigations: revealing victims' secrets to their families.

He didn't have to tell Dísa. He could wait until she found out at the trial. But it was inevitable she would find out, eventually.

Magnus had been in her shoes. Nearly twenty-five years before, his father had been murdered in the house in which they were staying in a small town on the shore south of Boston. The police had got nowhere. Magnus, a college student at the time, had demanded answers. There were none. He had tried to solve the case but hadn't got anywhere himself. Until, that is, he became a policeman and thirteen years later was transferred to Iceland.

Where the key to his father's death had been lying all the time.

He remembered the kindly local detective – Jim Fearon was his name – who had patiently answered Magnus's questions. And eventually, over a decade later, had helped him find the answers.

So he decided to answer Dísa's.

'You probably don't know this,' said Magnus, 'but it looks like your mother had an affair with Gunni. In the past.'

'I don't believe you,' said Dísa. She looked angry rather than surprised; she must have heard gossip. Despite her protests, she was really asking Magnus for confirmation.

'Your mother confided in someone a few years ago. And when we confronted Gunni with it, he admitted it.'

'I still don't believe you.'

'That's your choice,' said Magnus. 'But it is another possible motive.'

Dísa breathed in. 'Was this so-called affair still going on when she died?'

'We don't know,' said Magnus. 'Gunni says it finished in 2016, and at the moment we have no reason to doubt him. We're still working on it.'

'So why would that make him kill her?'

'The truth is we don't know the motive. Yet.'

'Yes, you do,' said Dísa. 'It's staring you in the face! Thomocoin. Gunni bought millions of dollars of Thomocoin from Mum and it's all worthless. So he was pissed off and he killed her. It's obvious, isn't it?'

'That may turn out to be the motive,' said Magnus patiently. 'But for the moment, we don't know.'

'Have you shut down Thomocoin yet? Have you arrested the people behind it? Sharp? Jérôme? The Swiss guy with the pointy beard?'

'No, we haven't.'

'Why not? It's a massive fraud. My family and Gunni aren't the only people to lose money from Thomocoin. Half of Dalvík has. And there will be loads of people in Reykjavík who have lost money too. What are you doing about it?'

'Thomocoin hasn't gone bankrupt yet.'

'Yet? Why wait until it does?'

Magnus decided to give Dísa an honest answer. 'It's political, Dísa. There are people in Iceland who want Thomocoin to succeed. There are others who think it will fail but don't want to take responsibility for it. I know that in some other countries Thomocoin is being investigated seriously. But not in Iceland. I'm sorry.'

'Which countries?'

'I can't say. It's an ongoing investigation. But one of them is big.'

'But not here?'

'Not here. I'm sorry.'

Dísa leaned back in her chair, her face torn with anger and frustration. Tears were forming in her eyes, but she controlled them.

'These people lied to me. They lied to my dad, to my mum, to Gunni, to lots of other people. And they are still lying. My mother died as a direct result. My grandparents are going to lose the farm that has been in their family for five hundred years. And you're not going to do anything?'

Magnus could see her point. 'I'm sorry. I can't.'

'Sharp is in Iceland. Did you even know that?'

Magnus shook his head.

'He had the nerve to show up at Mum's funeral. He says he's seeing the Central Bank in Reykjavík today. You could go and arrest him.'

'I can't arrest him. I have nothing to arrest him for.'

'You do! He's stolen millions of krónur from tons of people. And he killed my mum!'

'I'm sorry, Dísa . . .'

The contempt on Dísa's face struck Magnus. She just shook her head, stood up and left.

'She has a point,' said Vigdís from the desk opposite where she had been listening to the whole thing.

'She does,' said Magnus. 'She does.'


Thelma hung up the phone and smiled broadly as Magnus entered her office.

'You look happy,' he said.

'Just got our headcount raised,' she said. 'It's only by one, but that's a result these days.'

'Congratulations,' said Magnus.

Thelma was a few years older than Magnus, with short blonde hair, a pugnacious jaw, hard blue eyes that knew how to twinkle and a false leg – the result of a car chase gone wrong. She was not universally liked in the department: she was a bit of a hard-arse, and Vigdís in particular thought Thelma had a problem with women. But she and Magnus respected each other. Magnus got the results and Thelma took the credit. Win-win.

'What have you got for me?'

'Thomocoin,' said Magnus.

Thelma sat back in her chair and examined Magnus

over her reading glasses. It was an intimidating stare, but Magnus was used to it.

'Oh yes?'

'I just got a visit from Dísa Ómarsdóttir – it was her mother who was murdered in Dalvík. She holds Thomocoin responsible. Half the community up there has invested, including her mother and her grandparents. It's probably what motivated Gunnar Snaer to kill Helga. And no one here in Reykjavík is doing anything about it.'

'So?'

'So I thought I would ask around. Quietly. Dísa believes Thomocoin is on the verge of bankruptcy.'

'Was anyone from Thomocoin directly involved in the killing?'

'I don't think so. But I'd like to find out.'

'Let me put this another way. Is there any evidence that anyone from Thomocoin was involved?'

'Not yet.'

'Yet?'

'No,' Magnus admitted.

'And has Ólafur asked you for more evidence about Thomocoin?'

'No,' said Magnus. 'He doesn't think it's necessary. But if Thomocoin goes bust then a lot of people are on the line for a lot of money.'

'And who told you it's going bust? A nineteen-year-old student?'

'The FBI,' Magnus replied.

Thelma paused. Thinking through the angles.

'Let's say it does go bust. Then the shit really will hit the fan. And two things will happen. They will look around for who to blame. And they will look around for bodies to help them with the investigation. But they won't look to us on either count, because this has got nothing whatsoever to do with CID. It's not our job. It's not *your* job. It should stay that way.'

'Not even a couple of interviews?' said Magnus. 'I can write them up for Ólafur.'

'No.'

'All right,' said Magnus.

'Do you understand me, Magnús?'

'Of course.'

'Good.'

Magnus got up to leave.

'Oh, Magnús?'

'Yes?'

'How's that old guy you live with? Tryggvi Thór?'

'He's fine.'

'He avoided the virus in the spring?'

'Yes. He was pretty careful.'

'The numbers are ticking up again. We may get another wave. He should still be careful.'

'I'll tell him.'

'No, don't tell him,' said Thelma. 'He's a grumpy old git. Just keep an eye out for him, will you?'

'I will,' said Magnus. He left unsaid the question in his mind: Why do you care?

When he got back to his desk, he looked up the address for Fjóla Rúnarsdóttir. As Vigdís had said, Dísa had had a point. Magnus had been in her shoes once and he wasn't about to let her down. His mistake had been to try to get approval from his boss. Well, she need never know.

## TWENTY-THREE

TUBBYMAN: Hey Krak.

KRAKATOA: Hey Tubs.

TUBBYMAN: I'm hearing rumours about the FBI.

KRAKATOA: What rumours?

TUBBYMAN: They're asking questions. About Thomocoin.

KRAKATOA: They have been for a while. It's OK. We've shut up shop in the US. You know what the Americans are like: they don't care about anywhere else.

TUBBYMAN: There are threads on the boards that claim the Feds have been asking about Sharp and Jerome.

KRAKATOA: First I've heard. But we're expecting good news from Iceland. Any day now.

TUBBYMAN: For real?

KRAKATOA: For real.

TUBBYMAN: That's good. So what shall we do with the price today?

KRAKATOA: Put it up half a per cent. Show there's nothing in these rumours.

TUBBYMAN: I don't know. Maybe we take it down for a

couple of days. Show the rumours working through in
the price. Let them sweat a bit. Then snap the price up,
especially if we get good news out of Iceland. Give
them some relief. And also some regret that they didn't
buy more when it was cheaper. They'll like that.

KRAKATOA: Yeah. That's better. Do it.

TUBBYMAN: OK. I'll get to it. How's the COVID in
Canada? Are you getting a second wave?

KRAKATOA: Still not too bad. Nowhere as bad as the
States.

TUBBYMAN: They're getting a little worried here in
Germany. Stay safe.

KRAKATOA: And you.

Tubbyman was good. Krakatoa was always tempted to show
the price of Thomocoin rising inexorably upwards.
Tubbyman understood that Thomocoin was a gamble, and
that gambling was no fun unless there was a chance of
losing. That's what made the price rises, when they came,
sweeter.

Krakatoa looked up from his computer. Outside, the sea
shimmered silver as it reflected the low September light
which slipped under the clouds. It was a cold day here in
Iceland – whereas several thousand miles away on the west
coast of Canada the temperature was an unusually warm
twenty-two degrees Celsius, according to Krakatoa's
weather app.

He really must keep an eye on the COVID stats in
Canada. Here in Iceland, it was all fine so far.

# TWENTY-FOUR

Dísa turned off the National Ring Road at Mosfellsbaer and headed inland between mountains of bleak rock and scree. The road was good – it was the classic tourist route from Reykjavík to the site of the ancient outdoor parliament at Thingvellir – but with the virus, the usual coaches were absent, and Dísa could put Kata's Hyundai through its paces.

She was anxious to get to the lake.

She had been disappointed that the big red-haired detective had been so feeble, but part of her had expected it. On the long drive with Kata back to Reykjavík, a Plan B had slowly slotted into place in her head in case the police failed to act.

Ómar had built a tiny summer house of wood and glass next to Apavatn about fifteen years before, in the good times. It was at the end of a dirt track, which passed about a dozen larger summer houses. The track petered out at a stream that babbled and chuckled past the cottage. Dísa and Anna Rós had loved visiting the place in the summer as kids, both playing outside in the stream or the lake when it was sunny, or shut up cosily with both parents when the rain was driving horizontally against the wooden walls.

They'd still visited there with Dad and sometimes Jói after the divorce, but it wasn't the same.

She parked the car in front of the house but didn't go in. She didn't have a key.

Instead, she made her way through the grass to a thicket just a few metres away from the building, between it and the stream. The sunlight glittered on the blue lake, and hills slumbered on the other side. To the east, the powerful snowy shoulders of the volcano Hekla hunched under a solitary cloud. At this time of year, midweek, the other cottages were empty.

There, surrounded by willow and dwarf birch, stood a grey stone about a metre high and three metres long.

Dad had told them stories about that stone. The farmer who had sold him the land on which he had built the summer house had made him promise not to move it. A family of hidden people lived there. The farmer said that he wasn't bothered about them personally, but his mother definitely was and had almost blocked the sale of the land.

Ómar had promised. And had enjoyed telling his little girls all about them.

Dísa and Anna Rós had never seen the *huldufólk* but had played all kinds of imaginary games with them. The rock had become an important part of the attraction of the place to the little girls and hence their parents.

So Dísa hadn't been surprised when her father had told her that was where he had hidden his private key.

She had bought a trowel from a hardware store and clutched that as she ducked into the bushes. Unlike the stone at Blábrekka, this one wasn't surrounded by smaller rocks. Neither was there an obvious patch of bare earth.

Dísa considered the spot. Had Dad dug a kind of tunnel under the rock? Unlikely. There were about a dozen tussocks of grass. She yanked at these, but they didn't rise. But as she was bending down to tug at the last one, she saw a slit in the rock underneath it.

She went down on her knees. Gingerly, she slipped her hand into the hole. She felt dead leaves and moss and something else. Two something elses.

She pulled them out.

They were light metal tubes with writing in Spanish on them. It took her a moment to figure out what they were: cigar tubes.

She opened the first one and drew out a rolled-up scrap of torn paper. She laid it out on the stone. A large letter 'O' was written in blue biro, and underneath two long strings of letters and numbers that looked as if they had been produced by an inkjet printer. Above the first string were written in English the words 'private key'; above the second 'wallet address'.

Dad's cold wallet.

Dísa had considered taking a picture on her phone, but she didn't want the image floating around in the cloud where a hacker might find it. So she carefully copied out the characters from both keys on a card she had brought with her, and read them out loud backwards and forwards to double and triple check she had not made any errors. If just one character was wrong, then the whole key would be useless.

She opened the second cigar tube and extracted a similar scrap of paper, this one headed with the letter 'K'. Once again, she copied out the string of characters and read them back aloud to make sure she had got them down correctly.

She stuffed the papers back in their tubes and slipped the tubes under the tussock of grass.

Two wallet addresses. Two private keys. Two bitcoin wallets. One of them was clearly her father's. Whose was the other?

And how much bitcoin was in them? As she walked back to the car, she wondered whether there would be enough to repay all those investors in Dalvík. Even if Dísa couldn't repay them in full, even if she could just pay back a portion, it would be much better than doing nothing.

## TWENTY-FIVE

Fjóla Rúnarsdóttir lived on the sixth floor of one of the apartment blocks in the Shadow District that overlooked Faxaflói Bay. Those places were expensive. Fjóla herself was a tall woman with curly black hair, wearing a tight black top and black leggings. Her eyes, however, were blue and warm, and she gave a friendly smile as she welcomed Magnus into her apartment.

Friendly, though also nervous. But then a lot of people were nervous about talking to the police.

She sat him on a light grey sofa – the whole apartment was light grey and white, as if colour had been banished. Even the art on the walls was in black and white. Only the books were colourful; Magnus noticed a number with English titles on management and various self-improvement themes. Her windows looked down upon a narrow street of scruffy green and yellow metal houses that had not yet been devoured by Reykjavík's young professionals.

'How can I help you?' Fjóla asked, with a warm, helpful smile.

'I'm investigating the murder of Helga Hafsteinsdóttir.'

'Ah.' The smile left her face. 'I was so sorry to hear about that. But I understand you've caught the murderer?'

'We think so. But we're still gathering evidence.'

'Of course.'

'I take it you knew Helga?'

'Certainly. She was an investor in Thomocoin. More importantly from our point of view, she brought in plenty of other investors. She was one of my top customers. Actually, my top customer.'

'Because of all the commission those other investors brought in?'

'That's right. We use MLM to sell Thomocoin – multi-level marketing. It's perfect for the kind of thing that requires enthusiastic selling. Helga was very effective.'

'How many customers did she bring in?'

'I think about twenty directly, give or take. But they all brought in others, especially in Dalvík. I think there were probably another fifty or sixty in total.'

'And you earned commission on all of them?'

'I did,' said Fjóla. 'And so did she. That's how MLM works.'

'What form did this commission take?'

'You can take it either in Thomocoin or bitcoin.'

'How did Helga take hers?'

'Thomocoin. She was a true believer.'

'And you?'

'Bitcoin.'

Magnus raised his eyebrows. 'You aren't a true believer?'

Fjóla smiled. 'Oh, of course I believe in it! I wouldn't sell it otherwise. But I'm a professional. I don't think putting all my eggs in one basket is a good idea. I'd have preferred euros or dollars, but bitcoin is better than nothing. The price has been all over the place in the last couple of years, but it seems to be going up again now.'

'Are you aware that bitcoin is illegal in Iceland?'

Fjóla paused. 'I believe it's against the law to *buy* bitcoin. It's OK to own it. But I'd rather not discuss my own affairs unless it's relevant to your investigation. I hope you understand.'

Smart woman.

'I do understand,' said Magnus. He didn't want Fjóla to turn defensive. She seemed naturally helpful, and Magnus wanted to take advantage of that.

'The sale of Thomocoin in Iceland doesn't breach any current financial regulations,' Fjóla added. 'I got a lawyer to check.'

'I'm sure you did,' said Magnus, remembering Sigurjón in Financial Crimes and his instructions to look the other way. 'One of the investors Helga brought in was Gunnar Snaer Sigmundsson.'

'That's correct. He's the man you've arrested for Helga's murder, isn't he?'

'Yes, he is. Do you know how much Thomocoin he bought?'

'I can look up the exact number, but it was probably about three million dollars' worth.' She smiled. 'Actually, I do remember the number pretty accurately. Two million nine hundred and sixty-eight thousand dollars of Thomocoin. He was the biggest investor in Iceland.'

'Did you ever meet him?'

'Not directly. Helga handled him. But I did communicate with him by email recently.'

'What about?'

Fjóla paused. The smile disappeared.

Magnus waited.

'It was terrible Helga was killed like that.'

Magnus waited some more.

Fjóla blew air through her cheeks. 'Look. I've always believed Thomocoin is legitimate. I still do. I checked it out thoroughly before I signed up. I have no doubt that cryptocurrencies are the future, especially once they are approved for legal tender, and that's precisely what Thomocoin is aiming to do. To get approval.'

'I see.'

'If you are in the MLM business, you need a good product to sell. Amway, Avon, Herbalife – they all work because people want to buy the cleaning products or the cosmetics or the vitamins. And people *really* want to buy cryptocurrencies, once they're explained to them.'

'Provided they are worth something in the end,' said Magnus.

'Yes,' said Fjóla. 'And I believed Thomocoin would be. I'm trying to build up a network of loyal followers, people like Helga. The last thing I want to do is blow my credibility by selling them something worthless.'

'That makes sense.'

'Right. So Gunnar was concerned about the exchange that Thomocoin had promised to set up and hadn't.'

'I've heard that.'

'He was putting a lot of pressure on Helga. He was putting a lot of pressure on me. He was getting impatient.'

'Do you think that was why he killed Helga?'

'I don't know. But maybe. It's awful. If only he had waited.'

'Waited? Why?'

'Well, there's still a good chance that the Icelandic government will approve an exchange for Thomocoin.'

'Do you really believe that?'

'Yes,' said Fjóla. 'Thomocoin is in talks with the government now.'

'That would be Skarphédinn Gíslason? Otherwise known as Sharp?'

'That's right. He's in Iceland now.'

'Have you seen him?'

'I met with him yesterday. He had just flown back from Helga's funeral in Dalvík. They were old friends.'

'Tell me about Sharp.'

'He lives in London now. He used to work for one of the banks before the crash, in their London branch. He wasn't involved in any of the bad stuff. He's an entrepreneur in London who gets cryptocurrencies. He's an impressive guy. Inspirational.'

'Do you have his address in London?'

Fjóla hesitated and then decided being helpful to the police was in her best interests. 'Sure,' she said. She read out a London address from her phone.

'And he's the chief executive?'

'That's right. There's a French guy called Jérôme Carmin who is important too. Head of global marketing. He lives in Paris. I've got his address too.' She read it out.

'What about Krakatoa? Who is he?'

Fjóla smiled. 'Ah. Krakatoa. He's the brains behind the operation, supposedly. He lives in Canada, supposedly. British Columbia.'

'Have you met him?'

'No. Nobody has met him. He's a genius holed up in some secret lair in the mountains or something.'

'You sound sceptical?'

'I am. You can imagine that something like Thomocoin takes place online. It's the ultimate virtual company. And this guy Krakatoa runs it. Everyone is in awe of Krakatoa.'

'Except you?'

'I don't think Krakatoa is in Canada at all.'

'You don't?'

'I think Krakatoa is an Icelander.'

'Really? Why do you think that?'

'I don't know. It started off as just a feeling. His English is excellent, but I thought occasionally he sounded like an Icelander writing in English. And there's the name Krakatoa.'

'That's in Indonesia.'

'Yes. But it's a volcano. Volcanoes are really Icelandic. I bet he really wanted to call himself "Hekla" but couldn't, so he chose a foreign one instead. And Krakatoa sounds better than Vesuvius.'

'It's a bit thin,' said Magnus.

'Plus, he puts an accent on the "i" in Reykjavík. No foreigner would do that unless maybe they had lived in Iceland.'

'Hm,' said Magnus. 'It's not exactly conclusive proof, but I see what you mean. So in that case, who do you think Krakatoa is?'

'Sharp. It's got to be Sharp.'

'Have you asked him?'

'No. I was nervous to. And if you see him, please don't tell him I told you he's Krakatoa. It's just a guess.'

'Why are you scared of Sharp, Fjóla?'

'I'm not scared of Sharp, or at least the Sharp I know. But I am scared of Krakatoa. So if Sharp turns out to be Krakatoa . . .'

'I see. And why is Krakatoa so scary?'

'I don't know. He's decisive. Ruthless almost. You don't mess with him. He's at home on the dark web. All those drugs sites.'

'And Sharp isn't?'

'I think they are like Jekyll and Hyde. Sharp is the inspirational entrepreneur when he's in the real world. And Krakatoa is the enforcer on the dark web.' Fjóla raised her hands. 'Don't get me wrong. I don't think either Sharp or Krakatoa has broken the law. They're too smart for that. I just wouldn't mess with Krakatoa, that's all. And if he is Sharp, I am sure he had nothing to do with Helga's murder. There is no reason he would ever have even met Gunnar.'

'I'd like to speak to Sharp. Where is he staying in Reykjavík?'

'Just around the corner,' said Fjóla. 'At 101 hotel.'

## TWENTY-SIX

Magnus was due to meet Ási and Ingileif at five-thirty, but he had an hour before then, which should be long enough to interview Sharp. He called Agent Malley in New York first. Malley was insistent that Magnus avoid tipping off Sharp that the FBI were on to him. He expected a red notice to be issued in the next couple of days. But it would be useful if Magnus could discover Sharp's travel plans so they knew where to arrest him.

Reception at 101 hotel said Sharp was out, so Magnus decided to try again later on, after he'd seen Ási.

Magnus agreed with Dísa that Thomocoin bore some moral responsibility for her mother's death, but it was looking increasingly unlikely that it bore any legal responsibility, especially given the Icelandic government's approach to regulating it.

But he remembered his insistence on asking difficult questions of the authorities after his own father was murdered. He would give Dísa what answers he could. He would talk to Sharp.

And maybe he could help the FBI nab him. If Sharp

ended up spending ten years in an American jail, that should give Dísa some comfort.

Ingileif had suggested that they meet at a playground in Vesturbaer, a neighbourhood just above the old harbour where sea captains used to live in grand houses – grand by Icelandic standards.

Ási had changed, obviously: he was now nearly twice as old as he had been the last time Magnus had seen him, although he was recognizably the same boy. Thinner, taller, hair just as red, freckles spattering his nose. He gave Magnus a shy smile and then ran off to clamber over a high and complicated climbing frame.

Ingileif smiled. 'Perhaps this wasn't such a good place to meet. You don't get to talk to him, you just get to watch him.'

'He looks pretty fearless.'

'He's just trying to show off in front of you.'

'That's nice.'

'What, that your son is a show-off?'

'That he wants to show off in front of me.'

Ingileif looked as if she was about to say something – point out Magnus's neediness perhaps – but she thought better of it.

'Maybe we can take him for pizza later?' she said.

'That would be good. Thanks for this,' said Magnus. 'It's good just to see him.'

Ingileif didn't say anything, but watched her son. *Their* son.

They went for pizza at a place around the corner, Ási chatting happily, and then Ingileif invited Magnus back to her apartment for a cup of coffee.

It was the top floor of one of those old, white, metal-clad sea captain's houses, with glimpses of the harbour and the bay between the roofs. The apartment was decorated in what Magnus recognized as Ingileif's minimalist taste. Warm wooden floorboards, plenty of glass, dramatic vases, lots of curves. He recognized also a couple of paintings by one of the women who co-owned the gallery in Skólavördustígur with Ingileif: landscapes of waterfalls and lava fields in blocks of blue, white, green and gold. Magnus had always rather liked them. And candles – lots of candles.

But no cello. Magnus wondered what had happened to the cello.

'Why don't you show Magnús your room, Ási?' said Ingileif.

Ási proudly complied. It was a small room. Almost all the wall space was covered with books.

'Have you read all these?' said Magnus. 'It's a lot of books for a seven-year-old.'

'I like reading,' he said.

'What's your favourite?'

'I used to like Tintin and the Elstur books. But I've just started Harry Potter.'

'That'll keep you busy. And what are these?' Magnus pointed to a group of gruesome half-painted toy figures on his desk.

'Warhammer. My friend Binni plays with his brother. It's fun.'

'I can see that eating up his pocket money for the next few years,' said Ingileif.

The living room was a wide space – walls had been knocked down – and Ingileif and Magnus went to the kitchen area while Ási played some computer game on the sofa. It seemed to be something related to Warhammer.

'I said coffee, but I'm having a glass of wine,' said Ingileif. 'Would you like one?'

'I'm interviewing someone later,' said Magnus.

'OK,' said Ingileif.

'Well, maybe just one.'

Ingileif poured two glasses and they sat at the table. Magnus hadn't seen her for three years, and she looked older, but yet she looked exactly the same. He caught her eye. She was looking at him and thinking the same thing. He could tell.

'Thanks for letting me see him. It's been great.'

'I'm sorry,' said Ingileif. 'I should have done this sooner. It's just Hannes didn't want me to, and, well, I caved.'

'That seems unlike you,' said Magnus.

'I know.'

'When's he coming home? Hannes. Will I meet him?'

'No, you won't meet him,' said Ingileif. She lowered her eyes to her glass. 'He walked out three months ago.'

'Oh.' Magnus hesitated. 'I'm sorry.'

Ingileif shrugged and then looked straight at Magnus. 'I'm just not very good at staying with men. Am I?'

Magnus held her gaze and grinned. 'No.'

Ingileif laughed. 'You know I'm forty now?'

'I didn't. But I could have worked it out.'

'And I've got a string of bad relationships behind me. You would have thought I would have learned by now.'

'Ours wasn't a bad relationship.'

'I left you. Twice!'

'I know. But I'm glad it happened,' said Magnus. He realized it was something he had wanted to tell Ingileif for a long time. 'I'm glad we were together.'

'So am I,' said Ingileif.

They held each other's eyes. Something was going on in Magnus's mind, in his chest. His heart was pumping faster.

He was falling. Where, he didn't know.

She broke away from his glance and swilled the wine in her glass. She seemed to be thinking.

'What is it?' said Magnus.

Ingileif didn't answer; she seemed absorbed in her wine. Then she looked up.

'Can I show you something?'

'What?'

'Come,' she said. She led him along a hallway and opened a door. Magnus followed her into the room. Her bedroom.

She reached behind him and locked the door. Then she kissed him.

Magnus put his arms around her and held her. His senses exploded, her tongue playing with his, her smell, the feel of her wonderful arse beneath his hands, her chest against his. So familiar. So exciting. So *right*.

He was falling.

But then he clung to a branch on the cliff edge.

He pushed himself away from her.

'I'm sorry. I'm sorry, Ingileif. No.'

'Come on, Magnús,' said Ingileif with a smile. 'You want to.'

'I don't know whether I want to or not. But I know I can't. I'm with Eygló.'

'Do you want to be with her?' Ingileif gazed at him with hope; hope tinged with doubt.

'I don't know. But I *am* with her. So I can't do this.'

Ingileif's confidence crumbled before his eyes. 'What am I doing?' she said. 'I told myself not to do this. To leave you alone. To let you get to know Ási again. But just now in the kitchen . . . I thought . . . I thought . . .'

'I didn't mean to lead you on,' said Magnus.

'I know you didn't. And you didn't. It was me. Screwing

up again. I know you. I know you wouldn't do anything with Eygló around. I *knew* that. And yet I jump on you. I'm so stupid.'

'You're not stupid,' said Magnus.

Tears appeared in Ingileif's eyes. She wiped them and looked away, biting her lip. Magnus wanted to grab her, hold her, comfort her.

She turned back to him and sniffed. 'I think you'd better say goodbye to Ási and go.'

'Can I see him again?'

'Yes.' Ingileif nodded her head. 'Send me a text in a couple of weeks. No, a month. Leave it a month, please. But we'll fix something up. Now go!'

## TWENTY-SEVEN

Dísa drove straight from the summer house to Jói's apartment in Gardabaer to pick up her stuff. That was why she had borrowed Kata's car, although she had asked her friend if she could drive out to the summer house first, without explaining to Kata exactly why. She would pay her for the petrol.

She was desperate to log into her father's bitcoin wallet to see how much he had. Although she could have tried to do it on her phone, she thought it was safer to wait until she had some privacy with her laptop. It might be fiddly.

It didn't take Dísa long to pack up – she didn't have many things. When she had finished, Jói suggested a cup of coffee before she left. Petra was working in her coffee shop, so it was just the two of them.

'Thank you so much, Jói,' said Dísa. 'It's been great staying here.'

'It's been nice having you around. How are you doing now?'

'About Mum?'

Jói nodded.

'I was kind of looking forward to the funeral; I thought it would be an important step. And it was good to see all those people there, how they all liked and respected her despite the Thomocoin. But it doesn't really make much difference. I still miss her every second of the day.'

'Of course you do,' said Jói.

'Yeah.' Dísa sipped her coffee. 'They talk about the stages of grief, don't they? I'm not sure what they are or what order they come in. I think denial is one of them. But I'm in the anger phase.'

'With Gunni?'

'Yes, with Gunni. But more with Thomocoin and the people behind it. Dad. Sharp. Mum even. It's stupid, but I'm angry with Mum. I'm angry with myself for telling her about it.'

'Don't get worked up about that, Dísa. It'll just make things worse.'

'Maybe. Did you buy any?'

'Dad tried to get me to, but that stuff isn't my thing. You can make money, but you can lose it too.'

Dísa was tempted to tell Jói about her trip to the summer house – he knew it as well as she did – and about the private key she had copied down, but she held back. Although Jói had slotted into her family well – Mum had made sure of that – Dísa always got the impression that his loyalty was with his father. Which was fair enough. And with his own mother, Dad's first wife, a teacher in Breidholt whom Dísa had never met, which was even fairer.

'I asked the police about Thomocoin today,' she said. 'You know they're not even investigating it?'

'Why not?'

'Politics, apparently. Sharp has got to important people in the government. It makes me furious.'

'But do you even know that's why Gunni killed Helga?'

'That's just what the detective asked me.' Dísa hesitated. 'He said there might be another reason.'

'Oh?'

'You know, don't you, Jói? About Gunni and Mum. When I told you about the rumour I could see you weren't surprised.'

Jói winced. 'I wasn't.' Now it was his turn to hesitate. 'I caught them at it, you know.'

'What!'

'It was a couple of years before the divorce. I was about fourteen. I came home from school in the middle of the day, I forget why. I heard noises from her bedroom. I was old enough to know what that meant. I ran out of the house and spent two hours hiding behind a wall watching the front door to see who came out.'

'And it was Gunni?'

Jói nodded.

'And you didn't tell me?'

'Certainly not!' Jói protested. 'I didn't tell anyone. Except you just now.'

'Wow.' Dísa was about to tell Jói she didn't believe him, to stick up for Mum. But she did believe him.

'So that means that Dad wasn't the only one to cheat?' she said.

'She cheated on him first.'

'Do you think he knew?'

'No idea. But that's what happened with him and my mum. She cheated on him first too.'

Dísa frowned. 'You're just sticking up for him.'

'Maybe, a little bit. He did wrong too. He did have an affair with that woman, Bryndís. And he broke the law and went to jail. But he's paid for his sins.'

'Whereas Mum hadn't?'

Jói winced. 'She has now.'

Dísa shuddered. 'She was tough on Dad.'

'Look,' said Jói. 'Truth is, they both screwed up. But let's not take sides. You're my sister, Dísa. Aren't you?'

Dísa smiled. 'Yes, Jói. I am.'

Dísa's room in Kata's apartment was tiny; there was barely enough space for a single bed and a small table to act as a desk. But after all that had happened, it was good to be with an old, old friend.

As soon as Dísa decently could, she shut herself in there and opened up her laptop.

She knew her way around bitcoin, so with her father's wallet address and private key it didn't take her long to get into his wallet to see how many actual bitcoin he owned.

Three.

Or 3.116 to be precise. Dísa checked the price: $10,526. So that was over thirty thousand dollars. A reasonable amount of money, but not as much as she had hoped. Not nearly enough to save the farm. Or repay all those investors in Thomocoin Mum had suckered in.

But it was something.

Dísa hesitated. Was she really sure she wanted to do what she was about to do?

Steal from her father?

It wasn't theft. She wasn't going to take any of the bitcoin for herself. It was reversing a theft.

Restitution.

Carefully, precisely, she gave instructions to transfer the entire 3.116 bitcoin from her father's wallet to hers.

Ómar probably owned some Thomocoin as well, but

Dísa had no way of getting access to that. Not that there was any point. By this stage, Dísa was convinced Thomocoin was worthless.

Now, what about this other wallet? The one headed 'K'?

She carefully copied out the wallet address and then the private key she had retrieved from the summer house.

It worked!

She blinked. That couldn't be right.

She scribbled down a quick calculation of a piece of paper and counted up the zeroes.

It was right.

'K', whoever he was, owned 1,962 bitcoin in the blockchain.

Which, at a bit over ten thousand dollars each, worked out at about twenty million dollars.

# TWENTY-EIGHT

Magnus's head was spinning as he left Ingileif's apartment in Vesturbaer and his heart was churning. It was late to interview Sharp. On the other hand, Magnus really didn't want to return directly to Eygló's flat, so he drove over to 101 hotel, where Sharp was staying.

It was one of the hippest hotels in Reykjavík, but on a weekday evening in the middle of a pandemic, it was quiet. Fortunately, Sharp was in, although he said he had to leave for an appointment at nine.

They met in a corner of the empty bar, Sharp drinking one of the new Icelandic micro-brews and Magnus a Coke. Everything in the hotel was black, white and cool.

Except Magnus.

Sharp stood up and gave Magnus a friendly smile, but in those COVID times, no handshake. Magnus knew the type: well dressed in a studied, casual way, tall, good-looking, a smattering of stubble. The bankers had won a terrible reputation for themselves in Iceland after the crash. In many ways this was justified – the country had almost gone bust, after all – but compared to some of the seriously sleazy financial types Magnus had come across in Boston, the Icelandic banksters struck him as misguided optimists who had overreached themselves and paid the price.

Sharp seemed genuinely upset by Helga's death. He explained that they had become good friends in Reykjavík before the crash, and Ómar and Helga had stayed with Sharp and his wife Ella a couple of times after they had moved to London.

'Was your relationship with Helga more than just friendship?' Magnus asked.

'Oh, come on!' said Sharp, wrinkling his nose in disgust. 'What kind of question is that?'

'It's a question a detective should ask in a murder inquiry,' Magnus replied, deadpan.

'All right. No. She was my best friend's wife. That's all.'

'It's a long way to come for a funeral.'

'From Reykjavík?'

'From London.'

'I was in Iceland anyway. I've got some business with the government; I saw the Central Bank this afternoon. And I've been to see my parents in Hafnarfjördur. My mother isn't very well. So I took a day to go up to Dalvík for Helga's funeral.'

'I bet they weren't pleased to see you.'

'What do you mean?'

'I mean, half of Dalvík has invested in Thomocoin, and it's worthless.'

'It's not worthless. It was worth three hundred and sixty-eight dollars yesterday.'

'But if you can't sell it on an exchange, is it worth anything?'

'People can buy it. We're still selling Thomocoin every day. At three hundred and sixty-eight dollars.'

'"Still"? You sound surprised. Admit it, Sharp. Thomocoin is in trouble.'

But Sharp wasn't about to show any loss of confidence in Thomocoin. 'The roll-out of the exchange is taking longer than we anticipated, that's all. The idea is still a good one. Cryptocurrencies are moving up in price again. All those guys in Dalvík will be fine. Better than fine – they'll make a good profit.'

'How did it go with the Central Bank today?'

For a moment, the former banker's guard was penetrated. He blinked the fatigue from his eyes.

'Not as well as we'd hoped. But Iceland is still the perfect place to launch Thomocoin.'

'Because of the gullible investors?'

Sharp betrayed a flash of irritation. 'Because it's almost a cashless society already.'

'Gunnar Snaer Sigmundsson is a big investor in Thomocoin, isn't he?' Magnus asked.

'Big by Icelandic standards. There are plenty bigger around the world. He's the guy you arrested for Helga's murder?'

'That's right.'

'Well done. I hope they lock him up for a good long time. I hate the way Iceland lets murderers out after ten years.'

'Do you know him?'

'Not really. I think I met him a couple of times when he was an MP in Reykjavík. I haven't seen him since he made his investment in Thomocoin.'

'Did you know he was having an affair with Helga?'

'Really? No, I had no idea.'

'Does it surprise you?'

'How can I answer that? Helga was divorced. She never

spoke to me about her love life after Ómar and she split up. So I suppose not. Is he married?'

'Yes.' Magnus nodded. 'How much is Ómar involved in Thomocoin?'

'Not much,' said Sharp. 'He made a small investment when it was launched, so he will have made a profit on that. I suppose the biggest thing he did was introduce his daughter Dísa and through her Helga. Helga brought in a lot of investors.'

'Quite a catch,' said Magnus. 'Can you tell me something about Krakatoa?'

'Krakatoa? What's he got to do with this?'

'Isn't he the online boss of Thomocoin?'

'Who told you that? *I'm* the boss of Thomocoin. Krakatoa works for me.'

'Have you ever met him?'

'No.'

'Do you know his real name?'

'No. He operates online. Thomocoin is a virtual company. We employ people with computer skills throughout the world. Krakatoa is one of those.'

'How do you pay him?'

'Bitcoin.'

'Not Thomocoin?'

Sharp smiled. 'No. He prefers bitcoin.'

'Is he an Icelander?'

'No,' said Sharp. 'I think he's Canadian.'

'It's strange you know so little about such an important employee.'

'Oh, I know a lot about Krakatoa,' said Sharp. 'In the online world. He's good; he has a great reputation. He always delivers. Who he is or what he does in the real world is irrelevant.'

'Really?'

'Yeah, really.'

'Are *you* Krakatoa?' Magnus didn't expect a straight answer from Sharp, but he was watching his reaction closely.

'Hah! Where did you get that idea?'

Not an immediate denial, Magnus noticed, but a deflection.

'I have a witness who is convinced Krakatoa is an Icelander, that Krakatoa is you.'

'Who is this witness?'

'Who is Krakatoa?'

'I've told you: I don't know who Krakatoa is.'

'And I don't believe you.'

The two men stared at each other, Sharp's bright blue eyes unwavering. Had Sharp been unnecessarily evasive when refusing to respond to Magnus's question with a simple 'no'? Magnus wasn't sure.

Sharp leaned back. 'Can I ask *you* something?'

'Yes.'

'Did Gunnar kill Helga because of Thomocoin? Or was it the affair?'

'We don't know yet. Dísa thinks it's Thomocoin.'

'She's a smart girl, Dísa.'

'Why do you ask?'

Sharp took a sip of his beer. 'I genuinely believe Thomocoin is going to work. But if it turned out it was the reason why Helga died . . . Well, I'd feel bad.'

'Dísa thinks you should feel bad.'

'Does she? Poor girl. I didn't really get a chance to speak to her at the funeral. I spoke to Helga's brother, who was upset with me, but I think I squared him.'

'You know, Sharp,' said Magnus, looking him directly in

the eyes. 'I don't think you really believe Thomocoin is worth anything either.'

Sharp sighed. 'It was a bad day today. The meeting with the Central Bank really didn't go well. But if there's one thing I've learned in my career, it's not to give up. And I'm not giving up.' He glanced quickly at his phone. 'Look, I've got to go.'

'All right. Here's my card if you have any further information for me,' said Magnus, handing it to him. 'When are you flying back to London?'

'Tomorrow.'

'Can I get in touch with you there if I need to?' said Magnus.

'I suppose so,' said Sharp grudgingly. 'I'll be in England for a while. Travel is getting more difficult again, with the virus numbers ticking up everywhere. I've just heard the Brits have added Iceland to their quarantine list as from next Saturday.'

With that, he left the hotel bar and went out into the Reykjavík evening.

On the way back to Eygló's apartment, Magnus called Agent Malley in New York and told him of Sharp's travel plans. He also said that it looked as if Sharp's discussions with the Icelandic authorities hadn't gone well. Malley promised to get in touch with Magnus as soon as the red notice was issued.

'Where were you?' said Eygló when he arrived at her flat.

'At 101 hotel,' said Magnus. 'Interviewing a witness.'

He hadn't told Eygló he was meeting Ási and Ingileif. Why, he wasn't sure.

Well, maybe he was sure, he just didn't want to admit it to himself.

'At 101 hotel?' Eygló repeated. 'Very fancy. What was she like, this witness?'

'It was a he,' said Magnus, irritably. 'An ex-banker called Sharp. It's to do with the Dalvík case.'

'You look *so* guilty,' said Eygló, her tone teasing.

Magnus felt the guilt erupt within him. He ignored her and picked up his iPad, ostensibly to check the Red Sox results.

'You do look guilty,' Eygló repeated, all playfulness gone.

# TWENTY-NINE

Krakatoa stared across the water towards the mountains. It was a clear, breezy day out there, whitecaps skipping across the sea, which was, for the moment at least, blue.

He was going to have to pull the plug soon. There was no escaping it. Although, remarkably, Thomocoin was still pulling in money from China, Eastern Europe and Africa, the groundswell of disgruntlement was growing. The decision to abandon America had been a good one. But the European regulators were beginning to ask questions, and one of Thomocoin's investors in the Netherlands had received a visit from the police.

If they could have announced an exchange in Iceland, that might have turned things around, but the Central Bank had put paid to that. It wasn't going to happen.

They could maybe hang on for a few more days, maybe even a couple of weeks, all the while gathering in more money, but on balance, Krakatoa believed it was better to quit a few days early than a few days late.

Thomocoin had done what it was supposed to: lure

investors in. When he had been working on the concept, Krakatoa had given it the name FOMOcoin, for 'Fear Of Missing Out'. The idea was always to play on the fear of missing out on an easy fortune. That they had done, successfully. But FOMOcoin was not the ideal name for a hot new investment. Thomocoin was much better, especially if some made-up kid with leukaemia was thrown into the mix.

Whether Thomocoin would ever mature into a serious cryptocurrency had never been the main issue for Krakatoa. He hoped it would. He always spoke as if it would. He had successfully convinced his team that it would. But if it fizzled out in a digital puff of crypto-smoke, that was fine too. He had a plan.

Goodmanhunting had just warned him that the FBI hadn't dropped their investigation after all. Krakatoa had hoped that the agency would lose interest, once Thomocoin stopped selling in the USA.

Clearly not.

Krakatoa decided it was time to secure his bitcoin. He had balances in hot wallets with four exchanges. Time to transfer them to his cold wallet. This was held on a specialized USB stick, with a paper back-up tucked away in a remote part of Iceland where no one would ever think of looking.

There should be no reason why he would ever need to go there either. But it was a necessary insurance policy. There were too many stories of idiots who had lost access to millions in bitcoin because they had mislaid or forgotten their private key and hadn't made a paper back-up. It was estimated that 20 per cent of all the bitcoin outstanding had been lost forever in that way.

He plugged his cold wallet into his computer to check

his bitcoin balance, before transferring in some bitcoin from one of the exchanges.

He blinked. That couldn't be right.

Zero. A big fat zero.

The wallet should have had nearly two thousand bitcoin in it.

His fingers flew over the keyboard as he checked recent transactions.

One thousand nine hundred and sixty-two bitcoin had been transferred out of his wallet the previous day.

He sat and stared. The blood seemed to be seeping out of his body. He couldn't breathe.

He had lost twenty million dollars. Twenty million!

'Fuck!' he shouted. 'Fuck, fuck, fuck!'

Who could have broken into his bitcoin wallet?

There was only one person.

KRAKATOA: Where are my bitcoin?

Krakatoa waited. What if Lawrence wasn't online? Even though there was no point, Krakatoa repeated his question.

KRAKATOA: Get back to me. This is urgent. I don't know what's going on. Where are my bitcoin?

Still no reply. Krakatoa paced around his desk, swearing under his breath. What was he going to do now?

LAWRENCE: What do you mean, where are your bitcoin?

KRAKATOA: They've gone. They've all gone from my cold wallet.

LAWRENCE: Have you been hacked?

KRAKATOA: I can't have been. You are the only person who knows where my cold wallet paper back-up is. Unless you took them?

LAWRENCE: Of course I didn't take them.

Krakatoa was about to repeat his question with a threat attached to it when he forced himself to calm down.

KRAKATOA: OK. Can you check your wallet?
LAWRENCE: All right. brb.

Krakatoa waited. It was only three minutes, but it seemed to be an hour.

LAWRENCE: They've gone. My bitcoin have gone.
KRAKATOA: All of them?
LAWRENCE: Yeah. I had three point one. Have all yours gone too?
KRAKATOA: Yes. All of them.
LAWRENCE: How much did you have?
KRAKATOA: A lot. Everything. Almost everything.
LAWRENCE: Someone must have hacked it. How could they have done that? I thought these private keys were secure?
KRAKATOA: They are. Nobody hacked it. If we have both been cleaned out, it means that someone got hold of both our private keys. And there's only one way they could have done that. Find our cold wallets.
LAWRENCE: At the summer house?
KRAKATOA: That's right.
LAWRENCE: But that's impossible.
KRAKATOA: Is it? Have you told anyone where you hid the cold wallets?
LAWRENCE: Of course not.
KRAKATOA: Are you sure?

No reply. There was only one explanation. Lawrence had told someone. Unless he had stolen Krakatoa's bitcoin himself, and that was something Krakatoa found hard to believe.

Maybe he should believe it.

A message flashed up.

LAWRENCE: I did tell someone. Sort of.

KRAKATOA: Who?

LAWRENCE: Dísa.

KRAKATOA: What! Why did you do that?

LAWRENCE: It was back when I gave her the bitcoin. I was explaining how she needed a cold wallet. I think I mentioned where I kept mine. Something about the hidden people watching over it.

KRAKATOA: Why the fuck did you do that?

LAWRENCE: I don't know. It was just a joke. Anyway, Dísa wouldn't steal from me. It can't be her. Must be a hacker. Wait. Someone's at the door. Got to go.

# THIRTY

Ómar was not what Magnus had expected. Rather than a smooth banker, a mini-Sharp, he was faced with a pale, dumpy, balding man with a scrappy goatee, a Viking-rune dangling from his ear and half a neck full of ink.

'Inspector Magnús.' He held out his warrant card. Ómar examined it distractedly. 'May I come in?'

Ómar blinked. 'Yes,' he muttered. 'Yes, all right.'

Ómar's flat was small but tidy. Magnus sat on a beaten-up sofa, while Ómar took an armchair. The furniture had a second-hand IKEA vibe, with a touch of dumpster-rescue chic. Magnus guessed Sharp's apartment in London looked very different.

There were a few framed photographs scattered about the room. One of Dísa on a volleyball court, her brows knitted in concentration. And another of a group of five people standing in front of a lake. Two adults, one of which was Helga and the other a much slimmer, more confident version of the man sitting opposite. Magnus recognized Dísa again, gawky and shy, and the pretty little blonde girl who must be Anna Rós. The boy, with his own blonde curls, was no doubt Ómar's son from his first marriage.

Ómar followed Magnus's eyes and scowled. 'What do you want?'

'I'm investigating your ex-wife's murder,' said Magnus.

'Oh. All right.'

'First, please accept my condolences.'

'Thank you.' Ómar looked exhausted. Worried.

'I'd like to ask you about Thomocoin,' Magnus went on.

'And I'm not going to tell you.'

That surprised Magnus. 'This is a murder investigation, Ómar. You have to help me.'

'I thought you'd caught the murderer,' said Ómar. 'Look. I've been in jail; I know how you guys operate. I don't say anything about my financial circumstances without a lawyer present. And my financial circumstances include Thomocoin. And if you want to throw me in Building Number One at Litla-Hraun again, I'm fine with that. I could use the peace and quiet.'

Building No. 1 at Litla-Hraun was where suspects used to be held in solitary confinement pending trial. It had sometimes been used by the Icelandic police as a tool to extract confessions. They threw them in the new prison at Hólmsheidi now.

'Your daughter believes that Thomocoin is responsible for Helga's death.'

'Well, she's wrong.'

'She might be. But I have no way of knowing that unless I find out more about Thomocoin myself.'

'Do you think Sharp killed her?' said Ómar. 'Because that's crazy. It was this guy Gunni.'

'Do you know him?' Magnus asked. 'Gunni?'

'No. Never met him. But Dísa told me a little bit about him.'

'Did she tell you he was a big investor in Thomocoin? And that he believed that his Thomocoin was worthless?'

'Yes, she did. And I think he was the one who got Helga worried. I told your colleague, the black woman, that Helga came down to Reykjavík to ask me about the exchange. Until then I had no idea she was involved in Thomocoin at all.'

'What did you tell her?'

'That it was all going to be fine as far as I knew. Sharp had it all under control.'

'And does he?'

'Ask him.'

Ómar was drawing the lines. He seemed happy to talk as long as the discussion didn't involve his own investments. Magnus had gathered from Dísa that Ómar had invested in bitcoin several years ago, probably offshore, which was probably illegal, hence his reluctance to discuss it.

'Did you know Gunni had an affair with Helga?'

'No. Am I supposed to care? We were divorced nearly ten years.'

'Before the divorce. When you lived in Reykjavík. And he was an MP.'

That caught Ómar's attention. 'I don't believe you.'

'Gunni has admitted it. And Helga confided in someone.'

'Who?'

'I can't say.'

This was clearly new information to Ómar. 'Are you talking before 2008?'

'Yes.'

Ómar winced. Shook his head. 'Oh, Helga.'

Magnus waited.

'Actually, although it makes me angry, I'm also glad to hear that,' said Ómar.

'Why?'

'Because she cheated before I did. I had an affair with a woman from work, starting in 2008. It was stupid. It was one of the reasons Helga left me and went back to Dalvík. That and the fact I was in jail and not earning a salary any more. But if she was cheating on me, well . . .'

'You feel better?'

Ómar's shoulders slumped. 'There's nothing about any of this that makes me feel good.'

'Why are you protecting Sharp?' Magnus asked.

'He's a mate.'

'But your daughter thinks that Thomocoin is behind Helga's death. And Sharp is behind Thomocoin.'

'My daughter is wrong. And I've told you I'm not going to talk about Thomocoin.'

'I've read your record. You and four others went to jail, but none of you testified against Sharp. Why not?'

'Because he hadn't done anything wrong.'

'How did you feel when he was running around free in London and you were locked up? And now, when he has a nice flat in London and you live in this dump?'

'I'm happy for him. He's a mate.'

'A mate who gave you some bitcoin a few years ago? Who cut you in on Thomocoin?'

'I had a few thousand bucks of Thomocoin, that's all,' said Ómar. 'I introduced Dísa to it three years ago, but I specifically told her not to tell her mother about it.'

'Why did you do that?'

Ómar took a deep breath. 'Helga liked money, but she never understood it. She was always greedy. Whereas Dísa gets it.' He grinned. 'I don't know if she told you, but she did a phenomenal job turning a few thousand dollars' worth of bitcoin into hundreds of thousands.'

'She is a clever girl,' said Magnus. 'And her mother has been murdered. Your ex-wife. Which is why I want to help her find out what happened.'

Ómar shrugged.

'Was there anyone else from Dalvík who was worried about Thomocoin that you know about?' Magnus asked. 'Her father, perhaps?'

'Hafsteinn was always a true believer,' said Ómar. 'But I think her brother had doubts. Eggert. He gave me a hard time at the funeral.'

'Tell me about Eggert.'

'He was lined up to take over the farm, but he refused, which really pissed off his parents. He's an engineer. A smart guy. He got involved with some dot-com stuff many years ago, a website for individuals to offset their carbon emissions. It wasn't a bad idea. We talked about it, back when I was a banker; Sharp tried to put him in touch with venture capitalists in London, but it never got off the ground.'

'What went wrong?'

'Back then carbon offset was something corporations were more interested in than individuals. Something might have come out of it, but then the crash happened, and he retreated to Akureyri.'

'How did he and Helga get on?' Magnus asked.

'Pretty well. They're very different. I get the impression he was happy to leave the farm and the parents for her to deal with.'

'Did he understand Thomocoin?'

'I'd say yes. And, actually, his questions about the

exchange were good ones. He'd obviously read up a lot on crypto. Helga said he had made an investment in a bitcoin miner. Do you know what those are?'

Magnus remembered the shed near the airport with the open window and the ladder against the wall. 'Indeed I do. That's not very environmentally friendly for someone who set up a carbon-offset website is it? Those things use a load of electricity.'

Ómar shrugged.

'Do you believe Thomocoin is going to work, Ómar?' Magnus asked.

Ómar sat back in his armchair and didn't answer.

'Who's Krakatoa?' Magnus asked.

'It's a volcano in Indonesia,' said Ómar.

'It's also the name of the guy who runs Thomocoin.'

'I didn't know that.'

'Is he an Icelander? Is he Sharp?'

'I have no idea. And that really is all I'm going to tell you about Thomocoin.'

## THIRTY-ONE

LAWRENCE: It was a cop.

KRAKATOA: Did he ask you about Thomocoin?

LAWRENCE: Yes. He said he was investigating Helga's murder, but his questions were all about Thomocoin.

KRAKATOA: Did you tell him anything?

LAWRENCE: Of course not. I've been through this before. I told him nothing.

KRAKATOA: Did he mention the FBI?

LAWRENCE: Why would he mention the FBI?

KRAKATOA: Did he mention the FBI?

LAWRENCE: No.

KRAKATOA: You know how to operate the kill switch on your laptop?

LAWRENCE: Yes. You showed me.

KRAKATOA: Right. Next time the police show up, hit the kill switch before you answer the door. Otherwise they might seize the machine.

LAWRENCE: OK. I'll do that.

KRAKATOA: And then go dark.

LAWRENCE: What do you mean go dark?

KRAKATOA: Don't contact me. Or anyone else. Got that?

LAWRENCE: Got it. Do you think the FBI are on to Thomocoin?

KRAKATOA: Maybe. Bye.

Krakatoa sat back from his computer and exhaled.

It was happening.

There was no 'maybe' about it. The FBI *were* on to them. Goodmanhunting had just sent him a message that a red notice had been issued by Interpol and arrests would be made tomorrow. Probably at dawn.

Krakatoa had prepared for this. Although there had been the hope that Thomocoin might succeed on its own terms, Krakatoa knew it was always likely that he might have to bail. Hence the kill switch installed on everyone's computers, including his. It was activated by the simultaneous hitting of three keys, which would cause their computers to lock out all access to their hard drives forever.

Or actually until the year 2100. In a fit of whimsy, Krakatoa had decided to leave something for his grandchildren.

What about the twenty million? What about the twenty million fucking dollars Dísa had stolen from him?

That would have to wait. Not long, but it would have to wait.

Goodmanhunting's message had taken the decision for him. Time to pull the plug.

KRAKATOA: Scramble.

LINDENBROOK: Are you sure?

KRAKATOA: Certain. Arrest warrants issued today. Arrests likely tomorrow morning.

LINDENBROOK: OK. I'll contact you from Panama.
KRAKATOA: Good luck.

KRAKATOA: Scramble.
DUBBELOSIX: Shit. OK. Can I get a flight tomorrow
afternoon?
KRAKATOA: No. You've got to be out of France this
evening. Leave right now if you can.
DUBBELOSIX: But it's my wife's birthday tomorrow!
KRAKATOA: And do you want to be arrested on her
birthday? Arrests likely tomorrow at dawn. You need to
get out before the borders are informed. Are you going
via Madrid?
DUBBELOSIX: Yes.
KRAKATOA: Then kiss your wife goodbye and go!
DUBBELOSIX: When will I see her again? The kids?
KRAKATOA: It may be a while. I'm sorry. But it was
always a possibility.
DUBBELOSIX: I didn't think it would really happen.
KRAKATOA: Well, it's really happening. And unless you
leave now you will spend the rest of the decade in jail.
Comprends?
DUBBELOSIX: Je comprends. OK. I'll scramble.
KRAKATOA: Check in when you get to Panama. And
good luck!

Krakatoa hadn't expected Dubbelosix to flake. They
had been over the scramble scenario countless times. If
either Dubbelosix or Lindenbrook was arrested it would be
bad. They might talk, eventually; tell the FBI who he was.

There were a lot of people who worked for Thomocoin
all over the world. The cops would have a very hard time
tracking any of them down. And even if they did, none of

them knew who Krakatoa was, beyond the fact that he was Canadian. Which he wasn't.

But there were one or two of his most loyal employees that Krakatoa wanted to give a heads-up to.

KRAKATOA: Hey Tubs.

TUBBYMAN: Hey Krak.

KRAKATOA: You know you asked me about the FBI yesterday?

TUBBYMAN: Yeah. And you said it was just a rumour.

KRAKATOA: Turns out it was more than a rumour. They are planning to make some arrests tomorrow.

TUBBYMAN: Are they arresting you?

KRAKATOA: They'll never find me.

TUBBYMAN: What about me?

KRAKATOA: They won't find you either. I'm the only one who knows who you are or where you live, and they won't find me. But I thought I should warn you just in case.

TUBBYMAN: Thanks. I'm worried.

KRAKATOA: Don't be.

TUBBYMAN: What about the investors?

KRAKATOA: Their loss, I'm afraid. Give them a good last price today and then go dark.

TUBBYMAN: $400?

KRAKATOA: Why not give them $500? Your choice.

TUBBYMAN: What do I do if the police do knock at the door?

KRAKATOA: Hit your kill switch. And don't admit anything. Get a lawyer if you have to. You'll be fine.

TUBBYMAN: And you? You know the Mounties always get their man?

KRAKATOA: Not this one. Bye Tubs.

TUBBYMAN: Bye Krak.

Krakatoa had his own situation all worked out. But that had assumed he had twenty million dollars in bitcoin squirrelled away.

Someone had dug up his acorns.

Dísa.

He needed them back.

KRAKATOA: Are you still in Iceland?

TECUMSEH: Yes.

KRAKATOA: Good. Reykjavík?

TECUMSEH: Yes.

KRAKATOA: I may have something for you. Same rates as before.

TECUMSEH: Eighty thousand. Half now, half within forty-eight hours of success.

KRAKATOA: But that's twenty thousand more than last time!

TECUMSEH: And that's because it's twenty thousand more dangerous. Follow-ups are more dangerous by definition.

KRAKATOA: All right. I'll give you instructions tomorrow.

TECUMSEH: I'll be ready.

Krakatoa fought to control his anger. If he kept a clear head, this should all work out OK.

Dísa was sensible. Krakatoa had to create a situation where the only sensible thing for Dísa to do was to give Krakatoa his bitcoin back.

He could do that.

# THIRTY-TWO

Magnus returned to the station after seeing Ómar. What had he learned?

There was something very dodgy about Thomocoin. Regulators all over the world should have nipped it in the bud and not allowed it to take in millions from gullible investors. That certainly applied to Iceland. But Magnus wasn't sure that he had uncovered enough evidence to give investigators something to prosecute. Especially if those investigators were determined to look the other way.

He hadn't really learned anything that would help Dísa either. It was likely that Gunni's doubts about Thomocoin had played a big part in his decision to murder Helga. To put it another way, if Thomocoin hadn't existed, Helga would almost certainly still be alive today. But there was no sign that Sharp or Fjóla or anyone else at Thomocoin had assisted in any way in the murder, or that they bore any legal responsibility.

Gunni had decided to kill Helga of his own free will. That wasn't Thomocoin's fault.

Ómar was undoubtedly an investor in Thomocoin and

had a relationship with Sharp going back years. But Magnus doubted he was involved directly in his ex-wife's murder. Ómar had mentioned that Eggert had had dealings with Sharp in the past. But Eggert was hardly a major investor in Thomocoin. Enough to be upset, not enough to kill.

Sharp had put on a brave face, but from what Magnus could tell, Thomocoin's days were numbered. And with it the savings of dozens, probably hundreds of Icelanders.

There might be some vengeance for Dísa in that. But as far as Magnus was concerned, the loss of all those people's savings was bad news.

It meant a scandal was brewing. If Thomocoin did blow up, the regulators would have to turn around and look at the mess on their own doorstep.

Thelma had anticipated all this. Magnus realized that his interviews with Fjóla, Ómar and Sharp would come to light.

Magnus decided to prepare himself for that. He wrote up his interview notes carefully. He called Sigurjón in Financial Crimes to warn him that the shit was likely to hit the fan. He knew Thelma would not be at all happy with any of this when she found out, and she would find out.

Tough.

Then Magnus called Árni to fill him in on what he had learned and to find out how the investigation was going in Dalvík.

Gunni was still stewing in solitary at Hólmsheidi. The police were having trouble gathering further evidence against him. Ólafur was still confident of a conviction: it was certainly Helga's blood on the knife found in Gunni's shed, there was a motive in all the money Gunni thought Helga had lost him, and Gunni just about had the opportunity.

And that was it.

Magnus was about to finish the call when Árni dropped his voice to a whisper. 'Magnús?'

'Yes.'

'I'm not sure Gunni is our man.'

Magnus prepared himself for one of Árni's half-baked ideas. 'Why not?'

'It doesn't *feel* right.'

'And why is that?'

'Gunni strikes me as a smart man. A competent guy who doesn't screw up.'

'I'd agree with that.'

'So why didn't he get rid of the knife?'

'He did. He hid it.'

'Yes. But somewhere we were bound to find it.'

'Only if we were looking for it.'

'Yes,' said Árni. 'But if he *did* kill Helga, he must have assumed that at some point we would search his property.'

Árni had a point. 'Maybe he was hiding it before he got rid of it?'

'OK. Then why didn't he wipe it clean? Or wash it? It would have been dead easy to wash off that blood. He didn't even try.'

'Maybe he panicked. I've seen plenty of murderers panic and do dumb things in my time in Boston.'

'Yes. But Gunni doesn't seem like a panicker.'

Magnus was silent.

'Does he?' said Árni. 'He spent all those years captaining trawlers in the North Atlantic. Guys like that are good under pressure.'

'OK. He doesn't seem like a panicker. But if Gunni didn't kill Helga, someone must have planted the knife. Who?'

'The murderer. Maybe it was the guy seen hiking on the mountain with a backpack.'

'Seen by Gunni.'

'Yes. Seen by Gunni. Magnús, I don't know what to do.'

Magnus thought. Did Árni have a point? Maybe. Maybe there was some doubt.

'Have you spoken to Ólafur?' he asked.

'Yes.'

'And?'

'He called me an idiot. He said I was supposed to be helping the prosecution and not the defence. He told me not to mention my misgivings to anyone. He'd certainly be unhappy if he knew I was talking to you.'

It was Ólafur who was the idiot. Policemen who thought it was more important to secure a conviction than to convict the right man were all idiots who didn't understand their job. Árni might be wrong, but he had a legitimate question, and it needed to be answered, not squashed.

'OK, Árni,' Magnus said. 'You may be right. Or, more likely, the obvious may be true: Gunni killed Helga because she had lost him millions of dollars. Keep an open mind. Gather the evidence. Don't draw any preliminary conclusions, but if the evidence that Gunni is innocent builds, take it to Ólafur.'

'And if he won't listen?'

'Call me.'


Agent Malley phoned Magnus just as Magnus was about to leave the station.

'It's all go. The red notices have been issued.'

'For Sharp and Jérôme Carmin?'

'That's right. The French and British police know

where they live. The arrests will happen tomorrow morning. I'd be in London myself to talk to Sharp, but I'd have to go into quarantine, so I'll have to do it on a video link.'

'Are you publicizing the arrests?' Magnus asked.

'We will. Once we've got the cuffs on them.'

'That will mean the end of Thomocoin.'

'As it damn well should.'

'Have you alerted our people?'

'No way. Given your guys' lack of response to our requests, we decided not to. They'll see the red notice eventually. But I owed you the call. Don't talk to anyone else until tomorrow. We don't want Sharp tipped off.'

Would someone in Financial Crimes or any of the agencies regulating finance in Iceland really tip Sharp off?

Sharp no doubt had plenty of buddies from his heady days as one of Iceland's top bankers. So the answer to that question was a definite maybe.

'I'll keep it quiet. Keep me posted.'


'Maja saw you yesterday.'

They had finished supper – pad thai, one of Eygló's specialities – and Bjarki had sloped off to his room to do some homework.

'I didn't see her,' said Magnus. Maja was a friend of Eygló's from the University of Iceland.

'No, you didn't. She said she did wave. But you were too busy talking to a blonde woman. You were in a playground in Vesturbaer.'

'Ah.'

'Maja said she wondered what you were doing with this woman, who is quite attractive, apparently, and then she saw the kid you were with, who looks a lot like you, apparently, and she realized you must have been with your ex. Apparently.'

Eygló was trying to sound flippant, but there was an unmistakeable bite in her tone.

'Oh.'

'You didn't tell me.'

'No. Look, I'm sorry, Eygló. I should have done.'

'And was it Ingileif who you met at 101 hotel?'

'Of course not!' said Magnus, his indignation ringing hollow even in his ears. 'It was a banker. I told you. Skarphédinn Gíslason. He's the CEO of Thomocoin. Why would I take Ingileif to a hotel and then tell you about it?'

The moment Magnus uttered the words he regretted them, implying as they did that he would take Ingileif to a hotel and *not* tell Eygló about it.

'Can I believe you?'

'Of course you can believe me!'

'How many times have you seen Ingileif without telling me? Maybe you've been seeing her for years?'

'No. No, Eygló. This is the first time, I promise.'

'You promise? Einar used to promise.'

Einar was Eygló's old boyfriend. Magnus had seen at first hand how good a liar he was; he had had lots of practice.

'I'm nothing like Einar,' Magnus said. 'You know that.'

'I *thought* that. I *know* I'm too trusting.'

'Look, I've seen Ingileif, what . . . four times in the last eight years. There's nothing to worry about.'

'Isn't there?'

Eygló's eyes were angry.

'Hey. I'm sorry I didn't tell you I was seeing Ási yesterday. I really don't know why I didn't. I will next time.'

'Next time?'

'Yes. Ingileif said I could see him in a couple of weeks.' Magnus corrected himself. 'Maybe a month.'

'All right,' said Eygló. 'I know how important he is to you. And I'm glad she's letting you see him again. But don't hide it from me. OK?'

'OK,' said Magnus. He resolved to tell Eygló every time he met Ási. He resolved not to kiss Ingileif again. He didn't like feeling this guilty.

'I had my interview with Southampton.'

'Oh, great,' said Magnus. 'How did it go?'

'It went well, I think. It sounds like they'll make me a formal offer of a job.'

'Are you going to take it?'

'I don't know. Am I?' Eygló stared at him.

'It's really up to you,' Magnus said at last.

Tears appeared in Eygló's eyes.

'Eygló?'

She sniffed and rubbed her nose. Then her face hardened. 'I suggest you spend the night at Álftanes.'

# THIRTY-THREE

Dísa had shown up to one class at the university and spent the rest of the day in her tiny room in Kata's apartment, stewing about what to do next.

She had transferred the thirty thousand dollars' worth of her father's bitcoin and the twenty million belonging to 'K' to her own wallet. It had actually taken all night for the bitcoin to clear – it had to be verified by a 'miner' somewhere and added to the blockchain, a process that could take anything from a couple of minutes to a day or more, depending on how busy the system was. And the system was getting busier by the day; the pandemic had sparked a surge in crypto-trading from speculators trapped indoors.

Now the bitcoin was sitting in her wallet staring at her and she was staring at it.

She was scared. She had hoped that her father's wallet had contained a couple of hundred thousand dollars' worth of bitcoin, which she could take and distribute to the Dalvík investors. But twenty million!

That was more money than she could comprehend. It frightened her.

It would be enough to repay all the Icelandic investors in full. All the debts on Blábrekka; the farm would be saved. And there would be plenty left over for other investors in Thomocoin all over the world.

Who or what was 'K'?

At first, she had thought it might be a second wallet owned by her dad, but the more she considered that the more unlikely it seemed. With all that bitcoin, K was clearly high up in the Thomocoin hierarchy, probably at the very top, and that didn't sound like her father.

It did sound like Sharp. Sharp was a good friend of her father's. Although he lived in London, his friend's summer house in Iceland might well have seemed a good remote back-up.

How long would it take for Sharp to realize what had happened to his bitcoin? And what would he do once he had?

There would be no way for him to figure out who had taken it.

Unless he talked to Dad. And Dad remembered telling Dísa about the hidden people and the summer house. That was three years ago – maybe Dad would have forgotten.

Maybe not.

Dísa needed to figure out how to pay the bitcoin over to all the investors in Dalvík and Akureyri.

She had downloaded the list of names from Mum's computer on to her own machine, but she didn't have bank account details. All these investors would have had Thomocoin private keys, but not bitcoin, and there wasn't an exchange for converting one into the other – that was the whole problem.

She needed help. The truth was, she needed more than that: she needed an ally. Someone with whom to share the massive weight of responsibility of those twenty million dollars. Someone good with computers. Someone who knew about bitcoin or who was smart enough to figure out bitcoin. Someone she trusted.

Jói?

Trouble was, she wasn't sure she could trust Jói with what she had done. She had after all stolen bitcoin from their father. And it was clear Jói trusted Dad more than she did.

What about Uncle Eggert?

Dísa didn't know Uncle Eggert quite as well as she knew Jói. But he was good with computers: he was always giving Jói computer stuff for Christmas back in Reykjavík, she remembered. Although he knew Ómar a little, he had no loyalty to him, whereas he was Mum's brother. Dísa had heard he had invested in a bitcoin-mining company. Those companies must have figured out a way to sell their bitcoin legally. Maybe Uncle Eggert would know how, or could find out.

Her computer screen beeped. An email. She idly clicked to take a look. It was in English.

*From: Krakatoa*
*To: Dísa Ómarsdóttir*
*Subject: Your theft*
*You have stolen 1962.41634 bitcoin from me. Please return it.*
*If you don't return it within three days, someone close to you will die.*
*I am not bluffing. Your mother died. Now someone else will.*

*All you need to do is return my bitcoin and nothing
else will happen. You have my wallet address.*

*You may reply to this email address within the next
hour, after which it will become defunct. Then you
should download the Telegram messaging app using
the attached instructions and contact me using that.
Otherwise, I will contact you in twenty-four hours
from a different email address.*

*Don't tell the police about this message, or you
will die.*

*The easiest, most sensible thing to do is return the
bitcoin right now.*

*Krakatoa*

Jesus Christ! Who the hell was Krakatoa?

K. Krakatoa must be K.

So, who was K? Sharp, probably. It was Sharp who was threatening her.

Who was the 'someone else' who was going to die?

No idea. But it would be someone close to her, important to her.

Dísa's heart beat faster. What should she do?

Give the bitcoin back?

She really didn't want to do that after the risks she had taken to get it. She had this one chance to make amends for what she and her mother had done, to rescue Blábrekka and the savings of so many of her neighbours in Dalvík. Giving up on that one chance would be cowardly – once it was gone, it was gone.

She *had* to redeem herself. Redeem her mother.

Should she take Sharp's threat seriously? Maybe he was bluffing?

Killing someone was a very serious step. Threatening to kill someone less so. She could imagine Sharp threatening her. Could she imagine Sharp killing someone innocent? The 'someone else'?

She didn't think so. But the truth was she didn't know him at all.

What about going to the police? Bad idea. Although Inspector Magnús had seemed sympathetic, helpful even, he hadn't helped. She believed him that Icelandic politics had impeded his investigations, but that kind of bureaucratic obstruction wouldn't step out of the way over some unspecified threat. Besides, all she would be doing was removing a threat to someone else with what seemed to be a more certain threat to her.

At least she had been given a couple of days.

And Sharp might be bluffing.

She took a decision. She wouldn't respond to the email and she certainly wouldn't download Telegram. She would figure out how to return as much of the bitcoin as she could and then tell Sharp or Krakatoa or whoever that the bitcoin was all gone.

And then hide. Or something.

She needed to act quickly.


Krakatoa was pleased with his email. If Dísa was sensible, then the bitcoin would be back in his wallet within the hour. Realistically, she would stew over it for a day or two, which was why Krakatoa had given her three days.

Dísa was sensible. So no one would have to die.

But. If she held out, then Krakatoa would follow through on his threat.

Twelve months before, an American employee named Cryptocheeseman had ripped him off to the tune of two hundred thousand dollars. It had been a very public rip-off, a humiliation in front of everyone involved in Thomocoin. An organization like Thomocoin, which ran outside the normal auspices of contract law, had to have an enforcement mechanism.

Krakatoa had hired Tecumseh on the dark web to locate Cryptocheeseman and deal with him. Tecumseh had visited Cryptocheeseman in a suburb of Charlotte, North Carolina, persuaded him to give up his private key and then silenced him. Krakatoa didn't know how exactly, and he didn't want to know how, but the local newspaper's website that he checked to ensure Tecumseh had completed his task mentioned something about a stabbing during a street robbery.

No one in Thomocoin knew for sure what had happened to Cryptocheeseman. All Krakatoa had announced was that there was good news: the bitcoin Cryptocheeseman had stolen had been returned. The guys who worked for Thomocoin were smart. They now knew it was a bad idea to steal from Krakatoa.

Krakatoa had ordered the death of a real person. Yet giving that order hadn't seemed at all real to him. It wasn't just that the command had been transmitted in cyberspace, nor that the action itself had been committed on the other side of the world. It was also that the killer was Krakatoa. And that's the kind of thing that Krakatoa did.

Helga's death had been more difficult. Much more. But Krakatoa had really had no choice if he was going to stay out of jail. And, mostly, he had succeeded in convincing himself that it was Krakatoa who had ordered the killing. Not his real-life personality.

His phone rang.

He smiled when he saw the caller.

'Hi, Dísa.'

His sister's voice was trembling. 'Jói? Do you have Uncle Eggert's phone number?'

PART FOUR

# THIRTY-FOUR

Four days later, Tecumseh stood in the doorway of the small office building and watched the house fifty metres down on the opposite side of the street.

This was his second evening in that spot. The day before, the target had come back from the library at dusk and stayed in all night. He needed darkness to do his job, which meant he needed his target to go out after dark.

Krakatoa had been angry that he hadn't acted the previous night. But the one thing Tecumseh never compromised on was his own security, and he wasn't prepared to work in daylight. Not in a city.

He was an accountant by training, and that training meant he was careful. He planned everything meticulously, in code on his phone. He had a little spreadsheet app he found perfect for the purpose. With his lack of a relevant background, getting his first assassination gig on the dark web had been difficult. But he had received a good review on that first one, a cheating husband in Düsseldorf, and slowly, slowly business had picked up. The choice of Tecumseh as an online handle had helped, implying stealth and an ability to kill. His online reviews reflected his success: he was efficient, 100 per cent successful and a pleasure to deal with. He drove a hard bargain on the fee but always stuck to the deal once it had been agreed.

He tried to avoid organized crime if he could, although these days it was not always possible to tell the difference between an online drugs or arms market on the dark web and a violent crime gang. Krakatoa was the perfect customer. Internet savvy, concerned about his online reputation, ignorant of the market for killers. The North Carolina job had been satisfactory all round.

Tecumseh was a killer. He had become one at the age of seventeen in Kosovo, a period of his life he had managed to expunge from his memory until fifteen years later when, after moving to Germany, he had lost his wife and his job as an accountant at a plastics factory in Essen and he needed some money.

And, truth be told, some excitement.

He was well hidden in the shadows, away from any illumination of the street lights; nevertheless, he was worried about a passer-by noticing him. The only memorable item of clothing he was wearing was his green woolly hat, which hid his thinning dark hair and could safely be ditched once the job was done. The rest of his clothes were unbranded, nondescript. A dark jacket. Jeans. Brown shoes.

No one would see his face closely; if anyone saw him at all, they would remember him as a guy in a green hat. And glasses: not much he could do about those.

He had ditched the blue hat after the last job.

He hoped to God she appeared this evening. Tecumseh was getting nervous. This island was beginning to feel like a prison. Coronavirus infections were growing all over the world, and it wouldn't be long before cross-border checks grew with them. He wanted to be safely back in Germany with the minimum of tests and quarantines and the accompanying paperwork.

Do the job, collect the eighty thousand dollars and get out of here, preferably on an early-morning flight to anywhere at all.

The door to the house opened and the target emerged.

She turned towards his doorway and set off at a rapid pace, right past him.

Tecumseh removed his expensive glasses, gripped the cord in his coat pocket and followed her.

## THIRTY-FIVE

Magnus had barely got to his desk the following morning when his phone rang.

It was Thelma, summoning him to her office. She didn't sound happy.

She left him standing, never a good sign.

'Have you been investigating Thomocoin?'

'Not really.'

'Not really?'

'Just a little tidying up.'

'I see. Didn't you interview . . .' The half-moon reading glasses came on as she consulted a scrap of paper on her desk. 'Fjóla Rúnarsdóttir and Skarphédinn Gíslason last Thursday?'

'Um. Yes.'

'And hadn't I told you that very morning to stay well clear of Thomocoin?'

'You did. I'm sorry,' Magnus said. He had been rumbled.

'I did that for a reason. The shit has hit the fan, just like I said it would. Interpol has a red notice out for

Skarphédinn. The British police tried to arrest him in London over the weekend but missed him. Did you know that?'

'I did.' Magnus had kept in touch with his FBI contact Agent Malley.

'There is a very aggressive, nasty game of passing the buck going on in the ministries. I thought we were well out of it. Then, when someone from the Financial Services Authority questioned Fjóla Rúnarsdóttir, it turned out you had already been to see her. There are notes of the interview on the system.'

'In connection with Helga Hafsteinsdóttir's murder.'

'That's what I told them. But when the questions start flying around about who knew what when, I hope it won't turn out that you knew anything. That *we* knew anything.'

Magnus found his patience stretched. He knew it was Thelma's job to deal with this kind of crap, but someone had been murdered and as far as Magnus was concerned it was his job to know everything relevant.

He owed it to Dísa. He owed it to his younger self.

'Don't glare at me like that,' said Thelma. 'I'm covering your arse.'

'There *is* something bad about Thomocoin,' said Magnus. 'And that may have been why Helga died.'

'*May* have been? So tell me. What did you find? Apart from that Thomocoin was about to blow up.'

'Taking half of Dalvík with it.'

'Including Gunnar Snaer Sigmundsson who Ólafur has arrested for the crime.'

'That's true.' Magnus considered passing on Árni's doubts but decided against it. Not yet, anyway. He didn't want to harm Árni's already tarnished credibility with Thelma.

'So, did you discover any direct involvement by anyone at Thomocoin into Helga's death?'

'No,' said Magnus.

'Any evidence of a conspiracy with Gunnar?'

'No. The only person Gunni communicated directly with about Thomocoin was Helga, apart from a couple of emails from him to Fjóla worrying about the lack of a Thomocoin exchange. Neither she nor Sharp met him recently, although Sharp met him a couple of times when Gunnar was an MP in Reykjavík years ago.'

'So nothing, then?'

'The questions had to be asked.'

'Did they? When I had specifically told you not to ask them?'

'Sorry,' said Magnus, seeing no point in arguing further.

His phone rang. It was Vigdís. He raised his eyebrows to Thelma, who nodded for him to take it.

Vigdís's voice was urgent, concise. 'Homicide. Female, about twenty years old, near the university. Found under a hedge, naked.'

'Any sign of sexual assault?'

'Not yet, but they are looking.'

'I'll be right down.'

The body was stuffed under a hedge on the network of small roads between the university and the sea. Three police cars with flashing lights marked the spot, together with police tape. No sign yet of Edda and her forensics team; they wouldn't be long.

Magnus spoke to the constable who had been first at the scene. The police had been alerted by a dog walker, a man in his fifties standing a few metres away with his curious terrier, watching proceedings. Magnus and Vigdís put on their overalls, signed the log and approached the body.

No ID found as yet. Her wallet, if she had one, or phone – and she would definitely have had one of those – were gone.

She was so pale, a skin of white wax. Face down in the dirt. Magnus crouched and looked without touching. A bloody nose. Horizontal red line around her throat. Bruising at the nape of her neck. It looked as if rigor had set in throughout the body, including the legs. Carefully he touched her cheek. Cold.

No sign of bruising on the rest of her body, not even between her legs, from what he could see.

'Well?' said Vigdís. She was perfectly capable of drawing her own conclusions, but thanks to the years he had spent in Boston's Homicide Unit, Magnus had seen far more murders than she.

They had worked together off and on since Magnus's first assignment to Reykjavík in 2009. The mixed-race daughter of a black American serviceman at the airbase at Keflavik whom she had never met, Vigdís sometimes faced hostility or just bemusement in her own country. She was fed up with Icelanders assuming she was a foreigner and addressing her in English and so refused to reply to anyone in that language, ever. She was a very good detective and during the surge in virus infections the previous spring had proven herself adept at tracking and tracing people who had been in contact with carriers of the disease. Iceland's expedient of using police detectives to help with that effort had worked out well.

'Strangled with a ligature,' Magnus said. 'Probably last night. Probably moved to this spot.'

'Probably sexual,' said Vigdís. It was a statement, not a question.

'Probably. But let's not jump to any conclusions.'

They both stood up and exchanged glances. Vigdís was worried.

Murders were always worrying, but Magnus knew what she was thinking.

'Wasn't Albert DeSalvo from your old patch?' Vigdís said.

The Boston Strangler. One of the most notorious serial killers ever.

Iceland didn't have serial killers. Or, at least, not up till now. Magnus profoundly hoped that wasn't about to change.

'I said, let's not jump to any conclusions. We'll see what Edda comes up with. Get in touch with the university. And Missing Persons. We need an ID.'

'Magnús!'

It was the constable.

Magnus and Vigdís joined her outside the crime-scene perimeter.

'Got a missing person's report. From an address just around the corner.'

'Yes?'

'Katrín Ingvarsdóttir. Nineteen years old. Dark hair, blue eyes, about one-sixty tall.'

Magnus glanced at the body. It matched the description: a bit over five feet long, blue eyes staring in glassy shock, black hair matted with dirt. 'Come on,' he said to Vigdís.

They drove, but it was only a couple of hundred metres to the address, a grey concrete house broken up into apartments, a pile of bikes leaning against the wall indicating its student inhabitants. Magnus rang the bell, his warrant card at the ready, steeling himself to deliver the bad news. A female voice answered, barely comprehensible over the screech of static from the intercom.

A moment later a young woman appeared, her eyes wide with fear, fear for bad news she had already imagined.

But it was Magnus who was surprised.

'Dísa?'

## THIRTY-SIX

Dísa wiped the tears from her eyes as Vigdís handed her a mug of instant coffee. They were in Dísa and Kata's tiny student flat.

'Was she . . . raped?' Dísa asked.

'We think so,' said Vigdís. 'We won't know for sure until she has been examined. She was found naked.'

'Actually, we don't know yet,' said Magnus.

Vigdís glanced at him sharply. It was bad form to contradict a colleague. But Magnus wanted to stop the rape assumption taking hold.

Dísa noticed the look between the two detectives. 'How was she killed?'

'She was strangled,' said Magnus. 'With a cord or rope of some kind, probably. We think last night.'

'Oh, God.' Dísa stared miserably down at her mug.

'You reported Katrín missing at twelve-forty a.m.?' Magnus asked.

'Yes.'

'Why?'

'Because she hadn't come home.'

'Lots of students don't come home every night.'

Dísa nodded. 'That's true. She was going to see her boyfriend Matti – her ex-boyfriend. She told me she was going to explain why she split up with him. So I didn't expect her to stay the night.'

'They could have made up?' said Magnus.

'I know. That's why I called him. He said she had never shown up. So I called the police. They didn't seem very interested. I knew something had happened to her! I had to beg them to take her details.'

'It's not odd that the police weren't concerned about a student staying out all night,' said Magnus gently. 'What's odd is that you were.'

'What do you mean?'

'Why were you so scared something would happen to Kata?'

'Something did happen, didn't it?' she said defiantly.

'Something you were expecting?'

'No! Why would I be expecting something to happen to her?'

'That's a good question.'

'Well, I wasn't.'

Magnus paused. 'Do you think this attack may have something to do with Thomocoin? Or your mother's murder?'

'Of course not,' said Dísa. 'Why should it? You said it was rape, didn't you?'

'No,' Magnus corrected. 'We said it *looked* like rape.'

'I don't know why she was killed,' Dísa protested, another tear running down her cheek.

'There have been only two murders in the whole of Iceland this month,' said Magnus. 'Both involving victims you knew very well. That can't be a coincidence.'

'Can't it?' Dísa scrambled to collect her thoughts. 'Kata had nothing to do with Thomocoin. She wasn't interested in it at all whenever I talked about it.' Then a thought seemed to strike her. 'But that might be why I assumed the worst when she didn't come home. Because of what happened to Mum.'

That was possible. But it looked to Magnus like Dísa had stumbled on a plausible explanation for her fear for her friend's life.

'Have you done anything about Thomocoin?' Dísa asked.

'I made some inquiries,' Magnus said. 'It does sound dodgy. But I couldn't find any direct link between Thomocoin and your mother's murder, or even much of a link between Gunni and Thomocoin apart from some email correspondence with Fjóla.'

'What about Sharp?' Dísa asked. 'Did you talk to him? Is he still in Iceland?'

'I did. But he went back to London at the end of last week. The British police tried to arrest him, but he had already fled. As had Jérôme Carmin in Paris. Interpol thinks they both flew to Panama via Madrid.'

'So is that it for Thomocoin?' said Dísa.

'It looks like it,' said Magnus.

Dísa nodded.

Magnus wasn't sure how she was taking that news. 'Are you happy? That Thomocoin has blown up?'

Dísa sighed. 'They deserve it. But it means that all those investors have definitely lost their money, doesn't it? That my grandparents will lose their farm?'

Magnus nodded. His own father's death had blown up his family, although that had taken years. His grandparents, his uncle, his little brother: all had been damaged. Or caused the damage. Murders were messy and catastrophically destructive to the survivors.

Magnus was on the side of the survivors. He was on Dísa's side. But he needed her help.

'And now Kata's dead,' she said.

'Are you quite sure Thomocoin has nothing to do with that?' Magnus asked.

'Not that I know of,' said Dísa firmly.

Magnus let the silence hang.

But then he moved on. They needed information from Dísa: timings of Kata's movements the day before, details about her boyfriend Matti, her address in Dalvík, her closest friends at university, her professors.

And, lastly, they needed Dísa to identify the body *in situ*. The sooner they had a definite ID the better; if it turned out the victim wasn't Kata after all, they would avoid wasting a lot of time.

It was Kata.

Magnus's heart went out to Dísa as he saw her glance quickly at the body, still uncovered under the bush, and recoil. She had lost her mother. She had lost her best friend.

And, unless Magnus was very mistaken, she was scared.

'Sorry I contradicted you back there,' Magnus murmured to Vigdís. 'About the rape.'

'I see why now,' said Vigdís.

'Do you think she's hiding something about Thomocoin?'

'I'm damned sure she is.'


A major murder investigation swung into action. Magnus called Thelma to warn her to play down the rape angle with the press until it had been confirmed by a physical examination. He didn't mention Thomocoin to her. But he did when he called Árni in Dalvík and asked him to check whether Kata or any of her relatives were involved in the cryptocurrency.

Matti the ex-boyfriend was interviewed, as were his friends, as were Kata's friends. The international airport at Keflavík confirmed that Sharp hadn't slipped back into the country. The police search soon discovered a spot of blood on the pavement thirty metres away from where the body had been found, which indicated where Kata had been murdered. CCTV was examined, neighbours questioned. Although Kata's phone wasn't found, her computer and a tablet were, and by lunchtime keyword algorithms were swarming all over her online life.

# THIRTY-SEVEN

After the police had left her, Dísa sat on her bed and cried.

She cried for Kata. She cried for her mother. She cried for herself.

She knew that she was responsible for Kata's death, but she couldn't bring herself to face that fact. Not now. Not quite yet.

She told herself she hadn't received any threats from Krakatoa. She hadn't ignored them. Grandma was an expert at denial; maybe Dísa had inherited some of it. She would try.

Instead, she focused on Kata. On how they had become firm friends within weeks of Dísa moving up to Dalvík from Reykjavík when they were both nine. They just clicked. On Kata's sweet little puppy who had grown up and then died, run over on the road outside Kata's house the year before. On the hours spent talking in Kata's bedroom or her own. About Kata's first boyfriend. Kata's second boyfriend. Dísa smiled to herself. There were quite a lot of them and they all needed lengthy discussion, until Matti.

Kata had been going out with Matti for three years. It was serious.

Poor Matti. Dísa knew why Kata had broken up with him: Kata had spent her whole life within the confines of Dalvík where everyone knew everyone else. Now she had escaped to the big city, she realized she wanted to turn over a new leaf, reinvent herself at uni. It wasn't his fault, but Matti was part of the Dalvík Kata was trying to escape. Dísa and Kata had thrashed it out on the drive back to Reykjavík after Mum's funeral.

But Kata had never had a chance to explain it to Matti. That was what she had been planning to do the previous evening.

What had seemed to Dísa reasonable, sensible even, now appeared callous and cruel. She should see Matti.

She knew she had to talk to Kata's parents. She didn't know how long she could bury her own responsibility for Kata's death. Best to ring them now. Get it over with.

They had already heard. She spoke to Kata's mum, a woman she knew really well. An assistant to one of the top managers at the fish-processing plant, Kata's mum was calm, well organized, reliable.

But not now. Símon, the oldest and kindliest of the three local policemen, had just left, leaving a crater of emotional destruction behind him. Kata's mum was the wreckage. She wanted all the details Dísa could give her about what had happened. She was absurdly, illogically grateful to Dísa for reporting Kata missing so soon, as if it made any difference.

A voice was whispering in Dísa's ear, telling her that she was responsible for Kata's death, that she should tell Kata's mum, beg for her forgiveness.

Dísa tried to silence that voice, tried to ignore it. She succeeded, but only barely.

She was exhausted when she hung up.

She texted Jói: *Call me. Something terrible has happened. Kata has been murdered.*

He called a minute later. It was good to talk to him; he promised to come by later that afternoon.

The doorbell rang. It was three girls from Dísa's economics class. They had heard the news.

Dísa had only known them for a few weeks, but they were kind, they were sympathetic, and they took Dísa's mind off that insistent whisper: *You are responsible for Kata's death. You as good as killed your best friend.*

They went for lunch to a local café. On the way back, Dísa spoke to a couple of journalists who were staking out her flat, Kata's flat. She mumbled bland, factual responses to their questions.

Then she told the girls she wanted to be alone for a bit.

The time had come to face up to what she had done. What she would do next.

She made herself a mug of mint tea, sat at the kitchen table and looked around Kata's flat.

She was under no illusions that Kata's death was the result of a random, anonymous attack. It was Krakatoa.

She had to accept the fact that if she had given Krakatoa his bitcoin back as he had demanded, Kata would still be alive.

For some reason the idea that Kata would turn out to be the 'someone else' who might be killed hadn't occurred to Dísa until she was lying in bed, eyes open, at eleven-thirty the night before and she hadn't heard Kata return. Maybe she and Matti had made up?

Or maybe Kata was the 'someone else' Krakatoa had mentioned.

Dísa had waited, her fears growing, her imagination running amok. Midnight. Twelve-fifteen. She had called Matti. When he said Kata hadn't shown up that evening, she called the police. She had been frantic. The police officer who took her call was polite at first, then sympathetic, then irritated.

By that stage, it didn't matter how the police responded: Kata was already dead.

Krakatoa had killed her. Or had had her killed.

Dísa was pretty sure that Sharp was Krakatoa. If Sharp wasn't in Iceland, he could still have had Kata murdered by an accomplice or a hired killer.

An accomplice. Dad?

No. No way. She couldn't believe that.

She hadn't been in touch with him since she had taken his bitcoin, and he hadn't been in touch with her. She had been expecting a phone call or a visit, a demand that she return his coin, but nothing.

At first, she had hoped he hadn't realized that it was she who had broken into his trove. But if Krakatoa had figured out it was Dísa, then Dad must have too.

Did Dad know about Krakatoa's threats?

Dad knew Krakatoa really well. They must trust each other completely – why else would Krakatoa have left the key to his wealth at Dad's summer house?

Did that mean Dad knew Krakatoa had killed Kata?

The police had asked whether there was a connection between Mum's murder and Kata's. Was Dad that connection? Had he somehow murdered Mum? Or got Gunni to do it?'

The thought was unbearable. It was also ridiculous. Dad would *never* do something like that.

The whole thing was ridiculous.

But it was also real. Kata's death was real.

So what should Dísa do now?

She fetched her laptop and opened it up. Her phone had been overloaded with messages of sympathy and curiosity, and she expected a few backed up in her computer too.

But there was one that immediately caught her attention. An email.

*From: Krakatoa*
*To: Dísa Ómarsdóttir*
*Subject: Your theft*
*Dísa,*
*I told you what would happen. You ignored me. It happened.*
*You have until 5 p.m. tomorrow to transfer my 1,962 bitcoin back to my wallet. You have the details.*
*If you don't transfer the bitcoin, you will die. If you tell the police anything about me, you will die.*
*Is that clear?*
*You are a sensible woman. Do the right thing.*
*Krakatoa*

That was clear.

Oh, God!

She thought of the twenty million dollars' worth of bitcoin she held in her wallet. Twenty million! An unimaginable amount of money. A scary amount of money.

Too much.

Mum had died. Kata had died. Dísa was terrified that if

she didn't do what Krakatoa had demanded, she would die soon too.

There was only one answer.

She hit 'Reply'. She typed: *OK. You win.*

Her mouse hovered over 'Send'.

And hovered.

No. No.

No!

Krakatoa had killed her best friend and probably killed her mother. Krakatoa had ruined dozens of her neighbours in Dalvík, including Gunni. Krakatoa had taken Blábrekka away from her family after five hundred years.

Who knew how many people all over the world Krakatoa had ruined? The eager Chinese, the smiling Ugandans, the smug Dutch in the videos she had seen.

No, damn it. No!

She was glad Krakatoa had threatened her life and not another 'someone else' – Jói perhaps, or even worse, Anna Rós. Dísa was OK with being responsible for her own life. Someone had to stand up to Krakatoa, to stop him from sneaking off to Panama with other people's savings, other people's dreams. Other people's lives.

It was she. She was the one who had Krakatoa's twenty million under her control. The police couldn't stop him.

She could.

She had a little over twenty-four hours.

She needed to figure out how to pay out that twenty million to as many of the Thomocoin investors as possible, including her own grandparents.

For that, she needed Uncle Eggert.

She had called him several days before to ask him to help her figure out how to pay out the bitcoin. She had explained that she had inherited a small amount of bitcoin from her mother and wanted to repay something to those people Helga had encouraged to invest in Thomocoin, including Uncle Eggert himself.

Uncle Eggert had been happy to help, promising to call the management of the bitcoin miner in which he had invested and to do some internet research.

She dialled his mobile.

'Hi, Dísa. I just saw the news,' he said. 'Poor Kata!'

'Yes,' said Dísa.

'And poor you! How are you doing?'

'Not well,' said Dísa.

'Do they know who did it? Why?'

'No,' said Dísa. 'Reading between the lines, the police think it's probably rape, but they don't have confirmation yet.'

She didn't like to lie to Uncle Eggert, but she didn't want to scare him off either.

'Any luck with the bitcoin?' she asked.

'It's proving difficult,' said Eggert. 'I spoke to the people behind the bitcoin miner I've invested in, and they say we really need a bank account abroad to pay the proceeds from the bitcoin into. That's the tricky part. It's just about impossible to set up a bank account overseas just like that. At least for ordinary people like you and me. It's the anti-money-laundering rules. Banks need ID and they need to know where the money comes from.'

'But what about all those politicians with offshore accounts?' said Dísa. 'The ones in the Panama Papers.'

'They have contacts. And friends. I don't. Except maybe your dad. But you said you didn't want to go to him.'

'That's right. We can't go to him.'

'Because he's involved with Thomocoin?'

'Yes,' said Dísa. 'I'm afraid he is.'

'I see,' said Eggert.

'Isn't there anything more you can do?'

'Short of flying to Luxembourg or Switzerland and trying to open an account directly, no,' said Eggert. 'Even then, I'm not sure they would let me. Or you. They would be suspicious.'

'There must be a way.'

'I was thinking: maybe the easiest thing would be if you could get everyone to open their own bitcoin wallets and you could pay each of them individually in bitcoin. Then it would be up to them to convert it to krónur.'

'That doesn't sound easy,' said Dísa.

'I've got a bitcoin wallet,' said Eggert. 'You could pay me. And you could get your grandparents to open one. We could get the word out through them to the investors in Dalvík. You say you have a list of them?'

'I do. But I don't have their email addresses.'

'Maybe your grandparents have them, or some of them. If they managed to set up wallets to buy Thomocoin, they can figure out how to set up bitcoin wallets. Especially if it's going to get back their life savings.' Eggert hesitated. 'Are you certain Thomocoin is finished? Is there any chance they will come up with an exchange after all?'

'No chance,' said Dísa. 'The police told me they tried to arrest Sharp in London, but he had done a runner. They think he's in Panama. It's all gone, Uncle Eggert. All that Thomocoin is worth nothing.'

'Shit.'

'Yeah. Let me think.'

Dísa thought. Uncle Eggert's idea might work. But it would take longer than twenty-four hours. It would take at least a week to contact all those investors and get them to open bitcoin wallets. Some of them, the true believers, would still be believing and would need convincing. Including Grandpa.

She needed to keep the bitcoin somewhere safe for that week in case anything happened to her. If Krakatoa did catch up with her, her private key would be useless. And if the worst happened, no one would be able to access the bitcoin. Ever. Thomocoin's investors would never be repaid; Blábrekka would be lost.

She had to trust someone. And that someone turned out to be Uncle Eggert. At least he was family.

Dísa took a deep breath. And a leap of faith.

'Could I transfer the bitcoin to you, Uncle Eggert?' she asked. 'Then you could distribute it when I give you the investors' details.'

'I don't see why not. How much are we talking about?'

'Just under two thousand bitcoin.'

'OK. Wait a moment.' Eggert had done the calculation. 'Do you mean two thousand bitcoin or two thousand dollars' worth?'

'I mean two thousand bitcoin.'

'But that's twenty million dollars!'

'Yes.'

'That's not Helga's, is it?'

'No. It's mine. Or at least it's in my bitcoin wallet.'

'Where did you get it from?'

'Thomocoin.'

'You stole it?'

Dísa hesitated. She hadn't stolen it – that was the whole point. 'I took it back. It's not mine, and it's certainly not Thomocoin's; it belongs to all those people who trusted Mum and invested with them. That's why I have to give it back.'

'I see. Do Thomocoin know?'

'Probably.'

Silence.

'Is that why Kata was killed?'

Uncle Eggert wasn't stupid. 'Maybe.'

'I've got to think about this,' he said.

'OK. But please let me know. Soon.'

A plan was emerging. It wasn't a great plan, but it might work.

Transfer Dísa's bitcoin to Uncle Eggert's wallet. Get email addresses of the investors in Dalvík and Akureyri. Persuade them to set up bitcoin wallets. Get their details. Get Uncle Eggert to pay them.

That would take longer than twenty-four hours. But it could take less than a week.

Dísa had until 5 p.m. the following day. After that time she would have to disappear for a week. Somewhere outside Reykjavík. And away from Dalvík and Akureyri. Iceland was a big, empty country.

Kata's car was parked on the street outside. And her car keys were in a bowl right there on the kitchen counter.

Dísa reached into the bowl and slipped the keys into her pocket.

She plugged her cold wallet USB stick into her computer and logged into her bitcoin wallet. The bitcoin was all still there. If Eggert agreed, she would need his wallet address to pay him.

Could she trust Uncle Eggert? With twenty million dollars?

Probably. He had always been good to her. Dísa and he didn't have a strong relationship, but Mum had always trusted him, as far as she knew.

She couldn't be certain, but she didn't think he would just grab all the bitcoin for himself.

She didn't really have a choice.

More likely Uncle Eggert would decide to back away from helping her. He might decide it was too dangerous. It *was* too dangerous.

Then what?

The doorbell rang. It was Jói.

She gave him a big hug, COVID be damned. He held her tightly.

'God, I'm so sorry, Dísa,' he said.

It was good to talk to Jói. Not as good as it would have been to talk to Kata, but he was family. She needed family.

'You can move back in with me if you like,' Jói said, looking around the small apartment. 'I don't know, maybe you want to stay here. But if you need somewhere else . . .'

'Thanks, Jói.' For a moment, she wondered whether she would be safe in Jói's apartment. The answer was clearly not – Krakatoa would have no problem finding her there. 'Maybe in a week or two?'

'What's that?' Jói asked, pointing to Dísa's pink USB stick.

'Oh, it's my bitcoin wallet.'

'Hot pink?'

'I know.' She rolled her eyes. 'Dad gave it to me. I made him promise to switch it to a silver one, but he never did.'

'So you still have some bitcoin?'

'Mum had some.' Dísa lowered the lid to her computer. She didn't want Jói seeing how much.

'Do you have a back-up wallet?' Jói asked. 'Aren't you supposed to keep one somewhere, in case you lose that?'

'I do. But it's up in Dalvík. In a secret hiding place.'

'Where?' said Jói.

'I can't tell you that!' said Dísa. 'Or it wouldn't be secret!'

Jói grinned. 'I guess not.'

She had made light of it. But she wondered whether she should tell Jói where her paper wallet was hidden. Originally she had stuffed it under her old Barbie doll clothes in a drawer in her bedroom, but after her mother's death, she had moved it to Helga's hiding place by the elf rock behind the farm. Perhaps she should even give it to Jói for safekeeping.

But there was still a chance he might try to return his father's bitcoin to him, once he realized Dísa had taken it from him. And even if he didn't, Dísa would be putting Jói at risk.

It was bad enough that Uncle Eggert would be in danger. One relative at a time.

But if Uncle Eggert's answer was that he refused to help Dísa any further, maybe she should open up to Jói?


Later, half an hour after Jói had left, Eggert called.

'OK, Dísa,' he said. 'You're a brave girl. Those people deserve to get their money back, and I'll help you do it. I'll give you my bitcoin wallet address and you can pay them over when you're ready. You realize you'll be trusting me with twenty million dollars?'

Dísa smiled. 'I trust you, Uncle Eggert.'

# THIRTY-EIGHT

KRAKATOA: Well done. One more small job.

TECUMSEH: Not if it's in Iceland.

KRAKATOA: What do you mean?

TECUMSEH: I'm on the train from the airport.

KRAKATOA: Which airport?

TECUMSEH: It's not Keflavik.

KRAKATOA: You didn't tell me you were leaving the country!

TECUMSEH: Sorry. It was time to go. I'll expect the second forty thousand in my wallet by tonight.

KRAKATOA: But I didn't say you could leave Iceland.

TECUMSEH: You didn't have to. Pay me. I don't believe in outstanding debts. I have none. Everyone always pays me on time. Including you.

KRAKATOA: I understand. I'll pay you now.

TECUMSEH: Good. I hope you appreciated the quality of my work.

KRAKATOA: Yes. Yes, of course. Thank you.

TECUMSEH: You're welcome.

## THIRTY-NINE

Thud, thud, thud.

Ómar's heavy tread pounded along the pavement beside the bay, his gasps loud in his ears. A cold breeze bounded off the water, snapping at his cheeks. He tried to keep his eyes fixed on Mount Esja, a long slab of rock lurking beneath a dark cloud in the distance. No matter how hard he ran, the mountain was not getting any closer, although the grey cloud was slipping upwards, as if pulled back by a giant hand.

He switched his gaze to the sculpture of the Viking ship jutting out a couple of metres from the pavement into the bay, its bones burnished silver in the low sunlight. That at least was getting closer. And he knew there were benches there. He could do a stretch or two, like the responsible athlete he was.

God, he was unfit! This was his third day running and he wasn't sure he was going to keep it up. But his bulging stomach taunted him every day.

A tall grey-haired guy in tight black leggings loped past him. He had to be at least ten years older than Ómar.

His thoughts turned to Dísa, as they had constantly since Jói had warned him to check his bitcoin wallet. He had driven up to the summer house immediately. The two cigar canisters were still there, stuffed beneath the tuft of grass by the elf rock, and so were the private keys inside. At first, he had found no sign of anyone taking a look, but Dísa could easily have copied down the private keys and shoved them back in their hiding place. Then he spotted part of a fresh Dísa-sized footprint a couple of metres away on some bare earth.

Jói was right. There was no other explanation. Dísa must have stolen his bitcoin. Thirty thousand dollars of it.

She had as good as warned him, that afternoon by that other rock at Blábrekka. She had urged him to give his bitcoin to Dalvík's Thomocoin investors – more than urged him, virtually ordered him. No doubt that was what she planned to do with his hoard. And Jói's.

He had no idea how much Jói had stashed in his bitcoin wallet. He was sure it would be more than him, a lot more.

Part of him was impressed with what Dísa had done. She had tried to make him feel guilty about the Thomocoin mess and had succeeded. The message boards suggested that Thomocoin had imploded. The price on the website hadn't been updated since it had spiked up to five hundred dollars. There were rumours that Sharp and Jérôme were on the run, that Sharp was now in Moscow or Beijing. The believers were suggesting that the haters were trying to shut Thomocoin down, but that Sharp had escaped their clutches and, from the safety of Moscow or wherever, would resurrect the cryptocurrency.

Ómar knew it was bollocks.

So did Dísa. And she had done something about it.

It was partly for that reason, and partly because he

wanted to avoid a confrontation with his daughter so soon after her mother's death, that Ómar hadn't demanded the bitcoin back. Yet.

Neither had he been in touch with Jói. That was another confrontation he had been avoiding.

Thomocoin had been Jói's idea. It was Ómar who had put Jói in touch with his friend Sharp in London. Between the two of them, with some help from Sharp's French friend from business school, Jérôme, they had transformed Jói's original FOMOcoin into Thomocoin and turned it into what seemed to be a huge success. Ómar had kept out of it – he hadn't the nerve for that kind of thing any more – but from the periphery, he had been impressed and proud of the way that Jói, in the guise of Krakatoa, had asserted himself as de facto boss of the organization.

Now Thomocoin was in trouble, and so too was Jói, presumably. Unless his Krakatoa alias held. Ómar had been sceptical of Jói's insistence that Jói feign indifference towards crypto to people he knew in the real world. But now Ómar saw how smart his son had been to preserve his anonymity: Jói could look after himself, he had proved that.

Part of Ómar admired Dísa for what she had done, but a bigger part of him needed the money. The tourist season had been a complete washout that summer. Although Iceland had allowed tourists back in July, there were strict quarantine requirements, and not many had come. And those that had come had brought the virus with them. Two French tourists had just managed to infect more than ninety people after a little bar crawl in downtown Reykjavík; they hadn't understood the quarantine rules. And with the tourists had gone Ómar's income as a freelance guide.

He had found some work advising his various employers on dealing with their cash-flow problems, but for that he was mostly earning goodwill rather than hard krónur. He needed his stash of bitcoin. Especially since his small holding of Thomocoin was now worthless.

And he couldn't just pretend forever that he hadn't noticed what Dísa had done. It would be an unpleasant conversation, but he had to have it sometime, and it might as well be now. He would call her as soon as he got home.

Actually, he had a shower as soon as he got back to his flat in Nordurmýri. As he was drying himself he turned the radio on.

A student had been murdered not far from the university. She had been identified as Katrín Ingvarsdóttir, nineteen, from Dalvík.

That was Dísa's friend Kata, wasn't it?

Oh, God! Poor Dísa. First her mother and now her best friend.

Weren't they roommates now? Dísa had said she'd moved out of Jói's flat and in with Kata.

He pulled on some clothes and called her.

No reply.

He texted her.

No reply to that, either.

He remembered Dísa had sent him a message with her new address.

He scrolled back through his texts from her and found it.

# FORTY

After Jói left, Dísa put together her own spreadsheet of the names on Helga's computer that she had downloaded. She needed to gather together corresponding email addresses. Or maybe Facebook pages.

She recognized at least half of the names. She began googling, seeing if she could glean emails from the internet. It wasn't difficult, especially for the Dalvík names. Facebook pages were even easier. The medical staff in Akureyri posed a little more of a problem, but she was pretty sure she would be able to gather contact information for 90 per cent of them. The rest she could contact through the online phone book, or through their friends.

As she was working, she was composing in her mind the email or Facebook message she would send. She was concerned she would have to persuade some of them that their Thomocoin really was worthless, despite the fact that the website seemed to have gone dead.

She also realized that she shouldn't contact anyone with her plan before the five o'clock deadline the following day for fear it might somehow get back to Krakatoa or her father.

Her phone buzzed.

Dad.

She hesitated. Was he calling to see how she was? Or to demand his money back? Or to threaten her?'

She nearly picked up – she wanted her dad. She really wanted her mum!

But she didn't want a fight with him now.

Later maybe.

So she ignored it. And she ignored the three texts from him that pinged on her phone afterwards.

But not the one from Matti.

*Hey Dísa.*

*Oh Matti! I can't believe it!*

*Do you want to talk?*

*Yeah. Can I come round to your place?*

*Sure.*

*I'll be there in ten.*

Matti was sharing with two other guys in a place half a kilometre away. Walking distance. For Kata. And now for Dísa.

She shut up her laptop and hurried downstairs. As she opened the front door, she saw a figure approaching her.

Dad.

She hesitated.

'Dísa!'

She made to shut the door.

'Don't do that, Dísa! We need to talk.'

Dísa hesitated. Dad's expression was full of pain, and sympathy.

He smiled. 'Can I come in?'

The smile clinched it. She needed that smile. 'OK.'

Dísa went back upstairs, Dad following.

'I'm so sorry, Dísa,' he said when they were inside the apartment. He reached out to hug her. She stood back. Then she let him wrap her arms around her. It felt good.

They sat at the kitchen table.

'What happened?'

Dísa told him. The same story she had told many people that day. He listened. He seemed genuinely shocked.

As if he had nothing to do with it.

As she spoke, Dísa felt her anger rising. He sat there. Pale. Dazed. His straggly goatee seeming to droop with his shoulders. Weak.

Mum was right. Her father was weak.

Dísa didn't know what his exact role in all this was. She was sure he wasn't the leader. He was a follower. Dad was always a follower.

*Weak.*

Well, she felt strong.

She interrupted herself.

'Dad? You know I took your bitcoin? I drove out to the summer house and found the private keys hidden by the elf rock and I logged into your wallet and took all your bitcoin?'

Ómar raised his eyebrows. 'I . . . er . . . I suspected it was you.'

'Dad. Who is Krakatoa?'

'Krakatoa? I . . . I don't know. Who *is* Krakatoa?'

For someone who had spent so much time in prison, Dad was a pretty bad liar.

'OK. Who is K?'

'K?'

Yes. K. The second private key you hid under that rock belonged to K. I took his bitcoin too.'

Dad just blinked.

'K is Krakatoa, right? So who is Krakatoa?'

'I told you, I don't know.' Firmer now, but Dísa was unimpressed.

'Krakatoa is Sharp, isn't he?'

'What do you want me to say?'

'I want you to answer my question!' Dísa glared at her father.

Ómar looked down at his hands and then faced his daughter. 'All right. I thought it was you who took my bitcoin. And . . . K's. But I won't tell you who Krakatoa is. And I want my bitcoin back.'

'I'm going to give it back to those people who were foolish enough to believe Sharp and you and my mother.'

'Wait a minute! I didn't have anything to do with that! All right, I introduced you to Sharp and Thomocoin, and I'm very sorry about that. But I *told* you not to talk to Helga about it.'

'It was bitcoin you told me not to talk to her about, not Thomocoin,' Dísa said.

'You never said you had given your bitcoin to your mother when I introduced you to Thomocoin!'

That at least was true. Dísa had deceived her father, at her mother's request.

'Look,' Ómar said, aiming for sincerity. 'I'm not part of Thomocoin, I promise you. That bitcoin is what's left over from my trading. And I need it to get through the winter to next year's tourist season.' He leaned forward. 'Give it back to me, Dísa. It's mine. It's not yours. And it's not even those poor suckers' in Dalvík.'

'Poor suckers like Grandpa?' said Dísa.

'I didn't mean that,' said Ómar.

He clearly did. And, actually, he wasn't wrong.

Grandpa was a sucker. But he didn't deserve to lose Blábrekka.

'And if I don't give it back to you? What will you do to me?' Dísa asked.

Ómar seemed taken aback by that question. 'You should give back what you stole because it's the right thing to do,' he said. 'You know right from wrong, Dísa.'

'Oh yeah? And should I give Krakatoa his bitcoin back too?'

'Yes.'

'Because he said he would kill someone if I didn't?'

Ómar sat back. 'What?'

'You heard me. He sent me a warning a few days ago that if I didn't give him his bitcoin back someone would die. Then he sent another one twenty-four hours later. And someone did die.'

'You mean Kata?'

'She's dead, isn't she?'

'Oh, God.' Ómar's pale already skin went even paler – if that was possible.

'So, Dad. Who is Krakatoa?'

Ómar didn't answer. It was clear he had no idea what to say.

'He told me I'm next,' Dísa went on. 'That if I don't give him his bitcoin back by tomorrow at five o'clock, he will kill me.'

Ómar swallowed. 'So what are you going to do?'

An idea came to Dísa. She let her shoulders sag. 'I'll give it back. Right at the last minute. You can tell him that. Go and tell him that.'

Her father just sat there.

'Go!' she said.

He swallowed. 'What about my bitcoin? Will you return that to me?'

Dísa stared at him. 'Look me in the eye and tell me you will kill me if I don't give it back. And I will. But you have to threaten to kill me first.'

Ómar met her eyes for a couple of seconds. He scrambled to his feet and stumbled out of her flat without a backward glance.

Weak. So weak.

Dísa waited a couple of minutes and followed him out. The brief walk to Matti's place would be good to clear her head.

Jói sat in his car, watching Dísa's building. He saw his father go in and then come out again.

Ten minutes later, he saw Dísa emerge.

He was still hopeful that Dísa would do the sensible thing and return his bitcoin. But there was one other way to get his coin back. It was a long shot, but worth a try.

Ideally, he would have liked to pay Tecumseh to do it. But Tecumseh was gone and there was no time to line up a replacement. Jói had transferred the forty thousand dollars in bitcoin he owed him for the hit immediately. He didn't want Tecumseh as an enemy.

Jói would just have to do his own dirty work from now on.

He waited another ten minutes and then walked around the block to the road behind Dísa's. He had already checked the street and identified the right house.

He was strangely nervous. He had done a good job for months dealing with the vicissitudes of Thomocoin and had taken life-and-death decisions coolly. But that was from behind a computer. Out in the real world, a bit of breaking and entering in a Reykjavík street in daylight scared him.

He pulled himself together and boldly walked along the side of the house and through a small gate into a back garden. No furtive glances, no hesitation; he wanted to give the impression of a man with a perfect right to go where he was going. He swiftly crossed the small yard and slipped through the bushes at the back.

He had noticed the door with a window at the back of the hallway in Dísa's building. The building had three floors, presumably all containing students. Dísa's was the top. There were no lights showing on the ground floor, but he could see a yellow glow behind a curtain in the middle storey. He slipped on some gloves, both to protect his hands and wrists from broken glass and to avoid fingerprints. He smashed the glass and waited a few seconds.

If anyone came to investigate, he would run.

No one came.

He reached in and opened the door from the inside.

Quick. Up the stairs. Dísa's door wasn't even locked.

He had listed in his head the most likely places she would hide her pink USB wallet, accepting the possibility that she had kept it with her. It turned out it was still stuck in her laptop, which was lying on the counter in the kitchen.

He yanked the stick out of the machine, slipped out of the apartment, crept down the stairs and left the property by the front door.

In fifteen minutes he was back in his own flat.

He stuck the USB stick into the most powerful of his three computers.

Password protected.

He started with the obvious: '1234'; 'password' and its Icelandic equivalent '*lykilord*'. Dísa's date of birth in different formats. 'Dalvík'. 'Bonny'. 'Bonnie' – Jói didn't know how to spell Dísa's horse's name.

None of them worked, but that was OK. There was no sign that the USB stick had a finite number of tries before it would lock, so he fired up his favourite password cracker and set it to work.

He sat and watched it for a few seconds – it would only take that long to crack a simple password – but the password Dísa had chosen was clearly not a simple one, so Jói just let it run, chugging through the combinations of words and numbers.

The password cracker was top of the range; there was a good chance he wouldn't have to see his threat through.

# FORTY-ONE

Magnus heard the squeak and looked up to see Thelma approaching his desk with her habitual loping gate. Her false leg had started squeaking a few days before. Thelma refused to be embarrassed about it, but it clearly annoyed her. No one dared mention it; presumably, it would take more than a squirt of WD40 to fix.

'How's it going?' she asked.

It was late: everyone else had gone home.

Magnus nodded at his computer screen. 'Just going through the interviews today.'

'What's it look like?'

'Not sure yet. There are no physical signs of sexual assault or really much of a struggle. The attacker probably grabbed her from behind and strangled her with a cord, dragged her off and stripped her.'

'Why did he strip her if there wasn't a sexual motive? Could he have been disturbed?'

'It's possible.' Magnus shrugged. 'Maybe he was trying to put us off the scent?'

'Off the scent from what?'

'I remember a similar case in Boston,' said Magnus. 'It looked like a sexual assault. Turned out it was a professional hit.'

'You think a pro did this?'

'It's something to bear in mind.'

'Why would a professional killer be involved? Was she dealing?' There were drug gangs in Iceland, and they had the occasional turf war.

'No. She didn't even take drugs – her friends are adamant about that.'

'What about the boyfriend? I understand she had recently dumped him?'

'That's right. He was waiting in his flat all evening for her with his two roommates, so unless they are covering for him, he didn't do it. In theory, he could have hired a professional to do it, but he just doesn't look the type.'

'But you're keeping an open mind?'

'Always.' Magnus was thinking. Thelma let him.

'Yes?' she said at last.

'There's the Dalvík angle.'

Thelma listened. 'OK.'

'Kata came from Dalvík. Helga Hafsteinsdóttir was murdered in Dalvík. Helga was Dísa's mother; Kata was her best friend. There's a connection.'

'There could be.'

'I've got Árni checking whether any of Kata's relatives were involved in Thomocoin.'

'And were they?'

'So far, no.'

'So at least we know there's no Thomocoin connection.'

'We don't know that,' said Magnus. 'We need to look further.'

'I can see how there might be a Dalvík angle or a Dísa

angle,' said Thelma. 'Look for links between Kata and Gunni, perhaps. Maybe he had an affair with her in Dalvík? But don't get dragged into Thomocoin unless you are sure that there is a real connection, do you understand me, Magnús?'

'You know what murder investigations are like. You can't be sure there's a real connection until you go looking for it.'

'The Thomocoin scandal is going to be big; the press is going to be all over it. The last thing we need is for them to find you have been interviewing the scammers about murder. That would create the kind of shitstorm that could bring down governments.'

'But what if it's true, Thelma?' Magnus was doing his best to control his temper.

'If there is a link and you have proof, fine. But that's not the case, is it?'

'No,' said Magnus. He meant *not yet*, but he didn't say it. Thelma was right he was a long way from establishing a link. And the Gunni–Kata angle was worth pursuing. There was *some* connection between the two murders; he was sure of it.

'Why did you ask me about Tryggvi Thór the other day?' Magnus asked her.

Instantly, Thelma's expression changed, from aggression to wariness. 'Oh, I don't know. I was just curious.'

'I remember that when I first lodged with him three years ago, you said you didn't know who he was. You said he was bent.'

'You must be confused, Magnús,' said Thelma. She turned to stalk off back to her office, her leg squeaking all the way.

But Magnus wasn't confused. He recalled that conversation very clearly. Thelma had claimed she didn't know Tryggvi Thór, that he must have left the police before her time. She had also warned Magnus not to stay with him, given his reputation as a bent cop. But soon after that, Magnus had spotted Thelma and Tryggvi Thór leaving a restaurant together.

He didn't know what his boss's connection with his landlord was, but he did know she wanted to keep it concealed.

Not a big believer in openness, was Superintendent Thelma.

His phone rang. 'Magnús.'

'Good afternoon. This is Mark Grayson from the DA's office in Mecklenburg County, North Carolina.' The voice had a warm southern tang. 'Agent Malley of the FBI in New York gave me your name. He said you spoke good English?'

'I do,' said Magnus. 'How can I help you?'

'We're investigating a homicide from September last year. Victim's name was Corey Henning, forty-two. Online name Cryptocheeseman. Looked like a mugging – victim was knifed in the abdomen on a street close to his house. But we found computer evidence that Henning did work for Thomocoin, which I believe you have been investigating?'

'I have. And a couple of murders related to it.'

'Good. We think that the homicide may have been a professional hit ordered by a guy named Krakatoa. The FBI in New York have been investigating Krakatoa, and Agent Malley believes he might be an Icelandic national named Skarp . . . Skarp-herd . . .'

'Sharp,' said Magnus. 'I know the guy. I interviewed

him last week here in Iceland, but he went back to London the following day. Malley put a red notice out on him, but he had skipped town by the time the British police showed up to arrest him.'

'And gone to Panama. From where we have no chance of getting him.'

'How much evidence do you have that Krakatoa ordered the hit?'

'Just a few messages on Henning's computer. Veiled threats. Krakatoa seems to have believed that Henning stole two hundred grand in bitcoin from him. He was pissed and he wanted it back. We need more.'

'Have you found the bitcoin?'

'No.'

'Can't find the key?'

'That's right. We need to find Krakatoa and get a look at his computer. But we don't have hard evidence that Krakatoa is this Sharp guy, at least not yet. Do you?'

'Not yet,' said Magnus. 'He's definitely the favourite.'

'What are the murders you are investigating?'

Magnus described Helga's killing, and Kata's, and agreed with Grayson to share any information he had about Krakatoa.


As Magnus was driving home to Álftanes, Árni called.

'Sorry it's so late, Magnús.'

'No problem, Árni. What have you got? Did any of Kata's relatives say they'd invested in Thomocoin?'

'No. Her parents claim they don't have any spare money to invest in anything and never have. But you know what these small towns are like; Kata is related to half the population, so I haven't spoken to her entire extended family.'

'OK. So what's up?'

'I'm still not sure about Gunni.' Árni sounded hesitant.

'I know.'

'So I've been going back through the interviews. The house-to-house.'

'Yes?'

'And I came across something interesting. A man claims he saw someone out of his bathroom window sneaking around the houses by the church in Dalvík at about one a.m. the evening after the murder.'

'Sneaking around? What does that mean?'

'Precisely. He says a man was looking at the houses as he walked by.'

'Looking at them?'

'I know. It doesn't sound much. But people just don't do that in Dalvík at that time of night.'

'OK.'

'The thing is, that's where Gunni lives. Near the church.'

'Ah.' Magnus processed the information. 'Any description?'

'No. Just a man. Alone. Acting suspiciously. My guess is the constable who spoke to the witness didn't think anything of it at the time. The sighting was twelve hours *after* the murder.'

'But before you found the knife.'

'Precisely. We found the knife on the Monday morning. The witness was spoken to the day before – Sunday.'

'So the knife was planted?' said Magnus.

'Maybe.'

'Have you spoken to Ólafur about this?'

'No. I've only just read the report.'

'Do you think he's seen it?'

'Probably. I haven't, but then I haven't read through everything. It's not surprising it didn't register with Ólafur.'

It damn well should have done, thought Magnus. If not right away, then after the knife was found in Gunni's shed.

'What shall I do?' said Árni.

'Tell him tomorrow morning.'

'He's not going to like it.'

'Well, he should,' said Magnus.

As he hung up, he knew Árni was right. Ólafur wouldn't like that report coming to light. It would seriously screw up his case.

Because Gunni was innocent.

# FORTY-TWO

It was after eleven by the time Magnus got home. Tryggvi Thór was still up.

'Brandy?' he asked.

Magnus knew he should get some sleep so he could wake up again. But he also needed to wind down a bit.

'Sure.'

Tryggvi Thór poured two glasses and they sat in the living room. The brandy tasted good. Magnus let the day's events wash over him.

'Are you working on the murdered girl?'

Magnus had known Tryggvi Thór would ask. That was, after all, why he had stayed up and offered the brandy.

He nodded.

'Was it rape?'

'Almost certainly not,' said Magnus. 'But do you mind if we don't talk about it just now?'

Tryggvi Thór looked disappointed, but Magnus knew he understood. He understood Magnus quite well.

They sat in companionable silence, sipping the brandy.

For the first time that day, Magnus's thoughts slipped away from poor Kata. To Thelma.

Something bothered him about Thelma.

'My boss asked after you the other day, Thelma.'

'Oh really? Why did she do that?'

'I've no idea,' said Magnus. 'She asked if you were OK. With the virus. She said I should keep an eye on you.'

Tryggvi Thór bristled at this. 'Why should she care?'

'I asked her that. She just walked off.'

Tryggvi Thór grunted.

'How well do you know her?'

'Not very well.'

'When I first moved in here, she told me she didn't know you at all. In fact, she warned me off you. Said you were a bent cop.'

'Everyone said I was a bent cop,' said Tryggvi Thór matter-of-factly.

'But I saw you two having lunch together. Remember?'

Although Thelma hadn't seen Magnus watching her and Tryggvi Thór leaving the restaurant three years before, Tryggvi Thór had.

Tryggvi Thór was silent.

'You were attacked back then. Twice. Nearly killed both times. Then you had lunch with Thelma. And it all stopped.'

More silence. Tryggvi Thór's heavy dark brow was knitted in anger.

'What's going on, Tryggvi Thór?'

Tryggvi Thór took a deep breath. 'I told you back then that I wouldn't answer those questions. And I said it was a condition of living here that you didn't ask them.'

'You did say that,' Magnus agreed. 'And I complied. But I'm worried about Thelma. A woman was killed in Dalvík.

Her daughter's best friend has just been murdered in Reykjavík. This cryptocurrency Thomocoin links them both. Yet Thelma is telling me not to bring Thomocoin into the investigation. She says it's a political hot potato.'

'Maybe it is. You know it's the job of a superintendent to deal with politics. I'm sure it was like that in Boston. That's what they do.'

'"Dealing with" is OK,' said Magnus. 'Covering up isn't.'

'Do you think she's covering stuff up?'

'Maybe. And maybe you and she are covering stuff up too.'

The anger was growing. Tryggvi Thór clutched his brandy glass tight. 'Are you saying I'm a bent cop too?'

'Maybe,' said Magnus. As soon as he uttered the word, he regretted it. But he didn't trust Thelma and he needed to.

Tryggvi Thór pursed his lips. He was hurt. And he was angry.

'I had to leave the country twenty-five years ago. I came back to try to clear my name. And you're right, I nearly got killed for it!'

'And you stopped!' said Magnus. 'Right after you had spoken to Thelma, it all stopped. And she claimed she never knew you.' He shook his head. 'I know you told me to trust you and leave it alone, and I've done that. But this stinks. You've got to admit, it stinks.'

Tryggvi Thór's brown eyes glared at Magnus.

'I've got two women murdered,' Magnus said. 'And my boss is squashing an obvious line of inquiry. I'm going to have to stick my neck out in the next couple of days. And I need to know I can trust her.'

'Of course you can bloody trust her!' Tryggvi Thór said.

'If you trust me, you should know you can trust her.' His stare was firm, direct, uncomfortable.

'Even though she seems to have got you to back away from something? Something important enough for people to try to kill you?'

'Even though,' Tryggvi Thór said. 'Believe me when I tell you whatever case you are working on has nothing to do with her and me.'

'Are you sure?'

Tryggvi Thór nodded. 'I'm sure.'

Magnus shook his head. 'That's not enough. If she can cover up once, she can cover up again.'

Tryggvi Thór stared down at the brandy, which he swilled around his glass, his thin lips pursed.

Then he looked up.

'All right,' he said. 'I'll tell you this. There *is* a cover-up of a crime. But it's decades old. When I came back here from Africa four years ago, I intended to lift the lid. Some people clearly didn't like that.'

'Including Thelma?'

Tryggvi Thór nodded. 'Including Thelma. And she asked me to stop.'

'And you did?"

'I did.'

'But why would you do that?' said Magnus.

Tryggvi Thór hesitated. 'Because she was the one person with the right to tell me to stop.'

Tryggvi Thór held Magnus's eyes, willing him to understand. It took him a moment to figure it out; then he did.

'Thelma was the victim.'

Tryggvi Thór grunted. 'And that's all we're going to say about it.'

# FORTY-THREE

Magnus emerged from Tryggvi Thór's house in Álftanes the following morning to find a figure leaning against his car. A figure wearing a familiar cream-coloured woolly hat.

Ingileif.

His heart leaped when he saw her and then rearranged itself in its proper place.

'Hello,' he said.

'Hi. Have you got a minute?'

'Is it about Ási?'

'Partly.'

'Can you make it quick?'

'Sure. Can we walk down to the beach?'

'Look, I've got to hold a briefing at headquarters. There's been another murder.'

'Really, it will only be a couple of minutes. I'll say my piece and be on my way.'

They walked in silence down to the sand, both of them avoiding small talk, both waiting for whatever Ingileif had to say. The tide was out. Terns wheeled and cried above them. The black folds of the Reykjanes peninsula slumbered above the water. The sea slurped softly on the volcanic pebbles at their feet.

At last, Ingileif spoke. 'I've mismanaged my life, especially with men. I was going to say "screwed up" but I haven't screwed up. I've had fun. My relationships may have ended up badly, but they started out well. They were good men, most of them. I have Ási: that's good. That's very good. But I can't go on like this.'

'Like what?'

'Finding a man. Having fun. Then dumping him.'

'Uh-huh,' said Magnus neutrally.

'I feel different with you, Magnús. Safer. Secure. I trust you, and you, God help you, you trust me. Maybe it's because both our fathers were murdered, I don't know. But there's *something*. Don't you think?'

Magnus was reaching for an answer when Ingileif stopped him.

'Don't answer that. I told myself I wouldn't demand an answer from you on anything. I just want you to understand. Understand me.'

'OK. I was going to say yes, there is something, but OK.'

Ingileif flashed a quick smile at him and then looked out over the water to the lava field.

'All right. So I feel safe and secure with you. And from that security, I feel like I can have some fun. Fool around. Mess up . . . Back when we first met, I said you were hung up on relationships, that you were too serious, that monogamy was overrated.'

'I remember you saying that.'

'I did. I do think monogamy is overrated. But . . .'

'But?' Magnus was listening, fascinated.

'I don't know. I love Ási. I like you. Actually, I love you, I always have. But if I go back to you, if you have me, it will be great for me, and then I'll screw it up again unless I do something.'

'Do what?'

Ingileif looked straight at Magnus. 'Commit. Commit to you as a lover. As Ási's Dad. Commit myself not to have sex with anyone else. Commit and mean it. I hate to say this, but we'd probably have to get married.' Ingileif's lips twitched upwards at the absurdity of such a suggestion coming from her.

'Aren't you forgetting something?'

'That you have a girlfriend who is a hundred times better for you than I am? Yes, I'm kind of ignoring that. And that's why I'm not looking for a response from you.' She took a deep breath. 'I've finally worked out what's right for me. I'm not at all sure it's right for you. But I had to tell you. I *had* to tell you.'

Magnus didn't know what to say, how to respond. His brain was spinning. For so many years this was exactly what he had wanted Ingileif to say, but now she was saying it, he didn't know how to respond. Because she was right. He had a girlfriend who was good and kind and sexy and . . . not Ingileif.

'I'm going now,' said Ingileif. 'Text me when you want to see Ási again.'

She turned to head back up the beach to the road.

'Ingileif?'

She stopped. 'I told you I didn't want any kind of answer.'

'Thank you,' said Magnus.

'For what?'

'For talking to me. Telling me all that.'

She smiled quickly and was gone.

# FORTY-FOUR

As Magnus drove into Hverfisgata, Ingileif's words swirled around his head. They stirred up his thoughts into a mixture of excitement, nervousness and confusion.

He could feel Ingileif pulling him towards her. He had no idea whether he should let himself go, or fight it. Ingileif was dangerous, at least for him. She always had been. He knew he had an important decision to make, something that would alter the course of his life – and that of other people – but he didn't know how he was going to make it.

And what about Eygló? Eygló who trusted him. Eygló who wanted to build a family with him. Eygló on whom he could always rely. Eygló whom he loved.

Didn't he?

As he entered the conference room full of police officers, he firmly pushed Ingileif to one side. He had a murder to solve. Probably two murders.

He stood in front of the crowd and kicked off the briefing. The volume of information had built up in the previous twenty-four hours, but precious little useful had come out of it.

The autopsy showed no sign of semen or injury that could have resulted from rape. Death was by asphyxiation from strangling by a nylon cord. No signs of a struggle apart from the blood on the nose. No DNA from the attacker; nothing under the victim's fingernails. Some fibre that may have come from gloves; Edda's forensics team were working on pinning down the brand.

There were no CCTV cameras at the scene or even on the short route from Kata's apartment to where she was killed. But a camera situated a couple of hundred metres towards the centre of town from the apartment showed several single men walking that way, three of whom returned later in the evening. The police would try to identify these men; officers would be standing by the camera that evening in case it was a regular route for one or two of the three.

The jilted boyfriend was an obvious line of inquiry: Vigdís would interview him again that morning, as well as his two flatmates who claimed to be with him all evening.

Magnus mentioned that Árni in Akureyri was checking the Dalvík angle and any possible connection with Helga's murder. He didn't mention Thomocoin, or the call from the DA's office in North Carolina. Not yet.

Nor did he mention Thomocoin at the quick press conference he held after the briefing. But he did everything he could to scotch rumours that there was a rapist on the streets of Reykjavík.

'Are you sure you don't want to talk to Matti with me?' said Vigdís afterwards.

'No. I'm off to Hólmsheidi.'

'To see Gunni?' said Vigdís. Magnus had filled Vigdís in privately on his conversation with Árni.

'That's right.'

'Does Thelma know?'

'No. But if she asks, tell her I'm following up on her suggestion that there may be something between Gunni and Kata.'

'I don't think that's what she meant you to do,' said Vigdís.

Magnus grinned. 'Probably not.'

'What about Ólafur? He won't be happy. He's leaving Gunni to stew. He won't like someone else interviewing him first.'

'He may not,' said Magnus. 'So let's not worry the poor guy, eh?'

Vigdís rolled her eyes. 'Árni had better be right, or you are in big trouble.'

'Árni is *sometimes* right,' said Magnus.

'Oh yeah?'


Dísa got up early, made herself a cup of coffee and set to work on her computer. The flat was quiet and empty without Kata there.

For a moment that stretched to several, Dísa stared ahead, focusing on a scratch on the cupboard above the sink, and thought of her friend. How she would never see her again. How she always seemed to know what Dísa was thinking and how Dísa knew what she was thinking. How there would be no future boyfriends to dissect and analyse.

How Dísa would never now be able to persuade her that Taylor Swift was a good singer and not a commercial sell-out.

That last got to her. Yet another tear leaked from her raw eyes.

She was glad she had seen Matti the evening before.

The break-up with Kata had clearly hurt him badly, but obviously not as badly as her death. He was a wreck.

He had repeated that he had no idea why Kata had dumped him. Dísa tried to explain as gently as possible that it all had to do with Kata and her desire to reinvent herself, and not with Matti.

Matti didn't seem to understand. He also didn't understand why the police seemed to be treating him as a suspect when it should be obvious how much he loved her.

In the end, Dísa had said that Kata was an idiot to dump Matti, and in Dísa's opinion Kata would have realized that eventually. Dísa wasn't sure that was true, but it might have been, and it seemed to give Matti some comfort. The poor guy needed comfort.

She shook herself. She had a lot to do before five o'clock that afternoon. She still had some more email and Facebook addresses to compile, and she needed to draft messages to persuade the Thomocoin investors to set up their own bitcoin wallets together with instructions how.

She would send those at four that afternoon. And by that time she would be well out of Reykjavík. Where should she go? Not Akureyri or Dalvík. The Westfjords maybe? Or east to Höfn or Seydisfjördur, or somewhere even smaller. She should put some thought into that.

She went to check her bitcoin. The pink USB stick wasn't in the desk drawer where she usually kept it. A surge of panic leaped in her chest. Had she taken it with her the previous evening when she had visited Matti? She didn't think so. If she had left it stuck in her computer, it definitely wasn't there now.

She checked the pockets of her jeans. No.

She looked around the kitchen, the living area, her bed. No.

Could someone have taken it?

Krakatoa? Or Krakatoa's people?

She checked the flat for a sign of a break-in. She hadn't locked the door. No one locked their doors in Dalvík, and she didn't like doing it in Reykjavík unless she really had to. As it was, the door to the building itself was always locked, and she had nothing worth stealing.

Usually.

Now she had twenty million dollars of bitcoin.

She opened the door to her flat and stuck her head out into the narrow landing. A cold draught touched her face. She padded down the stairs in her socks.

The window of the back door was broken and had been roughly covered with a plastic bag.

She knocked on the door of the ground-floor flat. A bleary-eyed student, Nína, answered the door.

'What happened?' Dísa asked, pointing to the door.

'Someone broke in yesterday evening. We don't think they took anything. And we didn't want to disturb you because . . . well, you know. Did you hear them?'

'No, I didn't,' said Dísa. 'I was out.'

'Oh. Have you lost anything?'

'Maybe.'

'Should we report it to the police? Maybe you could tell them next time you see them?'

'Yeah, I'll do that.' Dísa was surprised at how casually Nína had taken the break-in.

She hurried back upstairs and fought the surge of panic that washed over her. She had lost the cold wallet. Krakatoa *had* stolen it, or arranged for someone to steal it.

The question was, could he get access to the private key?

The USB stick was password protected. Dísa had done

some research back in 2017 and had learned that the best passwords were four individual unrelated words strung together. These created a password of many letters that was nonetheless possible to remember.

Dísa had chosen *horse, dessert, philosopher* and *calm.* Except she had chosen the Icelandic equivalents: *hestur, eftiréttur, heimspekingur* and *logn*: *hestureftiretturheimspekingurlogn.* She knew that there were ever more sophisticated password-breaking programs around, but she doubted it would be worth anyone's while to program the Icelandic language into them.

Maybe there was a way that Krakatoa could bypass the password protection?

Perhaps there was. But there was nothing that Dísa could do about that now. Best to assume the password held and that the twenty million dollars of bitcoin were still there, untouched.

She had her back-up. The paper cold wallet that was buried next to her mother's beneath the stone at Blábrekka.

She needed to change her plans. It would take her all day to drive Kata's car to Dalvík if she set off right away. She could grab the cold wallet, send the messages to the Thomocoin investors and then drive off again, either west to the Westfjords or east, before Krakatoa realized she wasn't going to pay him.

It would be difficult to explain to Grandma and Grandpa at Blábrekka what she was up to, but she would think of something.

She packed a small suitcase, grabbed Kata's keys and left the apartment for the long drive north.

## FORTY-FIVE

It was shortly after 1 a.m. when Krakatoa realized what an idiot he had been. The password-cracking program was still chugging away. It operated in parallel using two different methodologies. One was brute force: checking every letter, number and punctuation mark in every combination. This worked well for short passwords, but not for longer ones – the number of combinations of truly random characters increased exponentially. The other was to combine numbers and letters from a host of dictionaries and lists of place names and proper names. It was almost impossible to memorize, say, twenty random characters; much easier to recall them if they combined words or dates or places.

If someone wrote down the twenty random characters and used that as a password they could beat the program, but why do that? You might as well just write down the private key itself. Yet it was beginning to look as if that was what Dísa had done.

Until Krakatoa realized that his program didn't speak Icelandic. Whereas a fifteen-year-old Dísa would have used Icelandic words for her password.

Shit!

Krakatoa thought, spoke and wrote in English. His online world was all in English and he kept it that way. He didn't want anyone to suspect that he was, in fact, Icelandic. Yet he really should have guessed that his own sister would pick Icelandic passwords.

He spent a frustrating hour trying various Icelandic words Dísa might have used, *blak* for example, which meant *volleyball*, but he didn't get anywhere. In the end, he gave up and went to bed.

He didn't sleep well.

When he got up at nine and logged on, there was plenty going on in the Thomocoin world for him to deal with. And not all of it bad.

Lindenbrook and Dubbelosix were safely ensconced in Panama. No one else in his globally dispersed network of employees had been bothered by the police. And, most surprisingly, Thomocoin seemed to be living on, at least in the eyes of some of its investors.

Thomocoin believers in India, England, the Netherlands and Iceland wanted to fight back against the haters. They were pleased to learn that Sharp had evaded the FBI and the CIA, who were trying to catch him and shut him up. The big banks wouldn't win! They would never shut down Thomocoin!

Tubbyman suggested posting prices again, at a much lower level. A price low enough to tempt the believers to invest more: $298 perhaps?

Krakatoa told her to give it a whirl.

These people! Really.

Krakatoa was more worried about his own situation. And his twenty million in bitcoin.

He was going to have to action his own evacuation plan

as soon as he could. He held the key to a safety deposit box on a small Caribbean island in which was stored a new passport in a new name. He had opened associated bank accounts. It was a name no one would know: not his father, not Sharp, not Jérôme. Not even Petra.

Krakatoa would live on. Jói would be gone. Forever.

Krakatoa had wanted to avoid this if he possibly could. He liked his life in Iceland. He really liked Petra. But he had to face facts. All that was over.

It had been over when he had decided to kill his stepmother.

At the time, it had looked as though he had no choice. She had flown to Reykjavík to see Dad to ask him about Thomocoin's prospects. One of her investors, Gunni Sigmundsson, was being difficult about the delays to the promised exchange. Helga had somehow got Dad to admit that Jói was involved; not only that, but Jói was Krakatoa, the guy who called all the shots.

So then she had come right across town to Jói's place in Gardabaer and confronted him, threatening to expose him. Jói had promised to pay her and all her investors back if things went wrong with Thomocoin.

The following day, Helga had called Jói from Dalvík and said she would go to the police if Jói didn't transfer the funds right away.

What bothered Jói wasn't just, or even mostly, that he would be identified with Thomocoin; he was still hopeful that Thomocoin might work out in the end. It was that he had got word from his man in the FBI, Goodmanhunting, that the police in Charlotte suspected Krakatoa of ordering Cryptocheeseman's murder. Until that point, only Sharp and his father knew Jói was really Krakatoa. He could trust them to keep quiet; Jói knew he couldn't trust Helga.

He would have to ensure she kept quiet himself.

So he had pleaded for a few days – enough time to activate Tecumseh and get him to Iceland.

Jói. Krakatoa. They weren't the same people. The only way Krakatoa could operate was by keeping them apart.

Jói was a mild-mannered, laid-back Icelander, a games developer with a girlfriend he liked, a few friends with whom he mostly communicated online, a father he loved, a mother he loved less, and a stepfamily who accepted him. He wouldn't hurt a fly. People who knew him knew he was clever. But they didn't respect him.

People respected Krakatoa.

In real life, Jói was never assertive. He had a low-grade craving for people to like him. He didn't want to offend.

Online, Krakatoa was ruthless, aggressive, decisive, effective. He had started messing around on the dark web in his late teens, getting involved as an intermediary in minor drug deals. By watching others, he learned to flex his online muscles, to earn respect, to lead.

And he liked it. No, he fucking loved it.

He wanted to build up his own online empire. At first, he had thought of drugs. Then of hacked personal details.

Then a cryptocurrency.

He had come up with the idea of FOMOcoin and through his father had approached Sharp. He had insisted from the outset on his anonymity as Krakatoa, claiming it was for security reasons, but actually because he knew that Krakatoa could do all sorts of things that Jói Ómarsson would never have dared. Krakatoa had outmanoeuvred Sharp and his friend Jérôme to retain 50 per cent of the profits of Thomocoin and, more importantly, to call the shots.

It was Krakatoa who had been ruthless enough to do

what had to be done with Cryptocheeseman when he had tried to rip off Thomocoin. Sharp had noticed. The dozens of people who worked for Thomocoin online had noticed.

They never asked questions. But they knew not to mess with Krakatoa.

Killing Helga as Krakatoa had been difficult, but Krakatoa had managed it. Through Tecumseh. Just as he had ordered Cryptocheeseman's death before her. But to go to his stepmother's funeral as Jói, to see his father and his sisters Dísa and Anna Rós so upset – that was hard.

Which was why, although he would miss Iceland, he wouldn't miss Jói and his scruples and his guilt.

Krakatoa had none of that. Krakatoa would live on. Krakatoa had a bright future, even if Thomocoin blew itself up. He had the skills, the reputation, the connections to build up something new, something bigger. He had some ideas already. A new angle on ransomware looked promising.

He could do all that, but he needed capital for his new life on a Caribbean island. He needed those twenty million dollars of bitcoin.

And now Tecumseh had left Iceland, only Jói could get it for him.

Jói would have to be brave. Jói would have to conquer his scruples.

He picked up his phone and selected a number.

'Hi, Eggert. It's Jói.'

# FORTY-SIX

The new prison at Hólmsheidi nestled in a wooded hollow just outside Reykjavík, a couple of kilometres off the main Ring Road and safely out of sight of any of the city's inhabitants. It was an isolated modern modular building of concrete, steel and glass, more akin to a secret defence-research establishment than a prison, facing eastwards across a blasted heath of desolation. It was a hell of a lot more convenient than Litla-Hraun, over an hour away from the capital on the south coast.

The traditional technique after a suspect was arrested in Iceland was to leave him alone in solitary confinement for three weeks and then present him with evidence of his guilt and get him to confess. International prison inspectors had raised eyebrows at this in the past, and the practice was much rarer than it used to be when Magnus had first arrived in the country, but Ólafur had persuaded an Akureyri judge to lock Gunni up for three weeks to sweat.

Those three weeks were nearly up. The last thing Ólafur would want was Magnus muscling his way in to speak to Gunni before he had had his chance.

Which was why Magnus hadn't told him.

Ólafur would be seriously pissed off, understandably. Magnus knew he was skating on very thin ice. If indeed Gunni was responsible for Helga's death, Magnus could be screwing up the prosecution. But Magnus was pretty sure Gunni wasn't.

Some men cope well with solitary confinement; some don't. Unsurprisingly, a tough old sea captain like Gunni could handle it. As he entered the small interview room in the prison he struck Magnus as calm, composed, but angry.

'Don't I need a lawyer to speak to you?' Gunni asked.

'You do if we discuss Helga's murder,' said Magnus. 'But I want to talk to you about something else. As a witness.'

The difference between 'witness' and 'suspect' was key in Icelandic law. Gunni wasn't a suspect yet for Kata's murder, and Magnus was pretty sure he wouldn't become one, but if he did, Magnus would have to stop the interview to allow Gunni to get himself a lawyer.

'Something else?' said Gunni.

'Have you heard that Katrín Ingvarsdóttir was murdered in Reykjavík two days ago?'

'No. Who's she?'

'She was a student from the university. She comes from Dalvík.'

'Ingvar Brynjólfsson's daughter? I know her. Poor Ingvar.' Then he frowned. 'Wait a minute. Are you here to try to pin that on me as well?'

'Did you have her killed?'

'No! I was in here, wasn't I?'

'Yes, you were,' said Magnus. 'But did you get someone else to kill her?'

'No! Why should I?'

'Do you know who did kill her?'

'Of course not! You said I'm not a suspect.'

'You're not,' said Magnus calmly. 'But I need to rule you out of the inquiry. Did you know Kata?'

'I know who she was. I've seen her about town. I'm not sure I've ever spoken to her.'

'You never had any sexual liaison with her?'

'What? No! Kata's young enough to be my daughter! She's younger than my daughter.'

'OK,' said Magnus. 'Thank you. I'm sorry I had to ask you those questions, but it is quite a coincidence that two women from Dalvík are murdered two weeks apart.'

'Well, I didn't kill either of them, and that's no coincidence.' Gunni's fierce stare reminded Magnus a little of Tryggvi Thór. Strong men angry at accusations against them.

Magnus let the words hang there. He watched Gunni with half a smile, trying to convey the idea that he believed him, without actually saying it.

'OK. Did you know that Kata was a good friend of Dísa, Helga's daughter?' Magnus asked.

'No. But I'm not surprised. They are about the same age, aren't they?'

Magnus nodded. 'Can you think of anything that might link Kata and Helga together?'

Gunni was watching Magnus carefully. Gunni was still suspicious, but he was also curious. 'Thomocoin. Was Kata involved with Thomocoin?'

'Not as far as we know,' said Magnus. 'Her parents say they didn't have any spare cash to invest.'

'I can believe that,' said Gunni. 'I never heard Ingvar talk about it, and I doubt he ever had much in savings. But Dísa was involved, wasn't she?'

'Yes,' said Magnus. 'Through her mother. But yes, she was.'

Gunni sat back in his chair. He grinned. 'You don't think I killed Helga, do you?'

Magnus kept his face expressionless.

'You think that Kata and Helga's murders are connected,' he continued. 'You know I didn't kill Kata. Which means you think I didn't kill Helga. Your job is to find out who killed Kata. The other guy – Inspector Ólafur – his job is to find out who killed Helga. Am I right?'

Magnus didn't answer.

'Unless you are just playing good cop to the other guy's bad cop?'

'I like to think I'm a good cop. Which is why I can't ask you about Helga's murder without a lawyer present.'

'But I can tell you why I didn't kill her?'

Magnus didn't move.

'That knife was planted, you know? Why would I leave a knife with blood on it lying around?'

Magnus didn't reply, waiting for more.

Gunni went on. 'I've got a little less than an hour unaccounted for the morning Helga was killed, when I was walking the dog. If I killed Helga up on the mountainside, I would have had to run there from my house with my dog running after me, stab her and sprint back. I know that mountain well; it's just not possible for me to do it in the time. And how would I know she would be at that spot exactly at the time I got there? Whoever did kill her must have been lying in wait for her, probably for at least an hour. It makes no sense! I've been thinking about it a lot over the last couple of weeks. I can't see how a judge can convict me, despite the knife evidence.'

'If you didn't kill Helga, who did?'

'I've got no idea. But I bet it's got something to do with Thomocoin. Some other poor sucker she talked into putting their life savings into it – that's my guess. Someone from Dalvík. Or maybe a doctor from Akureyri who worked with her. But not me.'

'And why Kata?'

'I don't know,' said Gunni. 'That's your job. But it seems to me it must have something to do with Thomocoin and something to do with Dísa.'

On the way back to police headquarters, Magnus called Árni.

'Did you speak to Ólafur?' Magnus asked.

'Just now.'

'And?'

'As we predicted. He's not happy. He says I shouldn't be wasting time trying to do the defence's job for them. I should be looking for evidence to incriminate Gunni.'

'Is he going to pass on the report to the defence?'

'He says it's not relevant. He says someone seeing someone walking along the street looking around is not evidence.'

Idiot.

'You think Gunni may be innocent, don't you?' Árni said.

'I'm damn sure he is,' said Magnus. 'From what Gunni told me, he would have had to run from his house with his dog to the spot where Helga was killed, stab her and run back immediately. And for that to work he would have had to know she would be there at precisely that time.'

'Yes. That's right,' Árni said.

'Well, that didn't happen, did it?'

'No. But wait a minute, Magnús! Have you just been to see Gunni?'

'Yes. In Hólmsheidi.'

'Does Ólafur know?'

'Not yet.'

'Jesus! He is going to go ballistic.'

'I expect so. Don't tell him, will you, Árni?'

'All right. But he *will* find out.'

'I know. I'll deal with it.'


Dealing with it meant talking to Thelma. Right away.

She looked up at him over her reading glasses as he entered her office.

'Any progress?' she asked.

'Yes, I think so.' Magnus took a seat.

'Tell me.'

Best to get it out quickly.

'Gunnar Snaer Sigmundsson didn't kill Helga. Helga and Kata's deaths are connected. The connection is Dísa and Thomocoin.' Best also to sound certain. Give Thelma any room for doubt and she would grab it and stuff it down his throat.

'What! I hope you've got evidence for this.'

'I have. One. The knife was planted in Gunni's garage. There is no reason why he wouldn't have cleaned Helga's blood off it before hiding it there. Árni has uncovered a report of a man prowling around Gunni's house the evening after the murder.

'Two. Gunni didn't have time to get to the scene of the crime to murder Helga. If he did somehow run there and back quickly enough he would have had to have known the precise time she would be there. What actually happened was that the killer lay in wait for Helga.

'Three. I have just spoken to Gunni in Hólmsheidi. He was very convincing to me. He didn't kill Helga.'

'You went to Hólmsheidi? You didn't tell me you were going to do that.'

'Just now, this morning. You suggested I check to see if there is a link between Gunni and Kata. There isn't, by the way.'

'What does Ólafur say about all this?'

'Ólafur is convinced Gunni is guilty.'

'I bet he is.' Thelma frowned. 'Assuming for a moment that Gunni didn't kill Helga – and I haven't heard enough yet to believe he didn't – what has Thomocoin to do with it?'

'There's an obvious link between the death of Helga and the death of Kata, and that's Dísa. Thomocoin has dominated Dísa and her mother's life in the last month or so. Her family have lost everything, including the farm that has been theirs for generations. We know Helga wasn't killed by a former lover. We know Kata wasn't killed in a random sex attack. Both murders must have been committed by a professional. They were hits.'

Magnus paused. 'I got a call last night from a district attorney's office in North Carolina. They are investigating a murder which they believe may have been committed by a professional killer under instructions from someone called Krakatoa, who supposedly runs Thomocoin.'

He looked Thelma in the eye. 'The connection is Thomocoin.'

Thelma's eyes were blazing. 'Magnús. I *told* you to leave Thomocoin out of this. I was clear; I was explicit. It's a political nightmare. But more important, much more important, if I tell you not to do something, I have to trust you not to do it! Now get out and don't bother me with these idiotic theories. And if you have screwed up the prosecution of Gunnar, I'll discipline you. It'll be back to Sergeant Magnús.'

Magnus sat there.

'I said go!'

'I know you did,' said Magnus. 'I spoke to Tryggvi Thór last night.'

'What has that got to do with anything?'

'I know you and he are covering something up. I don't know what it is, and I've told him I won't ask any more. But I did ask him whether I could trust you. He said I could.'

Thelma opened her mouth and then closed it.

'You've got a choice here, Thelma. If you spend a minute thinking through what I've just said, you'll see I'm right. You *know* I'm right. Two women have died and we need to do all we can to find their killers. That's what we do. Isn't it?'

The fire in Thelma's eyes had hardened. But she was listening.

'Politically it's a disaster. I get that. All kinds of ministers I don't know will be upset. Ólafur will be really upset – I would be if I was him and another cop trampled all over my investigation. But we shouldn't care about that, you and I. We should find the killer and the people who paid him, and we should arrest them.

'If you don't want me to do that, and you want me to walk out of here, I will. And I'll just keep walking.'

Thelma swung her artificial leg out from under her desk and paced over to the window.

Magnus waited.

She turned. She looked grim, but Magnus could tell she had made up her mind. 'All right. So what do we do next?'

'The link is Dísa,' said Magnus. 'She knows what the connection between Thomocoin and the murders is but she's not telling us. So we pull her in and we make her talk.'

Thelma nodded.

'Whoever set up Gunni must have known about Helga's affair with him. Which means it was someone who knew Helga well. It could be her ex-husband. There's her brother, Eggert – he was the one who told us about the affair. She has a stepson, Jói: we should talk to him. Ideally, we should talk to Sharp, who is Thomocoin's boss, but he's supposed to be in Panama.'

'And Gunni?'

'I suggest you go and talk to Gunni. Apologize to him. See if he has any further ideas.'

'Me?'

'Yes. He has been locked up for over two weeks for something he didn't do. That shouldn't have happened. He used to be an MP so he'll have powerful friends. You're the expert on the politics, but I'd have thought we want him on our side. And if you do this quickly, he might be happy. If we continue to pursue him and the judge throws the case out – which he will do – we will look really bad.'

Thelma sighed. 'There's something I don't get about the Thomocoin angle, Magnús. I see why Helga would be a victim. Or Dísa. But why Kata? What's her link to Thomocoin?'

'Dísa, I suppose,' said Magnus, feeling secure enough now to allow some doubt into his reply. It was a good question, and one he hadn't answered yet.

'Dísa was her friend. Was Kata working with Dísa on Thomocoin? Helping her?'

'Not that we've heard,' said Magnus.

'Then why would someone want to kill her?'

It was the right question. And as Thelma asked it, the answer came to Magnus. 'It's a warning. To Dísa. Someone has threatened her. To keep quiet, or to get her to do something. Which is why she's hiding something from us. She's scared.'

Thelma nodded. 'Well, go find her then. Find out what she's hiding. Now.'

## FORTY-SEVEN

Dísa drove fast on the empty road north – no tourists. She appreciated the time to think, to force her mind into some kind of order.

Helga had died. Kata had died. There was a chance she would die too, no matter how careful she was, and that scared the hell out of her. But she was determined not to panic.

Yet, for once she felt that she had gained some kind of control of the situation. She had a plan. She had asserted her will against her father. She had no illusions that Krakatoa wouldn't be after her once the five o'clock deadline had passed and he hadn't received his bitcoin.

Who was Krakatoa anyway? Perhaps Sharp. Or perhaps some nameless evil genius in a bedroom in Moscow or San Francisco or some other far-flung place, who had crept into Dísa's life through the internet.

Whoever Krakatoa was, he had killed before and he would kill again. If he could find Dísa.

The Westfjords were the place to go, with their twisty, slow roads and their scattered communities. Grandpa had a tent and some camping gear at Blábrekka – Dísa would borrow that. No hitman would ever find her.

Once the bitcoin had been safely distributed from her wallet to Uncle Eggert's, and from there to all the investors, she could re-emerge into the world. Or at least get in touch with the police. Perhaps wait until they had arrested Krakatoa or the hitman. If they could arrest him. While Krakatoa was loose, Dísa wouldn't be safe. She might need a longer-term solution to hide. Where could she go?

Perhaps she should keep some of the bitcoin back to help her go on the run. Twenty million dollars was surely more than the Icelanders had invested; she would also have to figure out how to return the rest of it to investors abroad. A website, or something, where people could make claims. But how to verify them? Tomorrow's problem.

Maybe Jói could help. After facing down her father, Dísa was a little less worried that Jói would grab her bitcoin and return it to him. Jói would probably be more use than Uncle Eggert in helping her find somewhere to hide.

She was placing a lot of trust in Uncle Eggert. Perhaps, before going to Dalvík, she should drop in and see him in Akureyri. She would need good Wi-Fi and a bit of peace and quiet to send out the string of emails and Facebook messages she had planned for the Thomocoin investors. It would be good to talk through the details with him. He would no doubt be at work, but maybe he could slip away for an hour.

She picked up her phone and called him.


Magnus took Vigdís with him to interview Dísa. They tried her doorbell, with no response. Magnus rang a couple of the other bells in the building. He was just about to give up when the door opened to reveal a tall, dark-haired woman with big bleary eyes, of about Dísa's age.

'Hi,' she said, blinking.

'Inspector Magnús Ragnarsson,' Magnus said, holding up his ID. 'Reykjavík police. And this is Sergeant Vigdís Audardóttir. Do you know where Dísa Ómarsdóttir is?'

'Have you come about the break-in?' said the student.

'What break-in?'

The student, who said her name was Nína, showed them the broken glass in the back door.

'We need to get forensics on to this,' said Magnus to Vigdís. 'Did whoever broke in take anything from any of the flats?'

Nína shrugged. 'I don't think so. I told Dísa about it this morning. She did seem kinda worried.'

'Do you know where we might find her?' Vigdís asked. 'Is she in class now?'

'I don't really know her,' said Nína. 'She hasn't been here very long. I did know Kata, of course.'

'So you don't know what class she might be in?'

'I doubt she's in any class.'

'Why?'

'Because I saw her leaving the building a couple of hours ago, dragging a suitcase behind her.'


They tried to call Dísa; unsurprisingly she didn't pick up her phone. Vigdís made some calls to secure the back door to Dísa's building and to get forensics over there. She also got the ball in motion to get a trace on Dísa's phone. That needed a warrant, and that would take at least a couple of hours.

Magnus drove to Dísa's father's house in Nordurmýri.

Ómar Baldvinsson looked, if anything, more strung out than the last time Magnus had spoken to him.

Vigdís and Magnus crammed together on the tatty sofa. Magnus noticed that Ómar had been working on a spreadsheet on his desktop computer when they had interrupted him. A laptop lay on a pile of magazines on a wooden chair.

'So, I've got the both of you, have I, this time?' Ómar said with a weak smile. 'How can I help you today?'

'We're investigating the murder of Katrín Ingvarsdóttir,' Magnus said.

'Ah. Dísa's friend. That's very sad.'

'It is. Did you know her?'

'Not really. I'd heard about her and I'd met her once or twice, but Dísa and she didn't become friends until Helga and the girls moved north to Dalvík about ten years ago.'

'When did you last see Kata?'

'Last week – at Helga's funeral. She was with Dísa. I'm not sure I said anything directly to her.'

'Where were you the night before last at about six p.m.?'

'Hah! You don't think *I* killed her, do you?'

'Please answer the question, Ómar,' said Vigdís.

'All right. I was here. Watching TV.'

'Alone?'

'Yes.'

'So no one can verify that?'

Ómar shrugged. 'You could ask the neighbours. They are pretty nosy. Especially the old bat downstairs. But I don't understand. Why would I kill Dísa's best friend? Wasn't she found naked anyway? Do you think I'm some kind of rapist?'

'We think she was stripped to put us off the scent,' said Magnus. 'As to why, we think the answer is Thomocoin.'

'Not this again,' said Ómar.

'We believe there is a link between Kata's death and your wife's.'

'I thought you had arrested Helga's killer? That guy Gunni?'

'New evidence has come to light which suggests he's innocent.'

'Oh. So you think I killed Helga as well? I thought you had already checked that I was in Reykjavík the day she died.'

Vigdís glanced at Magnus.

'We now think that both her murder and Kata's were committed by a professional killer,' Magnus said.

'Oh.'

'And that the connection between the two is your daughter. And Thomocoin.'

Ómar ran his fingers over his thinning scalp. 'Oh.'

'So we are trying to find the connection between Dísa, Thomocoin and the two murders.'

Ómar frowned. 'I told you, I can't help you.'

'Oh, yes you can,' said Magnus. 'This is a double-homicide investigation. I need you to tell me all about Thomocoin. We're not talking about fraud here. We're talking about murder.'

'I need a lawyer before I discuss Thomocoin.'

'The same professional may have killed a former employee of Thomocoin in North Carolina last year. Cryptocheeseman. Have you heard of him?'

'I won't answer any questions about Thomocoin without a lawyer.'

'Ómar.' Magnus leaned forward. 'We think your

daughter is in danger. We don't know exactly why your ex-wife was killed. But we think Kata's death was a warning to Dísa. To keep quiet about something, maybe. Or to get her to do something else. We don't know what. But we are pretty sure it has to do with Thomocoin.'

Ómar put his head in his hands. Magnus and Vigdís waited.

After a few seconds, he looked up, despair, anguish and fear filling his eyes. 'Have you talked to her? What does she say?'

'She's gone from Kata's flat,' said Magnus. 'With a suitcase.'

'I suppose that's good,' said Ómar. 'If she really is in danger.'

'We'll find her. But in the meantime, tell us what you know about Thomocoin.'

They waited while Ómar gathered his thoughts. 'I really don't know much about it. Sharp first described it to me a few years ago, and I took Dísa to a presentation he gave here in Reykjavík. She was impressed and so was I. She had made a lot of money trading bitcoin, and I thought this new Thomocoin would be a good way of converting her profits into krónur, which was very difficult back then with exchange controls. Actually, it's still difficult in Iceland. I thought she might make some more money out of Thomocoin. At that point, I hadn't realized she was giving it all away to Helga.'

'Would that have bothered you?'

'I would have warned her not to. Helga was always greedy. She was bad with money. I never realized she had got so many people involved with Thomocoin until after she died. She only did it for the commission.'

'Didn't your friend Sharp tell you about Helga's investments?'

'No. I had no direct involvement in Thomocoin myself, except a small investment.'

'How much?'

'About half a million krónur. Five thousand dollars at the time. It's all I could afford.'

'What might Thomocoin be wanting Dísa to do? Or to keep quiet about?'

Ómar sighed. 'I really have no idea.'

'And what about Krakatoa?'

'You asked me before. I don't know who or what Krakatoa is.'

'Really?' said Magnus, looking directly at Ómar. 'Because if Krakatoa is the guy who is really running Thomocoin, then Krakatoa may well be trying to scare your daughter, or even kill her.'

'You don't know that,' said Ómar.

'Is Krakatoa your friend Sharp?'

'No idea.'

'Kata's dead,' said Vigdís. 'Inspector Magnús and I saw her body yesterday morning. It was a terrible sight. Honestly. Horrible.'

This shook Ómar. 'Well, for God's sake find who did it then!' he said. 'Find this Krakatoa! Lock him up! But I've told you I can't help you.'

'I don't believe you,' said Magnus.

Ómar's shoulders slumped, as if the brief outburst of outrage had exhausted him and despair had reasserted itself. He shrugged.

'Do you have any idea where Dísa might be?' Magnus asked. 'We need to find her. If only to keep her safe.'

'No.'

'Think,' said Magnus.

'Does Dísa own a car?' Vigdís asked.

'No,' Ómar said. He hesitated. 'The only place I can think of is my summer house. It's on Apavatn. I used to take the girls there when they were kids. I don't know for certain she's gone there now. But I know she was . . . thinking about it recently. I can give you directions. She could have taken a bus there from Selfoss, although it would be a good walk to the summer house from the bus stop.'

'Do you believe him?' asked Magnus afterwards as they got into the car.

'No,' said Vigdís. 'He knows who Krakatoa is.'

'When we get back to the station, get someone from Selfoss to check out the bus and the summer house. We need to find Dísa. Put out an active alert. And get on to the airport – we don't want her leaving the country.'

'What about bringing Ómar in for more questioning?' Vigdís asked.

'I was thinking about that. But we need a warrant for his computer and phone first. See if he communicated with Sharp or Thomocoin, or Dísa for that matter.'

'I'll get on to it.'

'I wish we could speak to Sharp.'

'In Panama?' said Vigdís. 'We could. Instead of all that warrant stuff, I could fly out there and have a little chat. What about it?'

Magnus grinned. 'I'd have you on the next plane, Vigdís, but unfortunately, we have no jurisdiction there. Plus it's hurricane season.'

'I could wait it out. Lie by a pool until he cracked and confessed. It's got to be worth a try. And Panama in a hurricane can't be worse than Reykjavík on a windy Monday.'

'Actually, I have an idea,' said Magnus. 'I'll drop you at the station, and then I will go and see Iceland's Miss Thomocoin.'

'And who is that?'

'Fjóla.'

# FORTY-EIGHT

Ómar slumped down into his chair in front of his computer. The numbers on his spreadsheet – a cash-flow forecast for a little company that did glacier tours and was in a bit of trouble with its bank – swam in front of his eyes.

Of course he knew who Krakatoa was.

But he was only now beginning to understand what Krakatoa had done.

He had been so proud of Jói when he had come up with his idea for a new cryptocurrency, and proud when he had introduced Jói to Sharp. He had been hurt that the two of them had seemed to freeze him out of Thomocoin, as Jói's FOMOcoin was rechristened, but he thought it probably for the best. He had never been privy to the inner workings of the operation, and only recently had he realized that his son had the dominant role. He had been gratified when Jói had asked to stash his cold wallet at the summer house.

Ómar had been a banker. He understood the potential for Thomocoin, but he also knew there were risks. When they had failed to come up with the exchange they had promised which would convert Thomocoin into real money, these doubts had grown. He was glad he had only invested five thousand bucks: enough to make a decent profit if it all worked; not enough to wipe him out if he lost it all. His bitcoin profits had been good and he had taken most of those and spent them; if he lost all his Thomocoin, well, easy come, easy go.

He had become much more worried when Helga had started pressuring him for answers about the exchange and visited him in Reykjavík demanding answers and wheedling Jói's role in Thomocoin out of him. It was only then that he realized how she had bet everything on Thomocoin and suckered in so many other people as well. He didn't care about Helga, she deserved to lose her money, but he did care about Dísa and Anna Rós and their inheritance.

For a moment he had wondered about Helga's death and whether Sharp might be responsible for it, but he couldn't conceive of his friend doing anything like that to Helga, whom Ómar knew Sharp and his wife genuinely liked. So he was relieved when it turned out a local had done it. A local who had been his wife's lover, before he himself had strayed with Bryndís.

Kata was dead. And Dísa was convinced that Krakatoa had killed her, or had had her killed. Because Krakatoa had said he would.

And now Krakatoa was threatening to kill Dísa.

His son was threatening to kill his daughter.

His instinct had been to protect Jói's identity. Not to tell Dísa and certainly not the police who Krakatoa really was. Give himself time to think.

All right. Now was the time to think.

What he thought first was that Jói was incapable of killing Kata, let alone Dísa. Ómar's son was not a murderer.

First and foremost he needed to have faith in his son. Dísa, and the police, *must* be mistaken.

So, if it wasn't Jói who had killed Kata and was threatening Dísa, who was it?

Sharp? Either it was Sharp, or Sharp would know who it might be.

Ómar would really have liked to talk to Sharp on the phone, but he decided it was better to use the end-to-end encrypted messaging system that Jói had set up over Telegram on his laptop. He was glad he hadn't had time to hit the kill switch on that machine when the detectives showed up, as Jói had instructed him.

LAWRENCE: Are you in Panama?

LINDENBROOK: Hey, buddy. Good to hear from you. Yeah, got here last Sunday. Just in time. The British police raided my house the morning after I got out of London. I had to leave Ella and the kids there though. She's not a happy bunny.

LAWRENCE: Have you heard what's happening here?

LINDENBROOK: What do you mean?

LAWRENCE: Dísa's best friend was murdered two days ago.

LINDENBROOK: Oh no! I'm sorry. Was it the girl who was with her at the funeral?

LAWRENCE: Yes. The police think it was Krakatoa.

LINDENBROOK: Oh, ignore the police. They're just guessing.

LAWRENCE: Dísa thinks it's Krakatoa too.

LINDENBROOK: Tell her not to worry.

LAWRENCE: No. You don't understand. Krakatoa threatened Dísa. Said if she didn't give him his bitcoin

back, someone close to her would die. And someone
did. Kata.

LINDENBROOK: What bitcoin?

LAWRENCE: Jói's bitcoin. He and I shared a hiding
place for our cold wallets. She found it and took all his
bitcoin.

LINDENBROOK: I didn't know that. So Dísa thinks
Krakatoa killed her friend?

LAWRENCE: Yes. Did he?

LINDENBROOK: I don't know. I don't know anything
about this. But it doesn't sound right to me.

LAWRENCE: Nor to me. Are you sure you don't know
anything about it?

LINDENBROOK: 100%.

LAWRENCE: And is Krakatoa just one person?

LINDENBROOK: What do you mean?

LAWRENCE: I mean, does anyone else use the
Krakatoa handle? Apart from Jói?

LINDENBROOK: No. Just Jói.

LAWRENCE: But that means it must be Jói who killed
Kata.

LINDENBROOK: I don't know. I just find that hard to
believe.

LAWRENCE: So do I.

LINDENBROOK: By the way. I think Jói can read this. If
he wants to.

LAWRENCE: I thought it was super-secure encrypted.

LINDENBROOK: Yeah. But Jói set it up. He could have
set up an eavesdropping function without either of us
knowing. Be careful, Ómar.

'Hi, Dad.'

Ómar pushed past his son into the flat.

'What's up?' said Jói, his blue eyes wide in alarm at his father's expression.

'Did you kill Kata?'

'What?'

'Did you kill Kata? Dísa's friend Kata?' Ómar's voice rose to a shout.

'Of course not, Dad. Why should I? Look, sit down. And *calm* down.'

Ómar had decided that the only thing to do was to have it out with his son. Face to face, not over the damn internet where Jói could hide behind his Krakatoa personality.

He sat down at the kitchen table, and Jói sat opposite him. Ómar studied his son. Could he really have killed an innocent woman, his sister's best friend? He didn't look as if he could.

And yet the evidence was incontrovertible.

'Dísa took all your bitcoin. You wanted it back, so you threatened her with the death of someone close to her. She didn't give it back, so you killed Kata. Now you're threatening to kill your own sister! Dísa told me. The police told me – more or less.'

'The police?'

'Yes. They're just guessing. But they are on to you. Dísa doesn't know you're Krakatoa. But I do. I know *you* killed Kata.'

Jói sat, watching his father calmly.

'I had no choice, Dad,' he said eventually.

'You had no choice! What does that mean? You didn't have to do it. No one made you. Did they?' For a second Ómar saw a straw and grabbed at it.

But Jói didn't magic up an evil mastermind from nowhere. If there was an evil mastermind, it was he.

'Thomocoin is blowing up,' Jói said. 'I'm going to have to disappear pretty soon. Dísa has nearly all my money and I'm going to need it back.'

'But you killed someone, Jói! And the police say you killed Helga too!'

'I didn't kill her myself. And I didn't kill Kata. But I did arrange it. I had to.'

Ómar couldn't believe what he was hearing. His anger evaporated to be replaced by dismay. His son, whom he loved so much, in whom he was so proud, was a murderer.

'You got a hitman to do it?'

'Yes,' Jói said quietly. 'From the dark web. I've never met him.' He looked down at the table. He looked ashamed.

And so he bloody well should!

Ómar's son looked up. His expression was hard to read. He looked like the old Jói, the shy, innocent, clever boy he had always been.

But he was a killer.

'What are you going to do, Dad? Are you going to the police?'

'I don't know. You're not going to kill Dísa, are you?'

'Of course not! I'm only trying to scare her.'

'But you killed Kata.'

'Dad. I had to. I truly didn't want to. But I had to.'

'That's crap, Jói.'

Now Ómar was faced with the certainty that his son was a murderer, he didn't know what to do. He should report him to the police, he knew that. But he couldn't bring himself to do it. He just couldn't.

And Jói knew it.

But Ómar had to regain the initiative. He had to assert

some kind of authority over his son – stop him killing his daughter.

'OK. This is what's going to happen. You are going to disappear now. *Without* your bitcoin. You'll manage – you were always a smart kid. You are going to leave Dísa alone. I'll stay quiet for a day or two, then I will go to the police. If you haven't left the country by then, then that's your problem.'

Ómar took a deep breath. 'And I never want to see you again.'

Jói hung his head. 'OK, Dad. I'll go tomorrow. And I'll leave Dísa alone. I promise.'

'You'd better,' said Ómar.

He took one last long hard look at his son. The killer.

Then he left Jói's flat without saying goodbye.

Back in his car, Ómar called his daughter. She didn't pick up, which wasn't a surprise. So he tapped out a quick text: *Spoke to Krakatoa. He will leave you alone now. You can keep his money. Much love, Dad.*

## FORTY-NINE

Fjóla answered the door to her flat in Hverfisgata. She worked from home – but then everyone worked from home in these virus days.

'Oh, it's you.' She wasn't pleased to see Magnus.

'I've got some questions.'

'I'm sure you have. Do I need my lawyer?'

'No, it's not about Thomocoin,' said Magnus. 'Or at least not about your part in the fraud – if it is a fraud. I'm sure you've had plenty of questions about that.'

'Just one guy so far,' said Fjóla. 'He was from the Financial Services Authority. But I'm expecting more.'

'Has Thomocoin actually folded?'

'I thought it had,' said Fjóla. 'But they refreshed the price just now. It's down, but not out. And there are lots of enthusiastic people out there who refuse to let it die.'

'But not you?'

'I stopped taking any more orders a few days ago. If my clients want to buy, then they have to do it directly.'

'And do they?'

'Some of them.' Fjóla smiled. Much of the bounce and

energy had gone out of her, but there was still warmth. 'Have a seat. Coffee?'

'No, thanks. There's been another murder.'

'I saw it on the news. In fact, I saw you on the news.' Fjóla's hand flew to her mouth. 'Don't say this has something to do with Thomocoin. I thought it was a sex murder?'

'That's what the killer wanted us to think. But, yes, we do think it has something to do with Thomocoin.'

'Oh God.'

'Was Katrín Ingvarsdóttir an investor?'

'I don't recognize the name.'

'Can you check? She did live in Dalvík. And can you check her parents, Ingvar Brynjólfsson and Stefanía Jónsdóttir?'

'Sure. One moment.' Fjóla moved over to a laptop on a desk by the window overlooking the bay, tapped a few keys and tickled a trackpad. 'No. None of them. Thank God.'

'OK. I didn't think so.'

'So what's the Thomocoin connection?' Fjóla asked, returning to her chair.

'We're not sure precisely,' said Magnus. 'That's why I'm here. Kata was Dísa Ómarsdóttir's best friend. We *think* that Kata was killed to warn Dísa or to threaten her to do something. And we believe Dísa may have received a threat from Krakatoa.'

'I see where this is going,' said Fjóla. 'You think Sharp killed her?'

'If Sharp is Krakatoa. We're not certain of that, are we?'

'Not certain, no,' Fjóla said. 'But it's my best guess. And you can be sure that Krakatoa, whoever he is, will have paid someone to do it, not done it himself.'

'I've just been talking to Dísa's father, Ómar. He claims he wasn't involved in Thomocoin. Is that correct?'

'Yes. He made an investment, but nothing major. I don't think he was involved in the operations, although he is an old mate of Sharp from Sharp's banking days.'

'Can you check how much he invested?'

'One moment.' Fjóla checked her computer again. 'About five thousand dollars' worth at the price he invested. Maybe twelve now at today's prices.' She gave a hollow laugh. 'True value zero, more like. Don't quote me on that.'

Fjóla's brow furrowed as she processed what Magnus was telling her. 'You don't think I had anything to do with the murder you're investigating? Because, believe me, I never would. I wish now I'd had nothing to do with Thomocoin. I thought it was legit. I knew it was bending the rules, but I thought that was in a good way. That's how change comes, from bending rules. Murder is never good.'

'No, it's not.' Magnus leaned forward. 'Fjóla, I need your help.'

'I'll do anything I can to help you with that poor girl's death. What do you want?'

'I want to talk to Sharp.'

NEFERTITI: Hey, Lindenbrook.

LINDENBROOK: Hi.

NEFERTITI: Are you safe? I heard you had to hide.

LINDENBROOK: Yes, I'm safe. How are you?'

NEFERTITI: The cops are asking questions.

LINDENBROOK: Don't worry. We've done nothing illegal.

NEFERTITI: In fact I've got one with me now. Magnús. You've met him.

LINDENBROOK: Are you letting him see this?

NEFERTITI: Yes.

LINDENBROOK: Tell him to get off your computer and leave you alone.

NEFERTITI: He's asking me about the murder of a girl called Kata. She was Dísa Ómarsdóttir's best friend.

LINDENBROOK: That has nothing to do with Thomocoin.

NEFERTITI: It's Magnús here now. I've taken over from Fjóla. Can you confirm that Lindenbrook is Sharp?

LINDENBROOK: I'm not confirming anything.

NEFERTITI: I understand. We believe that Krakatoa may have warned Dísa that he would kill someone if she didn't do something. Kata is dead. We believe Krakatoa killed her.

LINDENBROOK:

NEFERTITI: So we need to know: who is Krakatoa? Is it you, Sharp?

LINDENBROOK: Krakatoa is not me.

NEFERTITI: Then who is it?

LINDENBROOK:

NEFERTITI: Is Dísa in danger now?

LINDENBROOK:

NEFERTITI: Are you still there?

LINDENBROOK: Dísa may be in danger. I don't know.

NEFERTITI: In danger from whom?

LINDENBROOK: Look. I didn't kill anyone. I don't believe there is any need for anyone to be killed. I have nothing to do with any of that.

NEFERTITI: You do now.

LINDENBROOK: You can't pin any of that on me. I told you I had nothing to do with it!

NEFERTITI: Maybe. Maybe not. But I do know that if

you don't give us the identity of Krakatoa, he may kill Dísa. And that WILL be your fault.

LINDENBROOK:

NEFERTITI: Won't it?

LINDENBROOK:

NEFERTITI: It's your choice: either you help Kata's killer, or you help me. There is no opt-out; doing nothing is helping a murderer. Maybe helping him to kill again. If you have any information about who might have killed Kata, or if anyone is planning to kill Dísa, contact me. You have my card.

# FIFTY

KRAKATOA: Hi, Lawrence. I've changed my mind.

LAWRENCE: Lawrence? Ég er pabbi.

KRAKATOA: I want Dísa to give me my bitcoin back.

LAWRENCE: Well, you can't have it back. We discussed this. If you touch her I will go to the police.

KRAKATOA: And if you go to the police I will have you killed.

LAWRENCE: What?

KRAKATOA: You read that right. Read it again.

LAWRENCE: Jói! You are telling me you will kill your sister and your father?

KRAKATOA: I'm not Jói, I'm Krakatoa. And I won't kill you, someone else will. But if you tell Dísa to give me back my bitcoin, then nobody dies.

LAWRENCE: What do you mean nobody dies? Helga and Kata have already died.

KRAKATOA: Nobody else dies.

LAWRENCE: You can't be serious.

KRAKATOA: I am serious. I'm not bluffing.

LAWRENCE: Dísa's gone, you know that?

KRAKATOA: Gone? Where?

LAWRENCE: I don't know. And neither do you.

KRAKATOA: I'll find her.

LAWRENCE: Then I'm going to the police.

KRAKATOA: Listen to me. This is Krakatoa talking, not your son. There's a difference – you know there is. If I'm going to get out of this, I'm going to need those bitcoin. Jói will be no more. So don't go to the police. And don't tell Dísa I'm after her. Or you will die. Is that clear?

LAWRENCE: Jói minn!

KRAKATOA: I'm not your Jói. And you are not my pabbi.

LAWRENCE: I won't do it.

KRAKATOA: Yes you will. Bye.

Krakatoa closed the Telegram window.

He had crumbled when faced with his father, and, actually, that had been a good thing. Because as Krakatoa, he could stand up to him.

It had been hard to write those words: *I'm not your Jói. You are not my pabbi.* But it was necessary. And he felt better having written them. Stronger.

Much stronger.

The essential difference between Krakatoa and Jói wasn't a negotiating tactic for his father. It was, Krakatoa had come to realize, his only hope of living with himself in the future. He had to become a new person, in a new country. He had to become Krakatoa.

Jói could never kill or even threaten to kill Dísa and his father. Jói was racked with guilt at what he had already done. Jói was worried about his girlfriend Petra and would miss her. The remainder of Jói's life would be hell: a mixture of regret and crushing guilt, as well as a long prison sentence.

So Jói had to go. And Krakatoa had to do whatever was necessary to make that happen.

The passport waiting for him in the safety deposit box in the small Caribbean island bore a Danish name, Anders Madsen, so people in the real world would call him Anders. He spoke Danish, but with a strong Icelandic accent, so that might lead to some awkwardness if he bumped into a real Dane in future, but he would deal with that when the time came.

Online, he would be Krakatoa. Online he would be powerful and successful and very very rich.

If only Tecumseh had hung around in Iceland. Because if any more killing had to be done, it was someone who looked a lot like the real-world Jói that would have to do it.

But it would be Krakatoa.

To carry out a credible threat, he needed to know where Dísa was. That was easy.

He picked up his phone and hit her number.

'Jói!'

'Hi, Dísa. What's up? Dad said you'd gone off somewhere?'

'Yeah. I need to go back to Dalvík. I'm on my way there now.' His sister's voice sounded strained. It also sounded as if she was in a car.

'What for?'

'I can't really say, Jói. I'm sorry.'

'Are you in trouble? Does it have something to do with poor Kata's murder?'

'It does, yes.'

'Can I help?'

'Maybe. Maybe you can, Jói. But not quite yet. I may need to call you later.'

'I'm here when you need me. Take care.'

'Thanks.'

Krakatoa knew why Dísa was suddenly driving to Dalvík. He glanced at her pink USB stick jutting out of his computer. Without that, she needed the back-up private key to her bitcoin wallet. And that must be at Blábrekka.

It wasn't necessarily a problem that Dísa was on her way to Dalvík. To pay him back, she needed that key, and that was the solution Krakatoa wanted. Then no one else had to die.

Whatever choice Dísa made about her bitcoin when she got access to them again, Krakatoa needed to be there too.

Krakatoa quickly packed a bag, which included two of his three computers. He hit the combination of keys that acted as the kill switch on the third, locking the hard drive from outside interference.

He was just about to leave the flat when the door opened and Petra walked in.

'Oh, hi, Jói. I got off work early.' She noticed his bag. 'Where are you off to?'

For a moment Jói looked at his girlfriend in something close to panic. She frowned. 'What's up, Jói? Where are you going?'

Then Krakatoa barged past her and down the stairs without a backward glance.


Ómar stared at his computer screen.

Here was proof that his son was a murderer. Proof that his son was perfectly capable of killing his sister.

And his father.

Ómar realized he was scared. Scared of his own son. Jói, the sweet, innocent nerd who would never hurt a fly.

He had to warn Dísa. He typed a text. *I spoke too soon. Krakatoa still wants his money back.*

Ómar hesitated before pressing 'Send'. Then he added: *Maybe you should give it to him.*

He sent that.

No response.

Ómar realized he could warn Dísa that Krakatoa was Jói, that Jói was after her. He could also tell the police.

If he did that, Jói had said that the professional hitman who had killed Helga and Dísa would kill him too.

Did Ómar believe Jói would do that?

Damn right he did.

He was absolutely correct to be scared of his son.

But he couldn't let Jói get away with it. Somehow he had to regain the initiative with his son.

How?

He didn't know. He just didn't know. Jói, he could deal with. But Krakatoa?

Krakatoa had him.

'Fuck!' He slammed his fist on his desk so hard the whole apartment seemed to rattle. It made no difference.

Ómar closed his eyes. There was still a solution to this – of a sort. Dísa gives Jói his bitcoin back. Jói disappears. Dísa is still alive.

It was the only way.

Warning Dísa that Jói was after her wouldn't save her. It wasn't Jói whom she had to look out for. It was whatever hitman Jói had dragged out of the dark web. A hitman who had killed at least twice before.

Ómar sent another text.

*For God's sake, Dísa! Please do as he asks. I don't want to lose you!*

A reply came.

*Don't worry, Dad. Krakatoa stole that stupid pink wallet you gave me, but it's password protected. Once I've got my paper back-up, I'll disappear. No one will find me. I'm going to pay the money back to the people who lost it in the first place.*

Ómar shook his head. This didn't look good.

Ómar couldn't help but admire his daughter's bravery. Dísa thought she could hide from Jói's hitman. And maybe she could – for a week or a month or perhaps even a year.

But not forever.

Which was why Ómar didn't call the police. He believed his son. Or rather, he believed Krakatoa. If he told the police about Jói, he *would* die, and Dísa probably would too.

But at least he knew where Dísa was going. There was only one place that her paper cold wallet would be hidden.

Blábrekka.

That was probably where Jói's hitman was going too.

Ómar checked his computer. There was a flight to Akureyri in forty minutes. He could make that if he was quick.

He might just be able to prevent his son from killing his daughter.

# FIFTY-ONE

It was only a couple of minutes' drive from Fjóla's apartment to police headquarters at the bottom of Hverfisgata.

Magnus had at least been able to get through to Sharp. He wasn't sure whether he had made the most of the opportunity. If Sharp was indeed Krakatoa, then he had no reason to respond to Magnus's questions at all. But if he wasn't – at least Magnus had opened up a line of communication.

As Magnus parked his car and walked towards the back entrance of the station, he recalled his conversation with Ingileif.

He had an important decision to make, once he had a moment to think about it. One that could change his life. And Ingileif's and Eygló's. And Ási's.

There was only one sensible answer, he knew that. Eygló was loyal. Ingileif was dangerous.

And yet. He felt an unexpected tingle of excitement course through his body.

'What are you smiling about?' said Vigdís as he sat at his desk. 'Did Fjóla come up with something?'

'Not really. I did message Sharp using her messaging app. His nickname is Lindenbrook, you know? The professor from *Journey to the Centre of the Earth*.' That classic story by Jules Verne had supposedly taken place at Snaefellsjökull, only a few kilometres from where Magnus had grown up.

'But not Krakatoa?'

'He wouldn't say,' said Magnus. 'Fjóla thinks he uses both handles, but she's not sure. And he didn't answer any of my questions.'

'So what were you grinning about?'

Magnus ignored her question. 'Any sign of Dísa anywhere?'

'Nothing. The Selfoss guys are on their way to Apavatn.'

'It's worth checking the buses to Akureyri. And flights from the City Airport.'

'I've done that.'

'She may just have gone to stay with a friend somewhere in Reykjavík.'

'What friend?'

'She hasn't been at the university very long: this is her first semester. Maybe a kid from her school in the north who's now at uni with her?'

'Before she moved in with Kata, she was staying with her brother Jói,' said Vigdís. 'Maybe she's gone back there?'

'That's not exactly hiding, but we should check it out. We need to question her friends in Reykjavík systematically. Find out who was close to her. Ask if anyone has seen her. We can use that list you put together of Kata's friends – there will probably be an overlap. How are the warrants for tracking her phone and Ómar's computer coming?'

'Still waiting.'

Two hours later, there was still no sign of Dísa, or, to Magnus's frustration, the warrants to locate her phone or to search Ómar's devices. They were piecing together a network of Dísa's friends in Reykjavík, but none of them had seen her. A detective had interviewed Jói's girlfriend at his flat; she said Dísa hadn't been back since Kata's murder.

Magnus's phone beeped.

A text. From a country code he didn't recognize: +507.

*Krakatoa = Jói Ómarsson. I am not a murderer. Jói is. Sharp.*

'Vigdís! Come with me! Now.'

It was ten minutes to Jói's apartment in a modern block in Gardabaer, next to the sea, or at least that's how long it took at the speed Magnus was driving.

A woman with dark hair and an un-Icelandic olive complexion answered Jói's door. Her eyes were red; she had been crying.

'Where's Jói?' Magnus asked in Icelandic, after identifying himself.

'I don't know,' the woman replied in Australian-accented English.

'Have you seen him today?'

'Yes. I told your colleague who was here earlier. He left a couple of hours ago.'

'Did he say where he was going?' Magnus snapped.

'No.' The woman looked as if she was about to burst into tears.

Vigdís interrupted. 'My name's Vigdís,' she said in slow,

clear Icelandic, avoiding speaking English. 'Now why don't we sit down and you can tell us what happened? What's your name?'

The girl seemed to understand. 'Petra.'

Vigdís sat on a sofa in the living room, and Petra sat opposite. Despite his impatience, Magnus knew Vigdís was right to take this slowly.

'Why are you upset?' Vigdís asked.

'Can we do this in English?' Petra said.

'Sure,' said Magnus gently. 'You seem upset. My colleague was asking why.'

'Is Jói in trouble?'

'He may be.'

'Oh, God.' Tears leaked from Petra's eyes.

'Does the name Krakatoa mean anything to you?'

Petra glanced sharply at Magnus. Clearly, it did. But Magnus waited.

Petra nodded.

'What?'

'It's Jói's handle. When he's online. When he's running Thomocoin.'

'Do you know about Thomocoin?'

'Not much,' said Petra. 'Except Jói spends almost all his time on it. He pretends he's working for some game-development company, but it's Thomocoin, Thomocoin, Thomocoin all the time.'

'Does he talk to you about it?'

'No. He knows I know that's what he's doing but he prefers to keep me away from it. It's taking over his life! He's changing. Especially in the last couple of weeks.'

'Since Dísa's mother died?'

'Maybe a bit before then.'

Magnus nodded. Vigdís was taking notes – he hoped

her English was up to it. Magnus knew her understanding of the language was better than her speaking, and better than she admitted.

'Petra. Do you know whether Jói had anything to do with Helga's death?'

The woman sobbed.

'Petra?'

'I don't know, no.'

'What about Kata, Dísa's friend?'

The sobs came louder. Magnus waited.

Petra recovered herself. 'He didn't kill them both, did he?'

'I doubt he did. But he may have gotten someone else to do it.

'Tecumseh.'

'Tecumseh?'

'Yeah. Sometimes I see Jói's conversations over his shoulder. Normally I don't pay any attention, Jói knows that, so he's stopped worrying about it like he used to. But there was this one guy, Tecumseh. He sounded like a genuine bad guy. You know, like a hitman, or something. I assumed it was just someone Jói knew acting tough – some kind of joke. I didn't think about it. But it scared me.'

'What did this Tecumseh say?'

'I don't know. I tried to forget it. Tried to put it out of my mind.'

'OK. I understand that. But try to remember now.'

'It was something about a knife. Hiding a knife. It was the day after Helga was stabbed.'

'Did you ask Jói about it?'

'No. I couldn't believe it really had anything to do with Helga's death. And . . . well . . . I am beginning to get a bit scared of Jói. So I played dumb. He likes it when I play dumb.'

'And you have no idea where he went? Or when he'll be back?'

'No. That's what upset me. He had a bag with him. And he didn't talk to me. He just blanked me.' She sniffed. 'I checked his stuff. He's taken his passport with him. Two of his computers. And his favourite leather jacket.' She looked at the two detectives. 'Jói's gone.'

'Where's his computer?' Magnus asked.

'He's got three of them. He left one of them here. But it's dead.'

'Can I take a look?'

The computer was in the corner of a large bedroom, with a view over the sea. The bed was a mess, but the desk was tidy. There were two screens, keyboard, mouse, high-end Bose headphones and a weird-shaped pink USB stick jammed into a tower under the desk.

Magnus's finger hovered over the keyboard, but he glanced at Vigdís, who shook her head. He knew she was right. Looking into Jói's computer without a warrant would be asking for trouble if there was a trial. Magnus might have risked it if there had been a chance of finding information that could save Dísa, but if Petra was correct, the computer was dead anyway.

A pad of paper lay on the desk, half covered with jotted notes: some words, mostly numbers. Magnus took a picture with his phone.

'What do you think that is?' he asked Vigdís, pointing to the numerals 1450.

'Could it be a time?'

'That's what I thought. A bus? Or a plane?'

'Does Jói have a car?' Vigdís asked Petra.

'Yes. It's a Nissan four-wheel-drive. Silver. But it's gone, I checked.'

'He doesn't need a bus if he's taken his car,' said Vigdís.

'A plane then?' said Magnus. 'He could have parked it at the airport. A plane to Akureyri, I'll bet.'

## FIFTY-TWO

Uncle Eggert met Dísa in the lobby of the town hall in Akureyri. She threw herself at him. He wrapped his long arms around her and squeezed.

'Come up to my office,' he said.

Fortunately, Eggert rated his own office, albeit a small one. It boasted a tiny meeting table, where Dísa dumped her backpack containing her computer, and half a view over the narrow fjord to the wooded mountain slopes on the other side.

'You've just driven from Reykjavík, I take it?' Eggert said.

'Yes. I borrowed a friend's car.'

'Does anyone know you're here?' Eggert looked concerned.

'I don't think so. I don't know what people know.'

'Sit down and tell me what's going on.'

So Dísa told Uncle Eggert as briefly and clearly as she could all about Thomocoin, Krakatoa's threats and Kata's death.

Eggert's concern deepened. It became more than concern; it became fear.

'Does this Krakatoa know anything about me?' he asked.

Dísa shrugged. 'He'll know you're an investor along with dozens of other Icelanders. He may know you are my uncle. But I don't think he'll guess I've come to see you. At least I hope not.'

'So do I. Who do you think he is?'

'I don't know,' said Dísa. 'Sharp, maybe? You remember him from the Thomocoin videos. Maybe it's someone else entirely. But he might be paying someone to do his dirty work.'

'You mean a hired gun?'

'Something like that. I don't know, Uncle Eggert. I'm just trying to keep one step ahead of him. Have you seen anything suspicious? Anyone try to contact you?'

Eggert paused. 'No. Nothing.'

'Keep your eye out.'

'Jói called me this morning. Asking how you were. He sounded worried about you.'

'Yeah, I saw him yesterday. What did you say to him?'

'Nothing. You asked me not to tell anyone you had been in touch. I didn't know if that included Jói, so I kept quiet.'

'Thank you,' said Dísa. She smiled at her uncle; she was extremely grateful to him. 'I might need his help later. But it's probably best if as few people know what's going on with all this as possible.'

For a moment she wondered why Jói had called Eggert, then she remembered she had asked him for Eggert's number – Jói had always been much better at keeping track of numbers and addresses than she. She had no doubt her brother was concerned about her.

'Can I use your table for an hour or so?' she asked.

'Sure. Have you got a list of investors?'

'Yes. I'm going to send out messages to them all, telling them to set up bitcoin wallets and to pass on to me their wallet addresses so we can pay them. I'll send you the list of names now, and then, as I get the details in, I'll forward them to you so you can make the payments.'

'What about all the bitcoin in your own wallet? When will you transfer that?'

'My private key is at Blábrekka. My plan is to go straight there and transfer the bitcoin to you right away. Can you send me your wallet address?'

'Yeah – I'll send you an email now,' said Eggert. 'You say that's twenty million dollars' worth?'

Dísa nodded.

Eggert swallowed. He looked nervous. Which just proved he wasn't an idiot. 'Then what will you do?'

'I disappear.'

'Where?'

'Best you don't know.'

Eggert nodded. 'OK.' He paused, clearly unsure how to say what he wanted to say. 'What if I don't hear from you?'

'I'll check in every day. If you don't hear from me, wait twenty-four hours and then get in touch with Inspector Magnús Ragnarsson. I've got his details here.' She passed Eggert a scrap of paper.

'I know him,' Eggert said. 'He interviewed me after Helga's murder. But what shall I do with the bitcoin?'

'Pay as much as you can out to the investors. Then get the police to take care of the rest of it. Get it out of your own wallet as quickly as possible; you'll be safer that way. We'll just have to trust that they can get it back to investors. Although God knows what the police will do with it. I'm hoping you'll never find out. I'm *hoping* our plan will work, and you'll be able to repay everyone.'

Otherwise, it meant Dísa was dead.

'Of course,' said Eggert.

'Thanks for doing this, Uncle Eggert,' Dísa said. 'I'm so grateful.' She didn't want to specify the risk that her uncle was taking, but she knew he understood it.

'OK.' He grinned. 'But the most important thing is that Aunt Karen must never find out. Otherwise we really will be in trouble. Deal?'

'Deal.'


Jói's flight had indeed left Reykjavík City Airport, right in front of the university, for Akureyri at 1450. Icelandair confirmed Jói Ómarsson had been a passenger, and Vigdís found Jói's car in the City Airport car park. Magnus checked his watch – it was four-thirty.

Jói's flight had landed at 1535. While Vigdís checked with car rental firms at Akureyri Airport, Magnus called Árni and asked him to check buses to Dalvík and send the local Dalvík cops to Blábrekka.

If Jói was going to Akureyri, it was probably to go on to Blábrekka. And the most likely reason for Jói to be going to Dalvík was that he knew Dísa was already there.

In which case, Magnus would go there too.

The next flight was at 1710. Magnus called Árni back and told him to meet him at Akureyri Airport.


Jói was waiting in Hafsteinn and Íris's bedroom, sitting on their bed, Hafsteinn's 12-gauge shotgun lying next to him, when he heard a car drive up towards the farmhouse.

Crouching, he approached the window.

A police car! Two officers in black uniforms climbed out and walked towards the house.

Wait here for them, or hide outside?

Outside.

He grabbed the shotgun and hurried downstairs as quietly as he could. He let himself out of the back door as he heard the doorbell ring.

He scurried across the farmyard to a boulder at its edge and squatted behind it.

A couple of minutes later, a grey-haired policeman emerged from the backdoor.

'Hafsteinn?' he called. 'Hafsteinn?'

He glanced at the small blue VW that Jói had rented from the airport, which was now parked by the side of the house. Jói hoped there would be nothing about it to suggest that it didn't belong to the farmer or his wife.

The policeman was forty metres away but, even from that distance, Jói could hear his radio bursting into life. The officer answered it and then turned to his younger colleague, who was sticking his head out of the back door.

'Hey! Símon!' the other policeman called. 'Did you hear that? Accident in the Ólafsfjördur tunnel. Suspected fatality.'

'Sounds bad,' said the older man. 'No one's here. Let's go.'

Jói waited until he heard their car drive off. He picked up the shotgun and emerged from behind the rock, heading for the large barn with its white concrete walls and red metal roof.

He entered through a side door and switched on the lights. The warm fug of a couple of hundred sheep enveloped him, the smell of their coats and their feed and their shit. The sea of light grey wool rustled and rippled as they acknowledged his entrance with muted bleating. The barn was divided by wooden railings into pens of different sizes, most of them full of sheep. He hurried along one of the raised aisles and then climbed into a pen at the end. He pushed his way through the animals to the far corner, where the farmer and his wife were slumped against railings in their his 'n' hers lopi sweaters.

Hafsteinn was still unconscious, blood streaking his cheek. His wife stared at Jói, her eyes wide with fear. Muffled squeaks and grunts emerged from beneath the plumber's tape over her mouth.

Jói squatted beside her, trying to avoid her eyes as he checked the knots of the cords that secured both of them to a railing. Hers were tight, and so were her husband's.

Hafsteinn was breathing, and the bleeding from his head had stopped.

Jói couldn't help it: as he moved away, he glanced back at the old woman. She was scared, but she was angry. Her eyes burned with hatred.

He was going to have to kill her. And her husband.

How?

It was going to be difficult.

It had been hard enough to shoot the damn sheepdog. Jói liked dogs, and this one was only doing its job, but there was nowhere to put it where it couldn't be heard barking.

Jói turned in shame. He forced his way back through the sheep and emerged into daylight, breathing hard.

He bent over. He fought the urge to vomit. This was as difficult as he thought it would be. If only Tecumseh hadn't scarpered!

He stood up straight.

He had to make a decision and stick to it. Was he Jói Ómarsson? Or was he Krakatoa?

Jói would admit defeat. Give up on his bitcoin. Free Dísa's grandparents. Turn himself in before anyone else was killed. Admit to the deaths of Helga and Kata and Cryptocheeseman. Take the consequences.

Even with Iceland's notoriously lax sentencing regime, Jói would be in jail for a long time. And when he came out, everyone in the country would know who he was and what he had done.

No one would forgive him. Why should they? His life would effectively be over.

Jói's life would be over.

So he should acknowledge that now. Jói was dead. He hadn't quite realized it at the time, but when he had given instructions to one man he had never met to kill another man he had never met in a country he had never been to, he had signed Jói's death warrant. From that moment on, there was no hope for Jói.

But there was for Krakatoa.

As far as he knew, the police weren't looking for him yet. If that was true, he still had time to transfer the bitcoin from Dísa's wallet – once he gained possession of her private key – get himself to Keflavík and fly off. Anywhere. Anywhere off this damn island.

Jói was beginning to understand Tecumseh's nervousness. Iceland was a prison, with only one exit: Keflavík Airport – if you excluded the weekly ferry from the east of the country, which you probably should. With enough money, he might be able to bribe a fisherman to take him on board and dump him on a foreign coastline, but an international flight was much the best solution.

As long as the police weren't looking for him.

That meant more people had to die. Dísa, for one, after she had been persuaded one way or another to give up her private key. Probably the two old people in the barn. And Jói would have to kill them.

He had the farmer's shotgun and a pocketful of cartridges. Gunshots from a farm in Iceland would cause a neighbour's head to rise in curiosity, an ear to be cocked, but nothing more.

Was he strong enough to do it?

Jói wasn't.

Krakatoa was.

Krakatoa entered the farmhouse, took up his position in the owners' bedroom and waited.

# FIFTY-THREE

Dísa drove quickly along the familiar coast road from
Akureyri to Dalvík. She was anxious to get her cold wallet
and transfer the bitcoin to Uncle Eggert. Five o'clock had
passed, Krakatoa's deadline.

Her life was now officially in danger.

She hoped that Krakatoa wouldn't act instantaneously.
That he would take a few hours to instruct whomever he
was using to carry out his dirty work. Dísa wasn't any use to
Krakatoa dead; with her would die his only hope of getting
his bitcoin back. He should have no idea she had transferred
it to Eggert.

Despite that logic, she was still scared.

Maybe she should keep hold of the bitcoin and trust
that Krakatoa wouldn't harm her? Too risky. The bitcoin
was safer with her uncle; she would feel much happier
when it was his problem and not hers.

Don't think about it. Find the private key. Transfer the
bitcoin. And then get the hell out of Dalvík.

She was keeping an eye out for lone figures on the
roadside who could possibly be hitmen – what did a hitman

even look like? Then she saw one, just as she was approaching the turn-off to Blábrekka, a couple of kilometres before Dalvík.

But this lone figure was very familiar. He was standing on the bridge by the junction, examining every car arriving from the south.

She considered driving on, but curiosity overcame her. So she slowed to a halt just past the bridge, and opened the passenger window.

'Dad?'

'Hi, Dísa.'

'What are you doing here?'

'Waiting for you. Can I get in?'

Dísa hesitated and then nodded.

Her father jumped into the passenger seat. 'I'm so glad to see you! For a while there, I thought you weren't coming.'

'How did you know I'd be here?' Dísa asked.

'I didn't. I just guessed. The police came to see me and said you had left Kata's flat with a suitcase. I thought this was the most likely place.'

'Did you tell them that?' said Dísa. 'The police?'

Her father smiled. 'No. I actually sent them to Apavatn.'

'So they don't know I'm here?'

'I don't think so.'

'Good. But I still don't know why you came.'

'To help you, Dísa. I'm worried. The police seemed to think that Helga and Kata were killed by a professional hitman. If that's true, and if you are determined to ignore Krakatoa's threats, then you're in danger. You need my help.'

A lorry barrelled past them. Dísa was happy to wait stationary on the side of the road while she spoke to her father. They were nearly at Blábrekka – she could see the farm on the lower slopes of the mountain from where the car was pulled over – and she wanted to figure out what her father was up to before she dealt with her grandparents.

'How are you going to help me?' she asked.

'By persuading you to pay Krakatoa his bitcoin.'

'It's not *his* bitcoin!' Dísa protested. 'That's the whole point! He effectively stole it. I want to give all that money back to the people he conned. Like Mum.'

'All right. I understand why you are doing this. But we have to take his threat seriously. I'm scared he's going to kill you.'

'I know. I'm scared too. But he killed my mother and my best friend – he deserves to lose his bitcoin. I will *not* give it him back. Do you understand me? Who is Krakatoa anyway?'

Ómar looked at his daughter and swallowed. Here we go, thought Dísa.

'I don't know,' he said.

'Dad! Of course you bloody know! How could you not know? You hid Krakatoa's back-up cold wallet for him. How could you do that without knowing who he is?'

'All right,' said Ómar. 'I do know, but I'm not going to tell you.'

'Well, get out of the car then,' said Dísa.

Ómar turned to his daughter, his eyes pleading. 'All right, we'll do it your way. You can pay the bitcoin to whoever you like. But I can't just let you go off by yourself. I'm scared for you, Dísa. I couldn't bear it if anything happened to you. You need my help. If there is some killer out there looking for you, you need my help.'

Dísa looked at her father with contempt. But the contempt was wavering.

She did need his help. He had come all this way to offer it. He was dead right: she was in danger.

'You *know* how much I love you, Dísa. You *know* I'd do anything for you. So let me. Please, let me.'

Dísa hesitated. Then nodded. 'All right. But this is the plan. My cold wallet is at Blábrekka. That's why I'm going there. Once I've got the private key, I'm going to transfer Krakatoa's bitcoin to someone else. That person is going to transfer it to the investors from Dalvík and Akureyri. I'm going to go into hiding for a week. And once the bitcoin has been distributed to all the investors I'm going to talk to the police – I don't want the cops grabbing it first. Are you OK with all that?'

'Who are you going to transfer the bitcoin to?'

'Who is Krakatoa?'

'Fair enough,' said Ómar. 'As I said, we'll do it your way. Let's go.'


Grandpa's old Land Cruiser and Grandma's even older Suzuki were parked outside the farm, together with a small blue car that Dísa didn't recognize. She hoped her grandparents didn't have visitors. It was going to be difficult enough explaining her arrival, now with her father, without having to go in for chit-chat with a neighbour.

She tried the doorbell. No answer, not even from the dog.

She glanced over the fields. No sign of her grandfather or any farm machinery on the move. Bonnie returned Dísa's gaze and, despite herself, Dísa waved to the horse. Anna Rós should be back from school in Ólafsfjördur by now, but there was no sign of her either.

She tried the doorbell again. Nothing.

She glanced at her father and pushed the door open. It was unlocked, but that didn't mean anything – her grandparents never locked the door.

'Grandpa! Grandma! Anna Rós!'

Nothing.

'They're not here,' said Dísa to her father. 'Come on.'

She led him down the hallway, through the kitchen and out of the back door.

'Grandpa!' Nothing. 'Perhaps they've gone for a walk together,' said Dísa, scanning the mountainside. Odd. That wasn't what her grandparents usually did.

'So where is your cold wallet?' Ómar asked.

Dísa grinned. 'You'll see. I actually stole your idea.'

She strode across the farmyard, with Ómar following, and climbed the slope on the far side. A pair of ravens watched her closely from their perch on the fence.

'Don't tell me,' said Ómar. 'Is that an elf rock?'

'It certainly is,' said Dísa.

'That's where we sat when I was talking to you at your mother's funeral.'

'Yeah. And I told you to give the bitcoin back. Well, the hidden people were my witnesses.'

Ómar laughed. Dísa found the familiar sound oddly reassuring.

Dísa squatted down by the rock and lifted up the stone. Underneath lay the plastic food container.

She carried it back to the farmhouse and set it on the kitchen table. 'Wait here,' she said. 'I'm just going to get my computer from the car. And then I'll make the transfer.'

Árni met Magnus at the foot of the steps off the plane.

'Blábrekka,' Magnus said. 'Now.'

They jogged to Árni's unmarked car, and he set off, lights flashing, blazing through the centre of town to the road to Dalvík.

'Are there any cops at the farm?' Magnus asked.

'I got a couple of the local uniforms to check it out. They saw no one there, not even the farmer.'

'Are they waiting for us?'

'No. They had to leave.'

'What!'

'There's been an accident in the Ólafsfjördur tunnel. Injuries. One killed, another critical.'

'All right,' said Magnus. 'But we need back-up. With firearms.'

'That means talking to Inspector Ólafur.'

'Then talk to him.'

'You talk to him. I'm driving.'

It was true; at the speed Árni was driving he needed all his concentration. As Magnus picked up his phone to make the call, it buzzed.

'Vigdís?'

'Yes. Are you in Akureyri?'

'Just leaving. On our way to Blábrekka. Jesus!' Magnus lurched to one side as Árni's car swerved past a car that was itself breaking the speed limit, narrowly missing a truck coming the other way. 'Although we may never get there, the way Árni's driving. What have you got?'

'Several things. Dísa's father Ómar is in Akureyri. He was on the same flight as Jói at 1450.'

'Together?'

'No. Separate bookings. Separate seats. Could be a coincidence?'

'Maybe. It's clear both of them think Dísa is up here somewhere. It must be Blábrekka.'

'They were right. Just got the data through from the phone company. Dísa was in Akureyri this afternoon, but the last read they got was from a phone mast near Hjalteyri.'

'Where's that?'

'Between Akureyri and Dalvík. She'll have got to Dalvík by now.'

'Blábrekka.'

'Or a friend? A relative?'

'True,' said Magnus. 'But Blábrekka has got to be our first shot. Could she have taken a bus? I thought we'd checked that.'

'Her friend Kata's car has gone. The cameras at Hvalfjördur caught it going north this morning. It's a white Hyundai Accent. I'll text you the registration.'

'Good work, Vigdís.'

'And Jói rented a car from Avis at Akureyri Airport. A blue VW Golf. I'll text you the registration for that too.'

'Great! Now I need to speak to Ólafur.'

Ólafur was not at all happy to hear that Magnus had arrived on his patch and was on his way to Dalvík. But no regional police inspector in Iceland could be impervious to the excitement of a request for armed police to hurry towards trouble. He called the district commissioner for approval, and within five minutes the armed back-up was on its way.

Árni was out on the open road now, the fjord flashing by on the right, the brute of a mountain above Dalvík approaching ever closer.

Magnus had an idea. There was no chance that Dísa would answer a phone call from the police. But she might read a text message.

He picked up his phone and tapped one out.

## FIFTY-FOUR

As Dísa went out to the car she felt the phone in her back pocket buzzing with a text. She ignored it and pulled out her backpack containing her computer from the rear seat.

She stopped at the entrance to the kitchen. There was someone else standing there, next to her father.

'Jói!' She dumped the backpack and rushed over to hug him.

He grinned, his blue eyes twinkling.

'What are you doing here?' she asked him.

'Same as Dad. Looking out for you. You told me you were coming here and, well, it all sounded a little dangerous. After Kata's murder.'

'So that's your car outside? The blue one?'

'Yeah. I rented it from the airport. I was out at the back of the barn looking for your grandparents when I heard your voice shouting for Hafsteinn.'

'Do you know where they are?'

Jói shrugged. 'They don't seem to be on the farm.'

'I'm so glad you're here!' She smiled at her father and her brother. 'I'm so glad you're *both* here.'

'What's that for?' said Jói, nodding towards the backpack.

'It's a long story,' said Dísa. 'But maybe you can help me. It turns out that Mum's murder *was* to do with Thomocoin, as was Kata's. Long story short, I've got twenty million dollars' worth of Thomocoin's bitcoin in my wallet, and I want to pay it back to the investors.'

'Twenty million!' said Jói.

'Yeah, I know. I lost my cold wallet, you know, the pink one Dad gave me. But I had hidden a back-up here.'

'Is that it?' said Jói, pointing to the plastic food container.

'Yes. So, my plan is to transfer the bitcoin somewhere safe now, and then get that person to transfer it on to the investors when they have had a chance to set up bitcoin wallets.'

'Sounds complicated,' said Ómar.

'It is, a bit,' said Dísa. 'Which is why you may be able to help, Jói.'

'OK. So who are you transferring the bitcoin to now?'

'Uncle Eggert. I've got his wallet address on my computer. All I need is to transcribe the private key. But it's really long. Look.'

Dísa extracted the two sheets of paper from the food container. One was her mother's and one was hers. She smoothed out the one covered in letters and numbers in her own handwriting.

'See,' said Dísa.

Suddenly she felt confident. The three of them, plus Uncle Eggert, could beat Krakatoa. Her family was there for her after all. There was still a lot to be done: she had to hide from a vengeful Krakatoa, and there was still a chance that a professional killer was right now on his way to try to find her.

But she would survive. With Dad and Jói's help, she would survive.

And she would get some justice for her mother, justice for Kata. She would make Krakatoa pay.

She opened up her computer and, as she waited for it to load, she checked her phone. She had been ignoring texts all day.

This one was from the policeman Magnús.

She read it. And froze.

*Krakatoa is your brother Jói Ómarsson. I think you are in danger. Where are you?*

She unfroze. It had only been a second; she had to move, to stop Jói from thinking there was anything untoward in the text. She shoved her phone in her back pocket.

'Who was that?' Jói asked.

'Friend from uni, wondering where I am. I won't reply.'

She sat down in front of her computer screen and opened and closed programs at random, trying to give herself time to think.

Was Jói really Krakatoa? No. That would mean it was Jói who had threatened her; Jói who had killed her mother and her best friend. Jói could never do that.

And yet, here he was, asking about Krakatoa's bitcoin. It was quite possible that Jói could have hidden his own private key at their father's summer house. It was possible that Jói could run an online business.

Jói knew Helga. Jói knew Kata. Jói knew her.

And she trusted Magnús.

'I'm just going to the toilet,' Jói said. 'I'll be back in a moment to help you with that.'

'OK,' said Dísa, head deep in her computer.

She lifted it once Jói was out of the kitchen.

'Dad, we've got to go,' she whispered, snapping her laptop shut and grabbing it.

'What do you mean?' said her father.

'Jói is Krakatoa. We've got to get out of here. Come on!'

She stood up to leave. Her father moved ahead of her to the front door and then turned to block her path.

'How do you know?'

'Just got a text from the police,' Dísa hissed. The downstairs toilet door was shut. 'Quick!' She tried to push past her father to the door.

'No, Dísa.'

'Dad!' She pushed harder.

He wouldn't move.

Then it hit her. She should have seen it right away.

'Wait a minute,' she said. 'You *know* Jói is Krakatoa, Dad, don't you?'

Her father inclined his head in assent.

Dísa took a step backwards. 'You and he came here together. From the airport.'

Ómar nodded again. 'We bumped into each other on the plane.'

There was a sound on the staircase. Dísa turned. Her brother was coming slowly down the stairs. Pointing Grandpa's shotgun right at her.

'No,' said Dísa. 'No!' she screamed and launched herself towards Jói, gun or no gun.

Strong hands grabbed her shoulders and held her back. 'It's OK, Dísa,' her father said. 'It's all going to be OK.'

The tears came as outrage overwhelmed her. 'What do you mean it's OK?' she yelled. 'You and Jói ganging up on me like that. Killing Mum. Killing Kata.'

'I didn't have anything to do with that, believe me,' said Ómar.

'But *he* did!' said Dísa, pointing to her brother.

'I had to,' said Jói reasonably. Quietly.

'Of course you didn't have to!'

Dísa stopped struggling.

'If I let you go, will you keep still?' her father said.

Dísa nodded. Anger wasn't going to get her anywhere. She needed to think.

But how could she think in the face of this betrayal? A betrayal that ripped at her heart, ripped at her mind, trampled on her very being. She knew she shouldn't be surprised that her father had let her down. Again. Yet she had always been sure of his love for her. For a second she had believed that his appearance in Dalvík proved that.

Idiot!

And she still couldn't believe Jói would kill anyone, let alone their mother. He had always liked Mum, for God's sake! And Kata. What had Kata ever done to him?

But the man pointing the shotgun at her didn't look like her sweet half-brother Jói. He looked perfectly capable of pulling the trigger.

She staggered back into the kitchen and slumped on to a chair.

'So it wasn't a professional killer after all?' she said to Jói.

'It was. I paid someone to deal with your mother and with Kata. But, unfortunately, he's left Iceland now.'

'So you have to do the dirty stuff yourself?'

Jói nodded.

'There doesn't need to be any dirty stuff,' Ómar said. 'You pay Jói what you owe him —'

'I don't owe him anything,' Dísa snapped.

'What you took from him,' Ómar said. 'Jói leaves. And once he's out of the country we tell the police what's happened.'

'And you think the police won't arrest you?' Dísa said.

'They probably will,' said Ómar. 'But you'll be alive. You'll both be alive. This is the only way I can figure out for that to happen. And if I end up in jail again, so be it.'

'Don't act the noble martyr with me, Dad. Claiming to sacrifice yourself for me. You need to stand up to Jói, that's what you need to do.'

'Well, I disagree. Jói, transfer Dísa's bitcoin to your wallet, and then we'll go.'

'Why didn't you warn me? That Jói was Krakatoa?'

'Because I thought he would get his hitman to kill you if I did.' Ómar swallowed. 'And me.'

'But the hitman has left Iceland. Didn't you hear him say that?'

'Yes. But I didn't know that. Until now.' Ómar looked away from his daughter.

Jói was still holding the shotgun. 'OK. Both of you stand over there, where I can see you.'

He pointed to the corner of the kitchen furthest away from the table, by the microwave.

'Jói?' said Ómar. 'You can trust me.'

'Possibly. But I'll be happier if I have you both covered.'

Ómar frowned. 'All right.'

He and Dísa watched as Jói laid the shotgun on the table, pointing towards them and tapped on Dísa's laptop. He pulled out his phone and tapped on that, glancing at them every few seconds. After a minute or so, he began to transcribe the characters from Dísa's private key into her computer.

'The police know you are Krakatoa,' Dísa said.

Jói looked up sharply.

'That was the text I read,' Dísa explained. 'From Inspector Magnús. They know who you are. You won't be able to get away.'

'I will with this money,' Jói said. 'You can do anything with twenty million dollars. I'll find someone with a boat or a plane who will get me out.'

'Stop him, Dad,' Dísa said, pleading with her father.

Ómar didn't answer. He didn't look at her. He was watching his son as he carefully typed the characters into Dísa's machine. Then, with a triumphant flurry of taps, Jói grinned.

'Done!'

'All right,' said Ómar. 'Now let's tie Dísa up and put her with the other two.' He turned to his daughter. 'I'm sorry, Dísa. I'll let you go once Jói's safely away. It's the only way for you to get out of this alive.'

Jói got to his feet and picked up the shotgun, waving it vaguely at them. At both of them.

'No,' he said, simply.

'What do you mean, no? We discussed this.'

'Dísa knows too much. She has to die.'

'What? Now?'

'Yes, now.'

'Jói? You can't do this.'

'I'm not Jói,' said the man holding the shotgun. 'I'm Krakatoa.'

Ómar stared at his son as if seeing him for the first time. A stranger. Dísa saw his face crumple as if in pain.

Then he straightened. He turned away from Jói and towards her.

She saw him wink. Once, long and slow.

He sighed. 'All right, Jói. But let me do it.'

'You?'

'Yes. I can't have my son kill my daughter. I'll do it. Give me the gun.' Ómar moved forward, extending his arm.

Jói took a step back. 'Do you think I'm an idiot? Stop. Or I'll shoot you,' he warned. 'In fact, I may just shoot you anyway.'

'OK,' said Ómar. He stopped. 'You do it. You kill her.'

Jói's eyes flicked from his father to Dísa and back again. The shotgun wavered between them.

'Run, Dísa!' shouted Ómar as he flung himself at his son.

The shotgun went off, the sound in the confines of the kitchen deafening.

Dísa did what she was told and bolted for the back door.

There was another explosion from inside the farmhouse as the second barrel went off.

Dísa sprinted across the farmyard. There were open fields above and behind the yard, with nowhere to hide except behind the elf rock.

That wouldn't work.

Then there was the barn.

She sprinted for the side door and, glancing behind to make sure that Jói hadn't emerged from the farmhouse, stepped inside, closing the door behind her.

The warm, familiar, safe smell of sheep and matured hay welcomed her. Thin daylight trickled into the barn through its small windows, illuminating hundreds of woolly backs. If the sheep made any noise at her arrival, she couldn't hear it; her ears were still ringing from the report of the shotgun inside the farmhouse.

She jogged down an aisle and then swung her legs over the railing into a pen. She dropped to her knees and crawled among the sheep. They looked bemused, but not frightened.

She noticed a leg, a human leg clad in denim. She crawled towards it. As the sheep parted, she saw Grandma and Grandpa pressed against a railing running along the back of the shed. Her grandmother was staring at her, eyes wide with alarm, mouth taped shut. She wriggled.

Her grandfather was slumped on the ground, out cold.

Oh, God! Was he dead?

Dísa was about to creep towards them and try to free them when she heard the barn door open. She raised her finger to her lips to tell her grandmother to be quiet and then crept away from her.

She slid through the railings into an adjoining pen and waited.

'Dísa?' It was Jói's voice, and he was getting closer. Her hearing was returning; she could make out his footsteps as they passed the pen in which she was lying. He stopped.

The sheep around her moved. Shifting.

One of them looked down at her quizzically. She recognized the ewe: unlike Anna Rós, she didn't know all of the sheep, but she knew a fair few of them. This one was Móey. She was one of the *forystufé* on the farm, the leader sheep who guided the others up on the hills in the summer. Smarter than the rest, they looked subtly different: longer-legged, skinnier. Móey had distinctive dark red patches on her wool, a black snout and a nice pair of curly horns.

She bleated. She recognized Dísa. The other sheep around her turned to look.

Dísa raised her finger to her lips. It might have been coincidence, but Móey shut up. She continued to stare.

Dísa could hear Jói moving towards the end of the barn. He was checking on her grandparents, only one pen away.

Dísa pressed her face close to the floor. The sheep seemed to gather around her.

She heard the sound of a body swinging over the rails between pens, the thud of feet landing on concrete.

She could see Jói's trainers coming towards her. Stopping. Turning to the right. Then turning towards her again. Then stepping her way.

'Oh, Dísa.'

She looked up. He was standing three metres away, pointing the shotgun directly at her.

She scrambled to her feet. She knew she was going to die, but she wanted to die upright, facing her brother, proud, not cowering on the floor. She successfully fought back the urge to cry.

'Did you kill Dad?'

'I think so. He has a big hole in his chest. He shouldn't have done that. You were never going to get away.'

'What now?'

'I kill you,' said Jói.

His voice was flat. His eyes were flat. They had lost their Jói sparkle. His expression was . . . expressionless.

Her brother Jói seemed to have gone. There was no one to appeal to. She couldn't appeal to this man standing before her.

There was a rustle and a loud bleat, almost like a roar, and a black head shot out of the woollen mass like a cannonball and hit Jói in the thigh.

The shotgun went off, causing the sheep to skitter and jostle, and the whole barn erupted into panicked cries.

Jói stumbled and fell.

The shot had gone high and to the left of Dísa's head. She leaned down to grab the shotgun and took a step backwards, pointing it at Jói.

Móey gave him another butt, this time on his arse. He

swore and twisted around to face his attacker, who glared back.

Dísa gripped the shotgun. It was double-barrelled, with two triggers. Dísa thought that the second trigger would fire the second barrel, but she wasn't sure. She assumed the second barrel was loaded.

By the look on Jói's face, so did he.

'OK, Jói. Stand up,' said Dísa.

Carefully, Jói pulled himself to his feet, the ewe still glaring at him.

'All right. We're going to leave this pen, slowly.'

Jói stood up straight and stared at his sister.

'Turn around and walk slowly to the railings.'

Jói didn't move.

'I said turn around!'

Still no movement.

In frustration, Dísa wiggled the barrel of the gun up and down in an attempt to show she meant business, that she would fire lead shot into her brother at close range.

Jói wasn't buying it.

'Put the gun down, Dísa,' he said quietly.

Dísa lowered the barrel a couple of inches. Her face puckered in frustration. What could she do? She couldn't shoot him in cold blood. She just couldn't. And Jói knew it. He was going to escape.

Worse than that, if she put the gun down, he would use it on her.

She should pull the damn trigger! But she couldn't.

She looked down at Móey for inspiration. But although the sheep was looking at her intently, she had no wise advice.

'Lay the gun on the floor,' Jói repeated.

'Shoot him!' The cry rang out loud from the other side of the barn, by the door.

It was the policeman, Magnús. Unarmed.

'Shoot him, Dísa! It would be self-defence. I'm a witness. You can shoot him.'

Dísa raised the barrel of the shotgun and aimed. Yes, she could shoot him. In self-defence.

Jói's eyes widened. He knew his sister well; he could see what she was about to do. He took a step backwards. Raised his arms. And turned towards the policeman.

'Jói Ómarsson, you are under arrest,' said Magnus as he approached the brother and sister.

Dísa waited until the detective had grabbed Jói, then she laid the shotgun down on the concrete floor and burst into tears.

# FIFTY-FIVE

Magnus caught a flight from Akureyri back to Reykjavík at about noon the following day.

He was exhausted. He had spent the morning on statements at the Akureyri police station before going to the hospital with Árni.

Ómar had survived: the focus of the shotgun blast had been on his left shoulder – the damage to his chest was less severe. They had operated the night before. He was awake but in a bad way.

Hafsteinn had regained consciousness but they were keeping him in hospital under observation for a couple of days.

His wife was murmuring nonsense at his bedside, flustered and shaken.

Dísa and Anna Rós were with their father. Dísa had told Magnus she was going to try to forgive him. In the end, he had risked his life for her. Plus he was the only father she'd got.

The hour after Jói had been arrested had been predictable mayhem. Árni had tried to staunch the flow in

Ómar's chest and called an ambulance. Anna Rós's bus from school had been delayed by the accident in the tunnel, and she had arrived home at the same time as the armed police back-up to find her father shot, her grandfather unconscious, her grandmother a wreck and her brother arrested. Not surprisingly, she was distressed.

Yet in the midst of all this, Dísa had pulled Magnus to one side and asked if she could take a couple of minutes to shut down her computer.

It had been more like ten. Dísa had had a grim smile on her face as she closed the lid of her laptop.

'All right?' Magnus had asked.

Dísa had nodded. 'Yes. All right.'

Magnus was impressed by the nineteen-year-old. It wasn't only that she had risked her life to try to make amends for her mother's folly. He suspected that despite having faced death down the wrong end of a shotgun barrel held by her own brother, that was exactly what she had just done. Made amends.

As Magnus had got off the plane at Reykjavík, Árni had forwarded him an email sent to him by a neighbour of Helga's in Dalvík, who had been an investor in Thomocoin. The email was from Dísa the day before, giving instructions on how to set up a bitcoin wallet so she could receive her investment back.

He would bet that was what Dísa had been fiddling with on her computer.

Magnus knew that the police should find out what Dísa was up to as soon as possible and put a stop to it. And yet . . . he trusted her. Thomocoin's assets, such as they were, would probably be tied up in legal limbo for years. As would Sharp's and Jói's, if anyone could find them.

Maybe that was what Dísa had done? Maybe she had

found those assets and was sending them back to where they belonged?

Magnus liked that idea.

The various Icelandic authorities had turned a blind eye to the activities of Thomocoin for too long. A little more of a delay would be entirely consistent with that policy.

Magnus had called Árni back and told him to leave it with him. He would look into it. In his own time.

He had called Agent Malley in New York and the guy from the DA's office in North Carolina the night before to tell them that Krakatoa had been arrested. Jói was going to be popular with the world's law-enforcement officers.

What happened to Sharp wasn't Magnus's problem either. The guy deserved to be prosecuted for the Thomocoin scam, but at least he had warned Magnus about Jói. That, Magnus was be grateful for. If they managed to extract him from Panama, Magnus would speak up for him.

If.

As he walked from the terminal at the City Airport to where he had parked his car, his phone buzzed.

Another text from Eygló. She had texted him three times the evening before, and once already this morning.

She wanted to talk to him. With all that was going on in Dalvík, he hadn't felt able to talk to her. At least not to say what he knew he had to say.

He unlocked the car, sat in the driver's seat and called her number.

'Hi,' she said. She sounded nervous rather than angry.

'Hi,' said Magnus.

'Where are you?'

'At the City Airport. Just got back from Akureyri. The Dalvík murder cases blew up.'

'Did you catch the guy who did it?'

'Yeah.'

'Good.'

'Hey, I'm sorry I didn't call you and tell you I wouldn't be at your place last night.'

'You said you would be. I told you it was important.'

'You did,' said Magnus.

There was a moment's silence on the phone. 'I said "yes" to Southampton.'

'I didn't know they'd even offered you the job yet?'

'They hadn't. It was one of those stupid "if we were to offer you the job, would you take it?" things. They said they needed to know right away – something to do with department politics or visas after Brexit or something. I didn't completely understand it. But I said "yes".'

Magnus knew a response was required from him. And he knew what it was.

'Good.'

More silence. Eventually, she spoke. 'Good for me or good for you?'

'Good for both of us.'

Silence.

'We should talk about this properly,' Magnus said. 'Honestly. I know we haven't up till now and it's been my fault. I'll see you at seven this evening, I promise.'

'Will you?'

'I will.' He hung up.

He felt guilty about Eygló. He hadn't spoken to her openly about how he felt over the last few weeks. He hadn't known how. But he was sure that her decision was best for both of them.

He was supposed to be going straight to police headquarters at Hverfisgata, but instead he drove to Vesturbaer.

He had no idea whether she would be in, but he had to try.

She didn't answer the bell on the first ring. But she did on the second.

He leaned into the intercom. 'It's Magnús.'

'I'll be right down.'

Magnus shifted from foot to foot; he found the thirty seconds he spent waiting at the door to her building an eternity.

Eventually, she opened it and shot him an anxious glance.

But then she saw his grin. Her grey eyes sparkled and a warm smile of happiness spread across her face.

'Come in,' she said.

# AUTHOR'S NOTE

It was unusually important to pin down the precise time at which the majority of the events in this book took place. During 2020 the coronavirus/COVID-19 pandemic broke out and bitcoin prices fell and subsequently exploded. I decided on September 2020.

Throughout that year, a blizzard of bewildering, ever-changing rules and regulations relating to the epidemic engulfed the world. After an initial first wave in the spring, Iceland had got the pandemic pretty much under control. During that summer life almost returned to normal, with the noticeable exception of the lack of tourists. Many of the regulations that were prevalent in other countries, such as the wearing of masks, were absent. There were some restrictions – large gatherings at funerals were controversial that September – but in general the virus and its attendant regulations were much less intrusive in Iceland than they were in other countries at the same time.

During the autumn cases ticked up, as they did in many other countries, and by the end of the year, Iceland suffered a new wave of infections and hospitalizations, which provoked a further lockdown.

Twenty seventeen was an extraordinary time for bitcoin. The trades I describe Dísa making in the book, which increased her investment sixtyfold, could have been made at real prices achieved by bitcoin and Ethereum during the year. The following year, 2018, prices fell 80 per cent.

Twenty twenty was if anything more of a roller-coaster. Prices of bitcoin fell to $4,000 in March at the beginning of the pandemic, then recovered strongly, breaking $10,000 at the end of September. But in the three months after this book ends, prices rose even faster, reaching $29,000 by the end of the year and $60,000 by March 2021.

As I write this, I have no idea what the status of the COVID-19 pandemic will be when you read it. Nor do I have any clue about the price of bitcoin: it could be anything from $1,000 to $200,000. Which uncertainty is great for gamblers who feel lucky, but should trouble the rest of us.

I should like to thank the following people for their help: Björk Hólm, Bragi Thór Valsson, Michael Olmsted, Richenda Todd, Liz Hatherell, my agents Oli Munson and Florence Rees, and my wife Barbara. None of the characters in this book are based on real people. In particular, Inspector Ólafur of the Akureyri police is not based on the real detective of the same name, who is, by all accounts, a charming man.

# FREE BOOK

A Message from Michael Ridpath
Get a free 60-page story

If you would like to try one of my stories about Magnus for free, then sign up to my mailing list. I will send you a free copy of *The Polar Bear Killing*, a 60-page story set in north-east Iceland.

> *A starving polar bear swims ashore in a remote Icelandic village and is shot by the local policeman. Two days later, the policeman is found dead on a hill above the village. A polar bear justice novella with an Icelandic twist.*

To sign up to the mailing list and get your free copy of *The Polar Bear Killing*, go to *www.michaelridpath.com* and click on the link for 'Free Download' of *The Polar Bear Killing*.

For more information on my other Magnus books, please read on...

## ALSO BY MICHAEL RIDPATH

### Where the Shadows Lie

One thousand years ago: An Icelandic warrior returns from battle, bearing a ring cut from the right hand of his foe.

Seventy years ago: An Oxford professor, working from a secret source, creates the twentieth century's most pervasive legend. The professor's name? John Ronald Reuel Tolkein.

Six hours ago: An expert on Old Iceland literature, Agnar Haraldsson, is murdered.

Everything is connected, but to discover how, Detective Magnus Jonson must venture where the shadows lie...

### 66° North (Far North in the US)

Iceland 1934: Two boys playing in the lava fields that surround their isolated farmsteads see something they shouldn't have. The consequences will haunt them and their families for generations.

Iceland 2009: The credit crunch bites. The currency has been devalued, savings annihilated, lives ruined. Revolution is in the air, as is the feeling that someone ought to pay the blood price... And in a country with a population of just 300,000 souls, where everyone knows everybody, it isn't hard to draw up a list of those responsible.

And then, one-by-one, to cross them off.

Iceland 2010: As bankers and politicians start to die, at home and abroad, it is up to Magnus Jonson to unravel the web of conspirators before they strike again.

But while Magnus investigates the crimes of the present, the crimes of the past are catching up with him.

## Meltwater

Iceland, 2010: A group of internet activists have found evidence of a military atrocity in the Middle East. As they prepare to unleash the damning video to the world's media, to the backdrop of the erupting volcano Eyjafjallajökull, one is brutally murdered.

As Magnus Jonson begins to investigate, the list of suspects grows ever longer. From the Chinese government, Israeli military, Italian politicians, even to American college fraternities, the group has made many enemies. And more are coming to the surface every day...

And with the return of Magnus's brother Ollie to Iceland, the feud that has haunted their family for three generations is about to reignite.

## Sea of Stone

Iceland, 2010: Called to investigate a suspected homicide in a remote farmstead, Constable Páll is surprised to find that Sergeant Magnus Jonson is already at the scene. The victim? Magnus's estranged grandfather.

But it quickly becomes apparent that the crime scene has been tampered with, and that Magnus's version of events doesn't add up. Before long, Magnus is arrested for the murder of his grandfather. When it emerges that his younger brother, Ollie, is in Iceland after two decades in America, Páll begins to think that

Magnus may not be the only family member in the frame for murder...

## The Wanderer

When a young Italian tourist is found brutally murdered at a sacred church in northern Iceland, Magnus Jonson, newly returned to the Reykjavik police force, is called to investigate. At the scene he finds a stunned TV crew, there to film a documentary on the life of the legendary Viking, Gudrid the Wanderer.

Magnus quickly begins to suspect that there may be more links to the murdered woman than anyone in the film crew will acknowledge. As jealousies come to the surface, new tensions replace old friendships, and history begins to rewrite itself, a shocking second murder leads Magnus to question everything he thought he knew.

## Writing in Ice: A Crime Writer's Guide to Iceland

An account of how Michael Ridpath researched his Magnus detective series set in Iceland: the breathtaking landscape, its vigorous if occasionally odd people, the great heroes and heroines of its sagas, and the elves, trolls and ghosts of its folklore; with a little bit thrown in about how to put together a good detective story.

Entertaining and informative, it's a guide to Iceland for the visitor, and a guide to crime writing for the reader.

# REVIEW THIS BOOK

I would be really grateful if you could take a moment to review this book. Reviews, even of only a few words, are really important for the success of a book these days.

Thank you.

Michael